PRAISE FOR

"James writes smart, taut, high ～～～～～～ his books are not for the timid. The e～～～～ ～～～ ～～～～ ～～～～ ～～～～
—MITCH GALIN, producer, Stephen King's *The Stand* and Frank Herbert's *Dune*

"A thought-provoking and thrilling mystery."
—NEW YORK JOURNAL OF BOOKS on *Placebo*

"The nail-biting suspense will rivet you."—RT BOOK REVIEWS

"[A] master storyteller at the peak of his game."—PUBLISHERS WEEKLY

"James delivers first-rate characters, dazzling plot twists, and powers it all with nonstop action."
—JOHN TINKER, Emmy Award–winning screenplay writer

"*Opening Moves* is a mesmerizing read. From the first chapter, it sets its hook deep and drags you through a darkly gripping story with relentless power. My conclusion: I need to read more of Steven James."
—MICHAEL CONNELLY, *New York Times* bestselling author of *The Burning Room*

"Pulse-pounding suspense."—FICTIONADDICT.COM

"Exhilarating."—MYSTERIOUS REVIEWS

"James clearly knows how to spin a yarn."—BOOKLIST

"His tightly woven, adrenaline-laced plots leave readers breathless."
—THE SUSPENSE ZONE

"James sets the new standard in suspense writing."
—SUSPENSE MAGAZINE

FURY

FURY

STEVEN JAMES

OLDHAM COUNTY PUBLIC LIBRARY
308 YAGER AVENUE
LAGRANGE, KY 40031

SKYSCAPE

SKYSCAPE

This is a work of fiction. Names, characters, organizations, places, events, and incidents are either products of the author's imagination or are used fictitiously.

Text copyright © 2015 by Steven James
All rights reserved.

No part of this book may be reproduced, or stored in a retrieval system, or transmitted in any form or by any means, electronic, mechanical, photocopying, recording, or otherwise, without express written permission of the publisher.

Published by Skyscape, New York

www.apub.com

Amazon, the Amazon logo, and Skyscape are trademarks of Amazon.com, Inc., or its affiliates.

ISBN-13: 9781477827468
ISBN-10: 1477827463

Cover design by Greg Stadnyk

Library of Congress Control Number: 2014918087

Printed in The United States of America
10 9 8 7 6 5 4 3 2 1

For
Elisabeth, Katherine and Mei Li

There are four government agencies that do not appear in the national budget. Officially, they have no staff. Their funding is not recorded.

The United States federal government continues to deny that they even exist.

One of those agencies searched for nearly a year to find an appropriate location to conduct its research.

And it found one.

Near a state prison in the isolated forests of northern Wisconsin.

PROLOGUE

"Do you know why you're here, Daniel?"

Daniel Byers found himself blinking and tilting his head to the side. A stark fluorescent light stared down at him. He was in a bed, on his back, disoriented. "What?"

"I asked if you know why you're here."

Looking around, he saw that he was in a hospital room. A window on the far wall had heavy shades drawn across it, letting only a muted smear of sunlight in around the edges. It was impossible to tell what time of day it was. He had a piercing headache, his thoughts twisting in strange, uncontrollable threads. But one thing he did remember clearly. "They said I hurt somebody," he mumbled.

Who? Who would you have hurt?

"Is that all?"

"Yes."

A looming man with a detective's badge stood beside the bed. The gaunt doctor next to him was wearing a white lab coat, but he remained silent as the detective spoke. "So you don't remember what happened with your father?"

"My father?"

Daniel thought hard, tried to remember, but all that came to mind were dim images of his high school basketball game the other night, of visiting a barn, of standing in the snow beside a dead wolf—twirling, merging worlds of waking and sleeping and dark nightmares cycling in on themselves.

There was no way to tell which images were memories and which were dreams.

You're still in a dream. This is a dream.

It has to be a dream.

Your dad's okay.

Nothing happened to him.

Daniel tried to sit up, but found it impossible. He looked down at the bed. His wrists and ankles were strapped down.

What is going on here?

"What did that nurse mean when she said I hurt somebody? Did she mean my dad?"

"So you don't recall anything about last night?"

"Tell me if he's alright. You have to—"

"Blood," the detective interrupted. "Does that jar your memory?"

"What?"

"Blood."

"I don't know anything about any blood."

He leaned over Daniel. "Who's Madeline?"

"Madeline?"

"We have your phone. We know about the texts. What did you do with him, young man?"

"With who?"

"Your father."

"I have no idea what you're talking about."

But he did remember the texts.

And he did remember the name Madeline.

"He needs to rest," the doctor said. "It's time for his medication."

"Tell me what's going on," Daniel demanded. "Is my dad okay?"

The detective looked severely at Daniel. "That's what we need you to tell us."

"I'm going to give you something to help you sleep." The doctor gestured toward the doorway and a nurse entered. She produced a syringe and handed it to him and he bent over Daniel.

"I don't want to sleep." He wrestled against the straps holding him down. "I want to remember!"

The detective finally stepped aside as the nurse held his arm still and the doctor stabbed the needle into it.

"No!"

But the world was already going bleary, fading out like a light on a dimmer switch that someone was slowly dialing off.

Daniel could only think of one word while the deep, sweeping nothingness swarmed over him: blood.

Then he remembered.

Yes.

He remembered the blood on his hands, the blood splattered everywhere.

What did you do to your dad, Daniel?
What did you do?
And then everything went dark.

PART I
TEARS OF BLOOD

48 HOURS EARLIER
FRIDAY, DECEMBER 21

CHAPTER ONE

Daniel stared at his locker.

Someone had taped a DVD of the old movie *Psycho* to the outside of it.

So. Someone knew.

Ty Bell?

Maybe. Probably. He was one guy who would do this. But how he might've found out what was going on was beyond Daniel.

Over the last couple months Daniel had done his best to keep what was happening to him a secret. His closest friends knew about it, yes they did, but he trusted them and he knew they wouldn't tell.

They wouldn't have left the DVD there.

He tore it off the locker and stuck it inside for the time being, then retrieved his books and headed to his first hour English class.

As he crossed through the hallway, the other students parted to let him by, the guys nodding to him, the girls smiling shyly and tipping their gaze to the side.

Sports were huge at his school and as their quarterback and all-conference point guard, Daniel was someone the guys respected and the girls tended to be drawn to—not that he was looking for a girlfriend, though. He was with another junior, Nicole Marten, had been since October.

Thankfully, things had been going pretty well lately, not just with her, but on other fronts too. A lot better than they had been.

The blurs—visions, hallucinations, whatever you wanted to call them—had stopped, at least for the time being. Everything seemed to have settled back to normal after what'd happened in September when the girl's body was found and he saw her sit up in her coffin, heard her beg him for help, felt her grab his arm.

That day at the funeral was the first blur, the first time reality had lied to him.

But it hadn't been the last.

That whole week had been weird, surreal, but once the guy who'd killed Emily and the two other girls from the schools in the area was out of the picture, the blurs hadn't come back.

All that was over.

All that was in the past.

The blurs died when the murderer did.

Today was the last day before winter break and Daniel had an AP Calculus final, but the rest of his exams were over and other than that one test, things were light, winding down for vacation. Their last basketball game before Christmas was tonight against Coulee High.

He mentally ran through his schedule for the day: go to classes this morning, grab lunch with Kyle rather than Nicole, since she had class that hour, then head to his doctor's appointment before swinging home. Finally, at four forty-five or so, return to school to leave on the team bus for the seven o'clock game.

Daniel glanced out the window. Snowflakes were falling lightly onto the foot of snow that had already accumulated over the past month. For some parts of the country it might have seemed like a lot, but this far north in Wisconsin they were actually behind what they'd gotten by this time last year.

People around here were used to driving on snow so it took a pretty serious storm for a game to be postponed or cancelled. Still, Daniel hoped the weather wouldn't get any worse.

He caught up with Nicole just down the hall from their English classroom.

Though she normally had walnut-colored hair, she'd dyed it red a few weeks ago. She'd always gone light on the makeup—she was one of those girls who didn't really need it. Today the sweater she'd chosen matched her perceptive, green eyes. Quirky and fun, she was someone Daniel had been friends with for years, even before they started going out a couple of months ago.

"Hey, you." He gave her a kiss.

"Hey." She seemed agitated.

"What is it?"

"Did you hear they found another one last night?"

"Another one?"

"Another wolf. Over by the lake."

"Was it . . . ?"

"Yeah. Shot and left for dead—just like the others."

"So, that's four," Daniel said half to himself.

"Four that've been found. Who knows how many others have been killed—you know, but that no one's come across. I can't believe someone's doing this."

Timber wolves, or gray wolves, were protected by law and had been making a comeback over the last decade or so in the wide, expansive forests surrounding the town of Beldon. But now someone was poaching them.

It wasn't for their fur.

It was just for sport.

If you could call it that.

An anonymous tip line had been set up at the forest ranger's station and Daniel's dad, who was the sheriff, had been working with local game wardens to try to find out who was killing the wolves, but from what Daniel had heard, they weren't making a whole lot of progress.

Nicole took caring for the environment seriously and ever since she'd first heard about the wolves being killed, it'd troubled her deeply. This latest news was only going to make that worse.

"It'll be alright," Daniel told her. "My dad's gonna find whoever's doing this."

"I hope they put 'em away for a long time."

They entered the room and headed for their seats. Daniel's friend Kyle Goessel was already there. He flicked back a strand of his shoulder-length blond hair and nodded to Daniel. "What's up?"

"Not much," Daniel replied distractedly, still thinking about the wolves.

He'd been following the news about the wolf shootings online, reading everything he could about them.

So, four had been found.

How many more were out there?

Why only wolves in this area? Does the poacher live nearby?

Questions that needed to be answered.

But that was going to have to wait until later.

The bell rang and English class began.

CHAPTER TWO

Miss Flynn liked it when the students called her "Teach." For some teachers it might have just been their way of trying to be cool, or to fit in better with the students, but it'd never seemed that way with her.

She was just a couple years out of college, hot enough for some of the guys in Daniel's class to have crushes on, and she tended to think of the horror stories of H. P. Lovecraft and Edgar Allan Poe as classics rather than the books most other English teachers assigned. All that, taken together, ended up making her one of the junior class's favorite teachers.

"So," she said, "I know you're about to start winter break and since you handed in your final papers already, you probably expected a free day, but based on what I've read of your work, we need to spend a little time discussing one aspect of literature that we apparently haven't covered as well as we should have—the forces that contribute to hinder the protagonist from reaching his goal or obtaining the object of his desire. You should all remember the term that refers to the person who interferes with the main character's journey through the story . . ." She gazed around the room. "Bradley?"

"The bad guy?" Actually, for Brad Talbot that was a pretty insightful answer.

"True enough. Or the . . . ?"

"Antagonist." Stephanie Mills had her hand flagged in the air but enthusiastically spoke up before Teach even had a chance to call on her.

"Yes. An unforgettable story needs an unforgettable antagonist. The strength of the protagonist is measured against the strength of the forces of antagonism he has to overcome. So when you're writing your stories, you need to make sure that the antagonist—the bad guy—is ruthless or persistent or cold-hearted enough to present a great enough challenge to reveal or develop the core characteristics of your protagonist. Make sense?"

A few nods around the room. Daniel jotted a couple things down in his notebook.

"Teach," Stephanie said, "can the protagonist also be the antagonist? I mean, is there some way for the main character to be both the hero and the villain?"

"That's a good question," she replied thoughtfully. "It might happen when the protagonist isn't aware that he's also the antagonist. So, perhaps in a story where you have an unreliable narrator—that is, he or she is telling the story but doesn't know the whole truth about what's going on yet. He might be crazy or delusional or both."

Daniel wasn't sure, but Teach seemed to glance in his direction for a moment before looking away. It was just that quick, hardly a look at all, but he saw it.

Maybe she knew more than she should.

He hoped not.

"But that's not all," she went on. "For example, in that Poe story we studied—'The Cask of Amontillado'—the main character is also the one who seals the other man alive in the crypt. I think that in that case, the protagonist is struggling against himself, against what he's capable of doing. So in a real sense, he is both the protagonist and the antagonist. It's also true in the story of Dr. Jekyll and Mr. Hyde. In fact, it could be argued that we are, each of us, both the protagonist and the antagonist of our own lives, in the stories we live out every day."

As she returned to her discussion of what makes a memorable antagonist, Daniel wasn't really listening. Instead, his thoughts had wandered back to an Ojibwe folktale his dad had told him after the events last fall when Emily was killed.

According to the legend, an old man was teaching his grandson the tribe's morals and values and he said that there was a fight going on inside of him between two wolves— one vicious and evil, filled with all the darkness of his soul; the other good and righteous, filled with hope and wonder. "Which one will win?" the boy asked. "The one I feed the most," his grandpa replied.

Then Daniel's dad had said, "That man who murdered Emily fed the wrong wolf for a long time until it was so strong that it finally killed off the other one."

And even then, Daniel had been aware that there were two wolves inside him as well.

Which one are you feeding, Daniel?

Which wolf will win?

It made him think of Nicole's favorite movie series—the *Star Wars* films—and Anakin Skywalker's descent into the dark side of the Force.

It calls to us all, it—

The bell at the end of class drew Daniel abruptly out of his thoughts.

He looked down and noticed that his notebook was covered with scrawled words in a script that didn't look anything like his own handwriting. Over and over, he'd written the words "Lost Cove is the key."

He had no idea what that meant.

Quickly, he closed the notebook, collected his things, and headed for the hall. Nicole had gone ahead to her next class, but Kyle was waiting for him.

His friend had him by a few inches and came across as a bit gangly and giraffe-ish until he took off running, and then everything came into sync. He could've probably sprinted past half the guys on the track or cross country teams, but he didn't go out for any sports. Daniel had always wondered why, but hadn't pressed the issue because it was pretty easy to tell that his friend didn't really want to talk about it.

Kyle lowered his voice. "Did you figure out who's sending you those texts?"

"Not yet. The number's blocked."

"Did you tell Nicole about 'em?"

"No. That might not be the smartest idea."

Daniel didn't think his girlfriend would be too excited to find out he was getting mysterious texts from someone named Madeline.

"Good point," Kyle agreed.

They started down the hallway.

Daniel didn't know any Madelines and none attended their school—at least as far as he could tell. There was a sophomore girl named Maddie, but that was as close as it came.

He'd even paged through the yearbook but hadn't found anyone with that name. Of course it was always possible that a freshman or a transfer student might have been named Madeline, but if that was the case, why would she be texting him? And how did she even get his number?

There were apps that could hide the number someone was texting from, so that part wasn't as big of a mystery. On the slightly stalkerish front, however, Kyle had reminded him that there wasn't even any proof that Madeline was a girl rather than some guy using a girl's name—or a girl using a different name. After all, online and in texts you can't know for sure if people really are who they say they are.

As they passed the gym, Kyle said, "Hey, at lunch I've got a puzzle for you. Made it up myself." He was always trying to come up with a logic or math problem that Daniel couldn't solve on the spot.

Hadn't been too successful so far.

Math and logic weren't things Daniel had ever tried to be good at; they were just second nature for him, like learning other languages is for some people. For a while he hadn't been into solving the puzzles his friend came up with, but lately Kyle had been getting more and more creative so he'd started to get into them.

Kyle paused in the hallway. "Bet you a Dr Pepper you can't solve it in one minute."

"I don't know, I'm feeling on my A-game today."

"You better be."

"You're on."

After Kyle left, Daniel responded to a few texts and by the time he was done he'd received a new one: *I'm here waiting for you, Daniel—Madeline.*

Madeline again.

Rather than delete her text, he archived it, hoping to eventually piece together who she was.

During his AP Calc exam he tried his best not to let the questions regarding her identity or the Lost Cove deal distract him, but that didn't work out too well, and it was a good thing calculus came easy for him or he would've really struggled with the test.

As it turned out, he was the last one to hand in his final, and his teacher, Mr. Corrigan, looked at him with concern. "You feeling okay today, Daniel?"

"Yeah." Usually Daniel finished his tests at least ten or fifteen minutes before anyone else so it didn't surprise him that Mr. Corrigan was wondering what was going on. "I'm good."

At lunchtime, Kyle sat across the table from Daniel in the back of the cafeteria. "My puzzle," he told him, "it's a liar's dilemma."

"I like liar's dilemmas." Today, rather than go for the cafeteria's mystery meat, Daniel had brought his own lunch from home. He took a bite of leftover chicken fajita. It was a lot better than anything they would have served here. "Let's hear it."

"Alright." Kyle set down the unopened can of Dr Pepper beside his food. "Picture this: There are four doors, two on each side of a hallway, each posted with a guard. Behind one of the doors is the princess; behind the others: a one-way ticket to the dungeon. Before choosing his door, our knight, Elvin—"

"Elvin the knight?"

"Sure. Why not?"

"Seriously?"

"Not medievally enough for you?"

"Well . . ."

"How about Elvinore?" Kyle offered.

Sounds more like the princess's name than the knight's.

"Sure. Whatever. Go on."

"So, Elvinore, he gets to ask each guard one question to try and find the princess so he can marry her and they can live happily ever after. But here's the deal: the guards in front of her door and one other door always tell the truth but the other two guards always lie."

"Gotcha."

"Alright, so he goes to the first door on his left and asks, 'Is the princess behind this door?' 'Yes,' the guard says. He moves to the next door on that side of the hall and asks, 'Is the princess behind this door?' 'Yes,' the guard replies."

"Two doors, two yeses."

"Right. Then he crosses the hall and asks the next guard, 'Is the princess behind the door I just left directly across the hall from you?' Again the answer is, 'Yes.' Finally, Elvinore goes to the last door. 'Is the princess behind this door?' 'No,' the guard tells him."

Kyle scrolled through his phone's home screens to bring up the timer. "Well, Elvinore thinks for a second and then walks confidently to the correct door and—" He tapped the screen. "Go."

"Door one."

Kyle stared at him. "What?"

"She was behind the first door."

"How did you . . . ?"

"The princess couldn't be behind that last door since her guard must always tell the truth and he said she wasn't there. If she was, he would've had to say so."

"Right. But . . . ?"

"She couldn't be behind the third door because that guard said she was behind a different door, and again, if he were guarding her, he would've had to be telling the truth. So that means it's down to the first or second door."

"But why do you think it was door number one?"

"If she were behind the second door, then three guards would have been telling the truth about where she was— the second, third, and fourth guards. But we know that only two tell the truth, so she had to be behind that first door. The first and fourth guards were telling the truth, the second and third were lying."

Daniel took another bite of his fajita.

It really was good.

Kyle shook his head, stopped his timer and slid the Dr Pepper across the table.

"You'll get me one of these days." Daniel glanced at the time, then hurried through the rest of his lunch, let Kyle keep the soda, and stood. "I gotta take off."

"Your doctor's appointment."

"Right."

He didn't need to tell his friend what kind of doctor he was going to see.

Kyle already knew.

And it wasn't a medical doctor.

"Hey," Kyle said, "Mia and I will be at the game tonight." Mia Young, Kyle's girlfriend, was into creative writing almost as much as he was and was even working on a novel: a horror story about ghosts who haunted an old monastery. The two of them had been together ever since summer and from what Daniel could tell they were perfect for each other. "Let's get together afterward. Bring Nicole. We can chill at my house."

"Sounds good."

"Play well. You own those guys."

"I hope you're right."

After leaving the cafeteria, Daniel stopped by his locker and grabbed the *Psycho* DVD that'd been taped to the outside of it. Then he swung by the school's office and turned in the note his dad had given him excusing him from his afternoon study hall and phys ed period. As he left school he was thinking about what he'd written in his notebook in Teach's class.

It was not a good sign that he had no memory of scribbling down that phrase, and it was even more bizarre that his handwriting looked like someone else's. What was all that about?

It's starting again.

The blurs are coming back.

He tried to tell himself that wasn't true as he drove toward his psychiatrist's office.

CHAPTER
THREE

They don't tell you that you're "going crazy."

Daniel had learned that on his first visit to the psychiatrist.

The guy had been very careful to avoid using that phrase.

But when you start seeing things, hearing voices, sleep-walking and digging up dead pets from the yard, there's obviously a cause for concern. That's what had sent Daniel to the shrink in the first place.

The MRI and CAT scans had come back negative. From what the doctors could tell, nothing was physically wrong with him—which was both reassuring and troubling at the same time.

Because *something* was definitely wrong.

And if it wasn't physical, then it had to be mental, psychological.

Which isn't exactly something a sixteen-year-old guy wants to hear.

This was Daniel's fifth visit to see Dr. Fromke. As he waited in the lobby, he pulled out his phone and Googled

"Lost Cove is the key." More than a million results came up.

Okay, that might be a bit much to check out at the moment.

He whipped through the first couple dozen, but didn't see anything that seemed particularly helpful.

After putting his phone away, he paged absently through the four-month-old issue of *Sports Illustrated* that'd been left on the coffee table beside his chair. A conversation he'd had with Nicole a couple weeks ago came to mind. She'd asked him what the difference was between someone who's a psychopath and someone who's psychotic.

"Well . . ." For obvious reasons, he'd done his share of reading on the topic since October. "Psychopaths—or sociopaths, whatever term you want to use—they know the difference between right and wrong. But someone who's psychotic doesn't."

"So . . . What about someone who has schizophrenia?"

"He doesn't always know what's real and what's not."

"But right and wrong?"

"From what I've read, he knows what's right, but since the difference between reality and his hallucinations is so unclear, he can't always be trusted to do it."

Now as he flipped through that magazine, he recalled the wolf legend and wondered if a person could be feeding the wrong wolf and not even know it, and if you could come to the place where you can't even tell the two of them apart.

"Daniel Byers?" the receptionist called, then informed him that the doctor was ready to see him.

He entered the psychiatrist's office: a cluttered desk with the pocketknife he used as a letter opener beside his inbox, a chair facing the couch, diplomas on the wall, a certificate for volunteering as a counselor at the Derthick State Penitentiary, a bookshelf with twenty-eight books on it with a total of four hundred and seventy-one letters on the spines. Daniel noticed the number, couldn't help but notice. It was just that way with anything dealing with math, with numbers.

Dr. Fromke looked like he was about the same age as Daniel's father, but was mostly bald and had a somewhat scraggly beard. He rose from his chair to shake Daniel's hand, then gestured toward the couch. "Please. Have a seat."

After Daniel sat down, the doctor settled back into his chair and said, "How are you feeling today?"

"I'm good."

"Any headaches recently?"

"No."

Dr. Fromke wrote something on his notepad, then dove right in: "And what about blurs? Have you been having any more?"

Actually, Kyle was the one who'd come up with the term "blur" for the times when fantasy and reality—or maybe it was sanity and insanity—merged for Daniel. The word had stuck, and back when Daniel first told Dr. Fromke what was going on, he'd found himself naturally using it.

Since then, the doctor had opted for it as well, rather than "hallucinations."

"No," Daniel told him now. "No blurs."

But what about what happened in English class? Writing that phrase over and over? Does that count?

No. That was just you being distracted.

But what about—

"I'm glad to hear that," Dr. Fromke said, drawing Daniel out of his thoughts.

He was hoping the doctor wouldn't ask him if he was taking his meds. He didn't want to admit that he'd been getting rid of them, flushing the two pills down the toilet each day, but he also didn't want to lie. It'd probably be better all around if the subject didn't come up.

Thankfully, Dr. Fromke didn't go there. "How have you been sleeping?"

"Good."

"No sleepwalking?"

"Nope."

"And things with your parents? Tell me how that's been going."

"Everything's going okay. With my dad, at least."

Daniel wasn't exactly sure how to explain how things were with his mom. That was a little more complicated.

She'd moved out last spring, hadn't told anyone why, and hadn't spoken with Daniel much at all since leaving. Then, in October, she'd come back for the first time from the Twin Cities, where she was staying, to see one of his football games.

That was awkward.

Very awkward.

Now, this weekend she'd flown to Anchorage, Alaska, to visit her brother, but she was planning to come back to the Midwest in time to see Daniel on Christmas this coming Tuesday.

He couldn't even begin to guess how that was going to go.

"And your mother?" Dr. Fromke asked.

"Pretty much the same."

She still hadn't told Daniel why she'd moved out. She wasn't seeing another guy and Daniel's dad hadn't had an affair or anything to make her mad—which basically meant that she preferred being alone to being with her husband and her son.

So there was that.

Everything was pointing toward them getting a divorce and Daniel was just surprised it hadn't been finalized yet.

He was torn.

On the one hand he wanted them to get back together, but on the other hand if his mom didn't want to be there with them, fine. He could deal with that.

He wanted her around.

He didn't want her around.

He wanted to forgive her for taking off.

He wanted to just forget about her and let her get on with her own life.

You get pulled in those two directions and sometimes you feel like you're going to snap because of it—but that wasn't exactly something he felt like he wanted to share with his psychiatrist right now.

Did he love her?

He wasn't even sure anymore.

"Have you been talking with her at all?" Dr. Fromke asked.

"A little. Yeah. Things aren't really any better, but they're not any worse either. Like I said—pretty much the same."

Dr. Fromke scribbled something down, then asked Daniel about his grades and how school and basketball were going, if he was feeling depressed or anxious, if he was finding it hard to concentrate.

Daniel assured him that things were fine. His grades were okay. Basketball was going well. No depression or anything. Figuring that the incident in English class was probably nothing to worry about, he didn't bring it up.

"So," the doctor concluded, "the medication must be helping."

It didn't really sound like a question.

Daniel said nothing.

They talked for another twenty minutes or so, Daniel reiterating that he was doing alright, Dr. Fromke looking pleased. "The last time you were in here we talked about your grandmother's death."

"Yeah." It was true, the topic had come up, even though she'd died when he was nine.

"How has that been for you?"

"It's good. I'm fine."

He explored Daniel's feelings about that for a couple minutes and then wrote out a new prescription and handed it to him. "Just give that to your dad. He can fill it at the pharmacy."

"Sure."

"Don't forget: Two pills in the morning. Take them with food."

"I won't forget."

He wasn't exactly sure why he'd bailed on taking the meds. Maybe it was because the blurs had stopped on their own. Maybe because he didn't want to chance coming up positive for anything if he was tested for drugs for sports, or that the meds would muddy up his thinking or slow down his response time.

Or maybe it was because he just didn't like the idea of admitting that he needed help.

Schizophrenia?

Yeah, it was possible that's what was wrong with him.

Or at least *part* of what was wrong.

For people who have it, the voices in their heads can be so real that they don't even question them. The hallucinations can be so convincing that people simply accept them as fact.

When he'd been having the blurs it was almost like reality was there around him, but there were fractures in it, tiny, invisible cracks that were letting through thoughts he shouldn't have been having at all.

Daniel was the right age for someone to be diagnosed with it.

He was exhibiting enough symptoms to make Dr. Fromke think that it might be schizophrenia, and that's why he'd prescribed the antipsychotic drugs.

But Daniel wasn't convinced.

There had to be something else.

After all, when the dead girl had grabbed his arm, it'd left a mark, red and swollen, in the shape of her hand, as if her fingers had burned their way right into his flesh.

That was real.

The pain was real.

The mark was real.

He hadn't imagined that.

Even if you start hearing voices that aren't real or seeing things that aren't there because you have schizophrenia, you don't have burn marks appear on your skin for no reason. Especially ones as severe as that, ones that miraculously heal on their own in less than twenty-four hours.

No, schizophrenia doesn't cause that.

Daniel wasn't sure what to believe about the paranormal, the supernatural, but he wasn't ready to discount anything. Something had happened to him that normal logic, normal reasoning, normal science couldn't explain.

After finishing up with the psychiatrist, Daniel left for home. The office was four miles outside of town and he had to pass the prison to get to his house.

Guard towers. Razor wire fence. The whole deal.

He always slowed down when he passed it.

Just curiosity, maybe.

Some people sped up.

Nerves.

After the Derthick State Penitentiary was constructed two years ago, it'd become one of the biggest employers in a county that had always depended mostly on outdoor tourism for jobs—guided fishing tours in the summer and snowmobile and cross-country ski rentals in the winter.

But people in the area had mixed feelings about it. Sure, they were glad for the jobs, but the idea of having a prison nearby didn't exactly thrill them, even though the government assured them that it was safe and there was nothing to worry about.

While Daniel had been in the psychiatrist's office, the clouds had parted and the snow had stopped. From what he could tell, maybe an inch or so had fallen since last night.

Unless Coulee High, which was an hour away, had gotten hammered with snow, the game would be on for tonight—which was good because Beldon High was 6–0 so far this season and this game was important for the conference standings going into the new year.

Besides, he would have already gotten a text if the game had been postponed.

The snow that covered the ground glistened in the emerging sunlight. Everything looked so pure and clean, just like it did after every snowfall.

Typically, when the plows went by—especially when the snow was slushy—they would kick up exhaust-stained snow along with the sand that the county sometimes put on the roads to help with traction.

Piles of snow got pushed up along the roadsides and when the fresh snow melted away it left a layer of grime on the crusty snow left behind. But a snowfall always covered that, so everything ended up looking pristine again, even though there was something ugly right beneath the surface.

There was probably some deeper meaning there; symbolism he didn't need Teach to point out to him—symbolism about the appearances of our lives and how they can hide what's really going on underneath.

We are, each of us, both the protagonist and the antagonist in the stories we live out each day.

Two wolves inside of us.

Battling it out to the death where no one else can see.

His dad's squad car was in the driveway.

Daniel had thought he might be out on patrol somewhere, but his hours weren't exactly nine to five and it wasn't really unusual to have him home—or gone—at odd times.

He was in the kitchen emptying the dishwasher when Daniel walked in.

"Hey, Dan."

"Hey."

His father avoided using the word "psychiatrist." It made it easier on both of them. "How'd the appointment go?"

Daniel handed over the prescription. "He wants you to fill that."

"Okay. Thanks."

They didn't have extra money floating around so Daniel wasn't excited about his dad having to buy medication that he wasn't even going to use, but he wasn't ready yet to tell him that he hadn't been taking the pills. He didn't really know how that would go over.

Maybe he would start taking them in the morning.

Yeah, maybe you should, since you're doing things again without remembering them, like writing mysterious phrases in your notebook—in someone else's handwriting.

"Anything I should know about?" his dad asked.

The question caught Daniel slightly off guard. "That you should know about?"

"From the doctor."

"Oh. Yeah. No—things are fine. It's all good. You need any help?"

"No. I got it." He put the last few dishes away. "So, you ready for the game?"

"Yeah. Hey, I heard they found another wolf."

His father nodded somberly and closed up the dishwasher. "We're looking into it. In fact, that brings up what I needed to tell you: I'm not going to be able to make it to your game tonight. I have to follow up on something related to the case."

"That's fine."

His dad had done a good job of balancing things out: coming to most of his games, but not hovering and coming to *all* of them. He made it clear that Daniel was important to him, but he didn't make it weird.

"Well." His dad dug his keys out of his pocket. "I should get going. Have a good game."

"I will."

"Text me. Let me know how it goes."

"Sure."

The headache started while Daniel was putting his books away.

It began in the back of his head and then moved steadily forward like a swarm of bees crawling through his brain, buzzing, stealing his attention, piercing his thoughts with their stingers.

Last autumn when he'd had the blurs, intense headaches had almost always preceded them, and he didn't take it as a good sign that he was having that same kind now again.

He told himself that it would go away on its own.

You know that's not going to happen until you see another blur.

Well, if that was the case, it'd be better if the blur would just come right away so his head would be clear during the game, but considering that the last time he'd had this kind of headache he'd seen a dead girl standing in front of him, he wasn't exactly sure he wanted that either.

After answering a few texts, Daniel grabbed his basketball uniform and shoes, stuffed them into his gym bag, and took off for the school parking lot where the team bus would be waiting.

CHAPTER FOUR

At this time of year in northern Wisconsin, days were short, and at five when the bus left for Coulee High it was already dark.

During the drive, a few guys on the team talked or joked around, but most of them texted, played games on their phones, or listened to music in their headphones or earbuds.

Stephen Layhe, who started at small forward and shared some classes with Daniel, was sitting next to him and asked him where he'd been that afternoon.

"Doctor's appointment."

"You okay?"

"Yeah, I'm fine. It was just sort of a checkup, you know, just to see how I was doing."

"Gotcha," Stephen said. "So, you ready to take these guys tonight?"

"I am."

"Just like last year in the playoffs."

"Just like last year."

They talked for a few minutes. The headache didn't go away, making it hard to concentrate. Finally, he told Stephen he was going to listen to some music.

Nicole had put together a pregame playlist for Daniel and now he scrolled to it. Rather than boy bands or top twenty pop tunes or anything like that, she was into electronic violin and techno music. A driving beat. No words. She liked to dance to it; he liked how it helped him get into the right mindset for his games.

He stared at the dark window, watching the reflection of the inside of the bus created by the greenish glow of people's phones merge with the moonlight coming in off the snow-encrusted landscape outside.

The two worlds passed across each other in the pane of glass: a snowy forest and the outline of the kids around him. Two images meeting there, becoming one. And if you didn't know any better, you might be confused about where one ended and the other began.

But you do know better.

You can tell what's real and what isn't.

The music pulsed in his head.

He turned it down, but that only made him notice the headache more, so he punched up the volume again to distract himself from it.

As he watched the black night mix in the window with the faint reflection of the inside of the bus, he found himself somehow drawn outside, standing in the snow.

It wasn't dark anymore. Daylight swept over him.

The snow was disappearing, not melting, but simply passing back into the land, and then it was autumn, the seasons cycling backward. Leaves covered the ground. Bare trees clutched at a wide open, steel blue sky.

It's a dream.

You're just dreaming.

But that realization didn't stop the images from unfolding before him.

He was walking along the edge of a fencerow paralleling a barbed wire fence. He'd made it about halfway to a barn at the end of the field when a girl emerged from behind one of the trees nearby.

He couldn't see her face, but based on how tall she was and how slight her build was, he guessed she was maybe ten or eleven years old.

She wore an old-fashioned white nightgown with lace fringes.

When she faced him, he froze.

She was opening and closing her mouth slowly, not speaking, not making a sound, just letting her mouth gape open as if there were words that wanted to come out but couldn't. Dark blood oozed from her eyes and trailed down her cheeks in two macabre streaks.

Tears of blood.

Daniel stumbled backward, but she moved toward him as if she were trying to keep the same distance between them. She raised one hand and pointed at him, then opened her mouth silently once again.

He wanted to ask her who she was, what she wanted—but then she turned and started toward the barn.

Both disturbed by her appearance and curious about her, Daniel followed.

He couldn't help it.

She seemed to walk slowly but also move swiftly and he knew it was because this was all a dream and dreams follow their own set of rules.

Then they were at the barn. She entered it.

Somewhat apprehensively, he went in behind her.

And found her standing ten feet away, staring at him with those terrible bleeding eyes.

She opened her mouth again and this time he could hear what she said. Her voice was scratchy and harsh, but was also somehow marked with the soft innocence of a child: "Madeline is waiting for you, Daniel. Madeline is waiting."

"Who is Madeline?"

The girl didn't answer, but rather lifted both arms and stared up at the barn's hayloft.

"Who are you?" he asked. "What do you want from me?"

The flames started at the bottom of her nightgown but rose quickly as they engulfed the fabric.

In his dream.

His dream—

Daniel rushed forward to push the girl down, to help her roll across the ground to put out the fire, but when he reached out to touch her, his hands passed right through her.

He felt his arms rage with pain from the fire and he nearly cried out as he drew backward.

Yet he didn't wake up. He wanted to, tried to, but he couldn't make himself wake up.

The fire was hungry and consumed the girl quickly until she was nothing but a blackened corpse standing before him as the flames flickered out. Thin curls of black smoke rose from her body and wisped off into the air.

She lowered her head, but kept her arms raised high. Somehow she managed to smile, revealing white teeth that contrasted sharply with her gruesome, charred skin. "Hurry, Daniel, you have to stop him," she said in that coarse, yet tender and childish voice. "Before it happens again."

And then she began to disintegrate.

"Stop who?" he asked her urgently. "Before what happens again?"

Small pieces of her face peeled off and floated away like dark sparks from a campfire, embers caught in the wind.

And then it wasn't just her face, but all of her—layer by layer, the black flecks that used to be that living girl swirled away until nothing was left.

Then, even though he wanted to stay and see if she would return again, he was drifting backward out of the barn and into the day where he heard the distant, lonesome howl of a wolf echo across the hills on the horizon.

A storm had moved in and the field, which had been sunny just a minute before, was draped in the gray shadow of a cold autumn rain.

Somewhere within the rumbling thunder he heard his name: "Daniel."

More thunder rolled across the landscape, which was transforming from a field to what looked like a ragged sea, or the waters of nearby Lake Superior or—

He felt a hand on his shoulder, someone shaking him.

"Dan?"

Lightning crackled across the sky while the rain sliced down at him and—

"You alright?"

Daniel didn't consciously open his eyes, but then they were open and he recognized that he was in the bus. Stephen was standing beside him. "You good?" Stephen said.

"Yeah." Daniel rubbed his head. He wasn't wearing his earbuds anymore. Either he'd taken them out without realizing it or they'd somehow fallen out on their own. "Must've dozed off."

The bus had stopped.

They were at Coulee High.

Daniel's headache hadn't completely gone away, but the bees weren't swarming as much as they had been earlier.

Usually, whenever he woke up, his dreams would fade away almost immediately, until he was left with only a dim impression of what they'd been rather than a specific memory of what he'd dreamt about. This time, however, the dream seemed to become clearer the longer he was awake and the more alert he became.

The girl.

Her eyes weeping blood.

The flames enveloping her.

Her corpse flaking apart and blowing away before his eyes.

All the guys in front of him were leaving the bus.

Daniel collected his things.

Last fall when the dead girl had grabbed his arm, it'd left that wound behind on his arm and now he looked uneasily at his hands to see if reaching into the flames in his dream had scarred him, had burned him for real, but thankfully, they looked okay.

The pain was gone.

The memory was not.

Since he was the captain, his teammates were waiting for him outside the bus.

Daniel tried to act like everything was fine, but noticed that his hand was shaking as he followed his coach and led the guys into Coulee High for the game.

CHAPTER FIVE

People talk about being in the zone, and they're right. It happens. It's a real thing.

There's a time to tinker with your shot and there's a time to just play the game. During practice you can tweak things, adjust your hand position on the ball, work on your form, but in the game you need to respond to what's happening on the court.

As soon as you start focusing on the technical aspects of your game rather than just being present and trusting your preparation, you'll be distracted.

But when you're in the zone, things flow naturally. You get into a groove; you respond without thinking. The noise of the crowd is there in the background, there at the edge of your awareness, but it becomes something that you somehow do notice and don't notice at the same time.

The game becomes the center of everything.

Tonight, despite the nightmarish dream of that girl, despite how things were starting to get weird again, Daniel was in the zone.

But the rest of the starters were not.

Coach tried different combinations of bringing in guys off the bench, but at halftime Beldon was down by eight.

In the locker room he didn't yell at them—not his style—but instead he told them they were too tense. "Pressure them in the back court. Set good picks. Don't get rattled. Execute your plays and we'll catch these guys."

The second half got off to a good start for Beldon.

They came back and even went ahead, extending their lead to six.

But Coulee played hard and powered past them again, until with one minute to go, Beldon trailed by four.

Daniel nailed a three-pointer from just above the top of the key to bring them within one, but Coulee scored on a lob to their post player.

Down by three.

Twenty seconds to go.

Daniel brought the ball up the court, faked left, drove the lane and when the defense collapsed, he kicked the ball out to Stephen who fired but missed, clanging a rushed fifteen footer off the rim.

Coulee snagged the rebound and was trying to eat up some time bringing the ball up the court, but Beldon pressured them. Raymond Keillor, Beldon's off guard, fouled their ball handler, putting him on the line—one and one.

Beldon's side of the gym went silent as Coulee's crowd erupted with cheers.

Twelve seconds to go.

The guy sank the first, but missed the second.

Stephen launched the rebound to Daniel who pushed up the ball.

Down by four.

Eight seconds.

Unless he could get fouled shooting a three, it was a two possession game so they needed to score.

Now.

A Coulee player who liked to try to block shots was guarding Daniel a little too closely and he decided to go for it, to try and draw the foul and stop the clock. With five seconds left he pulled up to shoot and, as the guy went for the block, Daniel fired, drew the foul, and managed to bury the three.

The foul meant he would be shooting one free throw, giving him a chance to tie the game.

The roar of the crowd edged in on his attention, but he closed his eyes and slid it aside.

Two seconds on the clock.

He just needed to sink this free throw, send the game into overtime and take things from there.

Daniel positioned himself with his toe an inch behind the nail that they put in the middle of the free throw line in every gym to let players know where the center of it is.

Eyed the basket.

The ref handed him the ball and started to count off the seconds—Daniel had ten to take the shot.

As he was taking a couple dribbles to get into his rhythm, out of the corner of his eye, he glimpsed the girl who'd been burned alive.

She was standing beside the end of the bleachers, a scorched, living corpse. She had one hand raised and was pointing at Daniel like she'd done in the field.

Somehow he heard her voice cut through the noise of the Coulee fans who were shouting to try to distract him from his shot: "You can't let him get away with it."

His heart squirmed inside him and he turned toward her to get a better look—he couldn't help it—but when he did, she was gone. He scanned that side of the gym, but everything looked fine. No dead girl.

You're imagining it.

She's not real.

Focus!

You need to hit this free throw.

He'd lost track and didn't know how many seconds had elapsed, but he figured he had less than five left.

He lined up his shot, but found himself thinking about the mechanics of it—keeping his elbow in, arch, rotation, palm off the ball, left hand there to guide the shot . . .

And thinking about the girl.

Letting out a deep breath, he brought the ball up just past his face and released the same way he'd done so many thousands of times in practice.

Even before the ball reached the rim he knew it wasn't going to go in.

As he watched it arc toward the hoop it was as if time slowed. He needed to wait until it hit the rim before he could go for the rebound, but as he tracked the ball's trajectory, something clicked in that hidden part of his brain, that math part, that part that calculated things—so many things—instantaneously, subconsciously. Instinct took over and he anticipated the trajectory the ball was going to take when it bounced off the rim.

It hit and he went for it. The Coulee player in front of him didn't box him out like he should have, and Daniel spun past him, found his way to the left side of the crowded lane, leapt, caught the ball just outside the block and, twisting in the air, put it up again before landing.

The buzzer sounded.

The ball glanced gently off the glass.

And went in.

Final score: 61 to 60.

Beldon on top.

Their side of the gym went crazy and the guys on Daniel's team rushed him, slapped him on the shoulder or fist-bumped him, congratulating him.

But he was only half paying attention because he was also scrutinizing the gym to see if the girl would appear again.

She wasn't real. Just like Emily wasn't real at that Homecoming football game.

She's not here.

But even if that were true, it didn't mean he wouldn't see her again. When he had these blurs, reality had very little to do with what he was experiencing.

He wasn't certain of it, but at least it'd *seemed* like he was asleep when he saw her on the bus ride to the game. He could write that off as a nightmare, but now, here in the gym, things were different because he'd seen her while he was *awake*.

Very awake.

Yeah. Things were getting worse.

Daniel had always been more concerned with putting hash marks in the win column than with worrying about stats, but his mind couldn't help but keep track of numbers and he knew, even without looking at the stat sheet, that he'd ended the game with eight assists, thirty-two points and three rebounds.

He'd definitely been in the zone—that is, until the girl who'd burned up alive had appeared to him.

Before heading to the locker room, he touched base with Kyle, Nicole, and Mia and they agreed to meet at Kyle's house at ten. Since Kyle didn't live too far from school, where Daniel had left his car, that sounded doable.

Curfew wasn't a major deal to Daniel's dad when there was no school the next day, but still, he typically wanted him home by midnight and Daniel did his best not to push things.

So, when he texted his dad the score, he also let him know he was planning to hang out with his friends, but that he would be home by twelve.

After showering and changing, Daniel was on his way down the hall from the locker room when he saw a man leaning against the wall near the school's trophy case. As he approached him, the guy looked his way, took a step toward him, and extended his hand.

"Nice game, Daniel."

Daniel shook his hand. "Thanks."

He couldn't remember ever meeting this man before and it was a little weird that he'd called him by name, but on the other hand, anyone watching the game could've found out who he was just by listening to the announcer.

He looked like he might be in his early thirties, had black, carefully combed hair, and a fiercely strong handshake.

Then the meeting was over. That was it. The guy was turning to go and Daniel was on his way, but a few seconds later he glanced back to get another look at him.

The man was gone.

Daniel paused.

It was possible that he might have slipped out another door, or hurried down the hallway and gone back to the gym, but it seemed unlikely. He would have had to really be moving.

A troubling thought hit Daniel: What if that man hadn't actually been there?

It wouldn't be the first time you've had a conversation with someone who wasn't real.

No—you shook his hand. If he was just in your mind you wouldn't have been able to touch him.

Outside the school, Daniel and the rest of the team piled into the bus.

He made sure he didn't fall asleep on the ride back to Beldon.

CHAPTER SIX

Daniel picked up his car from the parking lot and cruised over to Kyle's house.

Nicole hadn't arrived yet, but Mia had.

Tonight she wore torn skinny jeans and a faded Kurt Cobain T-shirt. Lank and willowy, she made it work. With her studded tongue and pierced lip she had an edgy look to her, but it was more emo than goth.

She pointed at him. "You, son, were smokin' tonight."

"Thanks."

"Yeah." Kyle was shaking some Tabasco sauce onto a bowl of cheese curls sitting on the coffee table. "You have mad skills, my friend."

"I should've hit that free throw, though. And I think that's enough Tabasco sauce."

Kyle gave the bottle one more hefty shake, set it down—then picked it up and dolloped a little more on before setting it down for good. "It was better this way—didn't go into overtime."

"That is true."

He offered Daniel some of the cheese curls.

"I'm good."

Mia declined as well, and Kyle shrugged and dug into them by himself.

Daniel assumed that Kyle's four-year-old sister, Michelle, was asleep down the hall. His mom had the TV on softly in her own bedroom, but came to the living room to say hi to Daniel. "I couldn't make it to the game, but Kyle said you played great."

"I'm just glad we won."

"Of course."

Kyle's dad had been killed in a car accident a couple years ago. Recently, his mom had started dating someone from the real estate company she worked at. Daniel didn't know how serious it was, but she seemed genuinely happy for the first time since her husband died, and he was glad she'd found someone.

Mrs. Goessel returned to her room and while Daniel and his friends waited for Nicole, Kyle noted that the curlazoids were much better with the Tabasco sauce.

"Curlazoids?" Daniel said.

"It's a new linguistics thing I've been working on. Just add 'azoid' to any noun or 'ify' to any verb. Voilà. Instant avant-garde word."

"So, you're saying that in basketball you could shootify a shotazoid?"

"Precisely."

"That's weird."

"Who knows. It might just catch on."

"Also," Mia added, "you could add 'anate,' or 'ification'—like, 'disqualifyanate,' or 'disqualifyification.'"

"So"—Daniel was thinking aloud—"digestify, digestanate, or digestification."

She nodded. "But not digestazoid."

"Definitely not," Kyle agreed.

"You two were meant for each other," Daniel said.

The conversation wandered briefly toward school and how glad they were that vacation was finally here. Mia mentioned Christmasazoid, which was just around the corner, and Daniel asked them what they were doing. Kyle replied, "Michelle, Mom and I are sticking around here. I guess Glenn is coming over."

"Is that the guy your mom's seeing?"

"Yeah. Glenn Kramer."

Daniel couldn't tell from his friend's tone of voice if he was excited about the prospect of spending Christmas with Glenn or not. "What is it?"

"Nothing. It's just . . . Well, I'm sick of him talking about his gun collection. I get it. He's into collecting antique firearms. It's this huge deal to him. Anyway." He waved his hand through the air as if he were erasing what he'd just said. "Whatever."

Mia said, "We're taking off to visit my grandma and grandpa in Eau Claire. I guess we're leaving Monday morning and coming back Wednesday around noon. Should be alright—as long as there's no more snow."

"I still can't believe you don't like snow." Kyle was working his way through the bowl of cheese curls. Halfway gone.

50

"Believe it."

"I'm just saying, living up here in the Great White North you gotta love snow. How can you not love snow? Inuit people, Eskimos, you know, they have dozens of words for snow."

"I heard that was just an urban legend sort of thing."

"One way to find out." Kyle pulled out his phone and did a quick search. "Okay. This one anthropologist figured out that different branches of their language really do have dozens of different words for snow. Even better: one group of people in Russia, the Sami, they have more than a hundred words for snow. So, there you go."

"Well, I have one word for it," Mia said.

"What's that?"

"Annoying. If God had wanted people to be outside in the winter he would've covered us with fur."

Kyle licked some cheese granules off his orange fingers. "You ever see Jason Berring's back? I saw him in the locker room after PE and I think God definitely made him for playing in the snow."

"Ew. Now see, that's just wrong."

A car pulled into the driveway.

While Daniel had been listening to Kyle and Mia, the nightmare of the girl bursting into flames hadn't left him alone.

Last fall, when the blurs started, he'd found that his subconscious was remembering things, piecing together what his conscious mind wasn't even aware of.

It was almost like an untapped part of his brain was rifling through the vast amount of information that sweeps past us each day, noticing things that no one else was noticing and then revealing them to him through the blurs.

He tried to figure out what the girl in the nightgown had been referring to when she said, "You have to stop him before it happens again," and "You can't let him get away with it."

Stop who?

Get away with what?

"You okay?" Kyle said.

Daniel looked up to see both of his friends staring at him. "Huh?"

"You zoned out there for a minute."

"I'm good." He went for some of the remaining cheese curls, carefully choosing ones that were not quite so Tabasco-sauceafied.

A car door closed and a few seconds later Nicole appeared in the living room doorway and motioned for Daniel to join her outside. "There's something I want to show you."

"What is it?"

"It's a surprise, silly. C'mon."

CHAPTER SEVEN

The night sky was clear of clouds, and even with the moonlight, this far out in the country the stars were bright. From where they stood he could see the sky in three directions but north was hidden from view by the house.

"What do you want to show me?"

By the light of the porch nearby, his breath was visible.

"Come here." She took his hand and led him around the side of the house where they had a clear view of the northern sky. "Look up."

He did.

Flickering green streaks shifted and shimmered high above them in the silent sky as the Northern Lights danced across the heavens. Elegant.

Mysterious.

Beautiful.

In this part of the state, especially without light pollution from being near a bigger city, you could see the aurora borealis pretty well, and the best time to check them out was in the winter.

Faint bluish and yellowish streaks flicked briefly before disappearing, but the rolling ribbons of green light remained there, whipping and curling through the sky as if they were alive.

"They're stunning," Nicole said softly. She was still holding Daniel's hand.

Which was okay by him.

"You know what causes them?" he asked.

"Doesn't it have something to do with the earth's magnetic poles?"

"That might be part of it, but from what my dad said, they're caused by electrically charged particles colliding. They come from the sun and hit particles in the earth's atmosphere."

Nicole eased closer to him. It was barely noticeable. Barely—but he could tell.

Also not a problem.

"So, when the two of them come together," she said, "sparks fly."

"Yes."

Okay, some more symbolism there that no one needed to point out to him.

The night embraced them and time meant nothing as they stood there beneath the ethereal beauty of the Northern Lights.

At last, the shivering braids of light faded away and the stars and the moon had the sky to themselves.

For a long moment neither Daniel nor Nicole said anything, then finally, still holding his hand, she led him out onto the lawn. "Make a snow angel with me."

"Well, you know, I'm not really a snow angel kind of guy. I'm more into snow snakes."

"Snow snakes? How do you make them?"

"I'll show you in a sec. First, you go ahead with the angel."

Nicole laid on her back on the blanket of snow covering the yard, with her feet together and her arms out to the side, then flared her legs out and drew her arms above her head and back down to brush the snow aside.

Then, she pushed herself to her feet and the two of them looked at the impression she'd left in the snow. Where she'd moved her arms it looked like wings; where she'd moved her legs it looked like a dress or gown.

"Okay," she said. "Let's see your snow snake."

"It's not just any snow snake. It's a snow *anaconda*."

"Oh." She was acting impressed. "Now you've got me curious."

Daniel walked forward, dramatically pulling one foot through the snow in a slithery pattern for about fifteen feet. Then he swept the snow aside at the end to make the head a little wider than the rest of the snake.

"That's it?"

"It's harder than it looks."

"Really."

"Yup. There's an art to it."

"An art to dragging your foot across the ground?"

"Takes years of practice."

"Is that so?"

"Maybe I can teach you—if you're willing to work with me, put in the long hours of practice."

"Hmm." She joined him near the snow anaconda's head. "And I would have to spend all that time under your tutelage?"

"Sounds like a Kyle word."

"Busted."

"So?"

"I might be able to *force* myself to do it."

"Is that so?"

"Mm-hmm."

Stillness nestled in between them.

Comfortable.

Sparks flying.

There was just enough light from the porch and the moonlight glistening off the snow for him to be able to peer into her eyes.

Gently, he brushed off some snow that had stuck to her hair when she was making the snow angel. "That's better."

"What are you doing?"

"Just taking in the view."

"You're not even looking at the sky."

"No. I'm not."

She didn't look away. Instead, closing her eyes, she nestled in closer for a kiss, but just as she did, the front door popped open and Kyle called, "Hey, kids." Nicole backed up slightly as Kyle and Mia appeared around the side of the house. "I hope we're not interrupting anything."

Actually—

"What's up?" Daniel said.

"Gina's having a party," Mia told them. "She invited us over. You know: a pre-Christmas, post-win sort of thing. We don't have to stay long. We'll just swing by, say hi to everyone and then we can bail. Come on."

Daniel and Nicole, who were both more interested in hanging out here alone beneath the stars, took a little convincing, but finally they agreed and the four of them hopped into Kyle's vintage Mustang and left for Gina Schroeder's house.

PART II
TRACKS IN THE
SNOW

CHAPTER
EIGHT

Nine cars were parked along the road when they arrived. Gina lived near the national forest, between Beldon and the Derthick State Penitentiary, without any neighbors nearby.

Multicolored Christmas tree lights were strung up in the living room. Near the fireplace, a tree was burdened with way too many ornaments, but not quite enough candy canes. A jumble of presents sat beneath it.

A few kids were dancing to the EDM tracks Gina had put on, but most were just hanging around. Some had beers in their hands.

There was a time when the people in Daniel's class had been nervous about the sheriff's son showing up at parties and then turning them in for using or drinking, but that wasn't his thing and tonight his classmates didn't bother to hide their beers when they saw him.

Brad Talbot and Stephanie Mills, who seemed like the most unlikely couple in the school, were on their way hand in hand down the hall toward one of the bedrooms.

It was clear by the atmosphere that Gina's parents were not around.

Though Daniel had sometimes been tempted to drink, with sports and college athletic scholarships on the line, there was just too much at stake if he would've gotten caught. Besides, it wouldn't have gone down that well with the local sheriff.

Gina greeted them near the kitchen. Preppy, a little too chirpy and a little bit tipsy, she gave Mia and then Nicole a friendly half-hug. "It's awesome to see you, girl," she said to Nicole.

"You too."

"What's up, Mia?"

"Life. Love. Terror. Joy. The enigma of existence. The usual."

"Um. Right . . . Good game, Daniel."

"Thanks."

"Hey, Kyle."

"Gina. Thanks for the invite."

"No prob."

At the kitchen table, a few guys were mixing liquid nicotine from e-cigarettes with energy drinks and chugging them.

When they asked Daniel and Kyle if they wanted to get in on some, Kyle reminded them of how this one girl had died from doing that in Milwaukee a couple weeks ago. "Not that that'd ever happen to anyone here, though," he added.

The kids who'd been downing the drinks looked at Kyle, then back at the liquid nicotine. In the end they opted for the energy drinks plain, followed by a beer, instead.

While their girlfriends caught up with Gina, Daniel and Kyle migrated to the basement.

The lights were low and the music not quite as loud as it was upstairs, but it seemed to be throbbing with a deeper, darker beat.

There were more couples here than there'd been up in the living room, apparently searching out the dimmer corners of the house for more privacy to make out.

At the far end of the room, Ty Bell and the three guys who usually tagged along with him had gathered around the couch.

"What are they doing here?" Kyle muttered to Daniel. "I can't imagine Gina would have invited 'em."

"Probably just crashing."

Daniel guessed that if Ty and his three buddies showed up at the door it would be a little intimidating for most people to turn them away, especially for someone like Gina who tried so hard to make everyone happy.

To a certain degree, there are guys like Ty at every school. But in his case, he wasn't just a bully. He had a cold, sadistic streak that intimidated most of the other students, and from what Daniel could tell, even the teachers and administrators.

Ty was a senior and had messed with Daniel a few times over the years, but seemed to have learned his lesson after he pulled a knife and Daniel disarmed him using a move his dad had taught him.

After that, rather than confronting him in person, Ty had resorted to posting stuff online to try to embarrass Daniel.

No big deal.

Daniel could deal with that.

Ty's dad was a game warden so, as it turned out, he and Daniel's father had been working together on trying to solve the wolf poaching problem and, after Ty ended up being the guy who found one of the wolves, setting up the tip hotline.

Daniel and Kyle crossed the room and it only took a moment for him to catch hold of what was going on.

Lisa Scalf, a girl in their class, had passed out and was slumped on the couch. Ty had a black Sharpie marker and was leaning over her, about to write something on her forehead. His friends stood by snickering, with their phones out to take pictures of her.

None of the other kids in the basement seemed ready to confront Ty or stop him.

Daniel could guess some of the phrases Ty might write on Lisa's forehead, but writing on her was only the start of what he imagined Ty and his friends might eventually to do to her if they were left down here with her unconscious like that.

Daniel stepped forward. "Ty, leave her alone."

Ty turned to face him. "Oh. Hello there. Daniel."

"Put down the marker."

Ty offered his friends a sly half-grin and said to Daniel, "Did you get the present I left you?"

"The DVD."

"So you did get it. We all know about your little visits to the shrink."

In a small town it was entirely possible that someone Ty knew had seen Daniel entering or leaving Dr. Fromke's office. Either way, it didn't matter at this point.

"I appreciate the gift," Daniel said. "It's nice to know you were thinking of me, but you're not going to impress me with presents. Besides, I already have a girlfriend."

Ty's eyes became daggers. His hands balled into fists.

Except for Kyle and the guys with Ty, everyone else in the basement eased back, giving them space. More kids pulled out their phones.

"I'm not going to ask you again," Daniel told him. "Step away from her and put down the marker."

"Or what?"

"Or I'll take it from you." He gestured toward the group of people with their phones ready. "And they'll catch it all on video."

Daniel didn't want to fight Ty, but he wasn't about to back down and let him humiliate Lisa.

Ty gazed at the people holding out their phones. For a moment he looked defiant, like he was about to push things further with Daniel, but he must have thought better of it because, instead, he tweaked the marker though the air at Daniel, who caught it just before it would have hit him in the chest.

At last, Ty motioned for his buddies to join him, blew Lisa a mocking kiss, and led his friends up the stairs.

Kyle, who'd been a lifeguard last summer and knew about first aid and CPR, went to wake up Lisa and make sure she wouldn't somehow throw up and choke while she was passed out.

Once Ty was gone, a few of the people in the basement thanked Daniel. Others didn't seem to care and just went back to what they'd been doing in the low lights before the confrontation with Ty had distracted them.

Daniel and Kyle hung around for a little while talking with a few guys from their class, then Daniel checked the time. "I told my dad I'd be home by midnight. We should fly."

On the way back upstairs, Kyle asked Daniel, "What DVD was Ty talking about?"

"Something he left on my hall locker. A copy of an old movie. Somehow he must have found out I've been seeing that psychiatrist."

"What movie was that?"

"*Psycho*."

"I've heard of it, never saw it."

"Me neither, but I think the name speaks for itself."

They found Nicole mingling in the living room and Mia grabbing a smoke outside. After explaining to Gina that they needed to go, they took off for Kyle's house.

Not far from the party, however, they saw that a car had slid off the road. Its front end was wedged into the snowbank that the plows had pushed up along the shoulder.

The guy at the wheel was trying to back onto the road, but his front tires just spun uselessly in the snow.

After parking, Daniel and Kyle approached the driver's door. Daniel tapped on the glass to ask the man if he was okay and if he needed a hand.

He lowered his window.

It was the same guy who'd shaken his hand in the hall-way after the game.

CHAPTER NINE

"Hello, Daniel," he said.

"Hi." Okay. This was weird. "You alright?"

"I'm fine, except my car doesn't want to move. Maybe you two could give me a push?"

"Let me have a couple of your floor mats."

"Floor mats?"

"I'll put them next to the tires. It'll give us the traction you need."

"Oh. Right. Gotcha."

He handed them over.

Daniel had a medium-sized shovel in his trunk to use in case he ever went off the road into the snow. He thought about getting it out, but figured he'd try the floor mats first and see if they did the trick.

He and Kyle positioned the mats as far under the tires as they could, then tromped into the snowbank and leaned their weight against the front bumper. "Okay," Daniel called to the man. "Go for it, but don't overdo it."

He gave the engine some gas to reverse out of the snow and, with the floor mats there for traction and Daniel and Kyle pushing from the front, he was able to get back onto the road again.

Once the car was free, they gave him back the mats and he reached for his wallet. "How much can I give you?"

"No," Daniel said, "you don't have to give us anything. Just glad we could help."

"Are you sure?"

"Yeah."

"Well, thank you. I guess I'll owe you one."

He wasn't quite sure how to respond to that. "We should probably be going."

"Of course. Well, thanks again."

"Sure."

Back in the Mustang, Kyle asked Daniel, "Who was that guy?"

"I have no idea."

"He knew your name."

"Yeah, he congratulated me after the game too, but I've never seen him before tonight."

"Okay, but that's a pretty huge coincidence, though, don't you think?" Mia exclaimed. "I mean, that he would end up in the ditch right ahead of us here, an hour from where you saw him at the game?"

"Yes. It is."

In Kyle's headlights Daniel could see that the car had a Georgia license plate. If the driver was from the south, it might explain why he'd gone into the snowbank on a night when the roads weren't even icy.

But that doesn't explain why he would be driving out here right in front of you.

The man took off into the night.

He made them a little uneasy and they thought it might be best to just avoid him, so at the next intersection, even though it was a little longer, Kyle chose an alternate route home.

On the way, Nicole asked what everyone was up to tomorrow and Kyle told them he had to work at Rizzo's for a couple hours during lunchtime, from eleven to one.

The pizzeria was the best place in northern Wisconsin to get a pepperoni and jalapeño pie, and Rizzo had been teaching Kyle how to toss and spin the dough in the air. It hadn't gone too well so far and Kyle had landed a ton of dough on the floor over the last couple months.

Good thing Rizzo was a patient man.

Kyle mentioned a movie that was opening that weekend. "It's this dystopian fantasy about a world where everyone only gets so long to live. Money's worthless, but you can barter with the time of your life—that's their currency, time. You can buy anything you want, but it costs you a few minutes or hours or years each time. I heard it was pretty good."

"Big news: life is time, time is life," Mia said reflectively. "What you spend on one, you've spent on the other. So it is, so it'll always be."

"Profound," Kyle said. "So you interested?"

She shrugged. "Why not."

Beldon was so small it only had a second-run movie theater, so the four of them decided that driving to Superior or Duluth up on the Lake Superior shore tomorrow night to check out the flick sounded like a plan. It was a little over an hour away, but living out here in the middle of nowhere they were used to the drive.

At Kyle's house, Daniel asked Nicole if she wanted to get together before the movie.

"Sure."

"I'll text you in the morning."

A quick kiss, a quick goodnight, and they were on their way.

With the trip to Gina's house, the extra time spent helping that man out of the snowbank, and the longer route back to Kyle's place, it'd gotten a little later than Daniel had anticipated. He hadn't been keeping a close eye on the time and only after he left Kyle's house did he realize it was already a quarter after twelve.

He texted his dad about what'd happened and figured that, since they were "assisting a stranded motorist," being a few minutes late wouldn't end up being that big of a deal.

CHAPTER
TEN

His father was sitting at the dining room table scrolling through a news feed on his iPad when Daniel arrived home at 12:35.

"Hello, Dan."

"Dad."

"Your text said you were helping someone out of a ditch?"

"Well, the snowbank along the shoulder. We were on our way back to Kyle's house."

"On your way back?"

"We stopped by Gina's."

"Gina's?"

"Yeah. Gina Schroeder."

Tell him it was a party or not?

Probably best if you don't.

"We'd gone over there to hang out for a little while," he explained somewhat ambiguously.

"And this man who hit the bank, he went off the road on a night like this? It wasn't even snowing."

"I guess he must've just lost control of the car."

"Going around a curve, maybe?"

"No. It was on a straightway."

"Well then, he was perhaps braking to avoid hitting a deer or something."

Is he questioning your story? Does he not believe you?

"His plates were from Georgia. Maybe he's not used to driving on snow."

This conversation pooled off into silence.

But it wasn't the comfortable kind.

"But you won?" his dad said.

"Yes."

"And you played well?"

"Yeah. I guess." Daniel didn't really want to give a full rundown of what'd happened, especially regarding why he'd been distracted and missed that free throw.

But at least you were able to put the rebound back in.

Even though his dad knew about the blurs from last fall, Daniel wasn't excited about the idea of letting him know they'd come back. It would've just made him worry.

"I'm glad," his father said, referring to the game.

Daniel thought about asking him if he'd found out anything about the wolves, but decided it might be best to bring things to a close. "So. I should probably be heading to bed."

"You texted me that you were going to be home by twelve."

"Yeah."

"I need you to keep your word, Daniel."

Since he hadn't said anything about him getting home late until now, his blunt words and cold, detached tone surprised Daniel. He wasn't sure what to make of it. "I told you we were helping that guy."

"Yes. But I don't want to wonder if you're going to be home when you tell me."

"Right. I get it."

He didn't realize how defiant his reply probably sounded until it was out and he expected a rebuke, but his dad simply stood and without a word left for his bedroom.

Alright, that was odd. And a little perplexing.

Daniel kind of wished that his dad would've argued with him a little more. He wasn't into the silent treatment so it only made it even more clear that something was up.

Whatever was on his mind, Daniel guessed it was something more than just his son getting home later than he'd said he would.

The last he'd heard, his dad was going to look into the wolf poaching tonight.

Maybe something to do with the case had upset him.

In his room, Daniel found a new plastic bottle full of his medication on his dresser. Apparently, his dad hadn't wasted any time picking it up from the pharmacy before they closed that afternoon.

The blurs are back.

Maybe you should take the meds.

During his first visit to the psychiatrist back in October, the guy had told him that it would take a week or two for the medication to work its way into his system and really be effective, so even if he did start taking them in the morning, they weren't going to solve things right away.

A step in the right direction but not a solution.

Thinking back through all the odd things that'd happened during the day, he got out his English notebook and flipped to the page where he'd written "Lost Cove is the key," over and over.

How could he have done that in this handwriting style? He tried to think of a time he might have seen this handwriting before, and though he had the sense that he might have, he couldn't come up with anything specific.

For whatever reason, most of the time he could tell just by looking at someone's writing if it was done by a guy or a girl.

This looked like a guy's handwriting, but it was definitely not his.

Then whose?

He Googled "Lost Cove is the key" again, just as he'd done at the shrink's office while he was waiting to be seen.

Scrolling through some of the top results he found out there was a town named Lost Cove in North Carolina, a supposed ghost town by that name in Tennessee, and lots of businesses, campgrounds and things like that, but he couldn't see how any of them might be the key to anything that was going on here this week.

And it certainly didn't explain how he was able to write the words down in a style that didn't look anything like his own.

He stared at that page in his notebook.

And as he did, the letters began to change, to wiggle free of the paper and move toward each other, becoming living scribbles, slinking across the page and combining with each other, creating bristling, wormlike creatures that moved swiftly off the notebook and onto his fingers.

He dropped the book, but the dark worms were already on the back of his hand and had started skitching up his wrist.

He swatted at them and managed to squish two of them, but the three remaining ones immediately burrowed into his flesh, sending a sharp, tearing pain up his arm as his skin split open to accept them.

But that wasn't anything compared to the pain he felt as they writhed up his arm, just beneath the skin.

He actually thought about getting a knife and slicing open his arm to dig them out, but then he realized how irrational that was, because the narrow, black worms that were crawling under his flesh could not possibly be real.

No, they could not be.

But they are.

They slid across his biceps.

They can't be!

They are!

At last, the ridges flattened out and the creatures worked their way into the muscles of his shoulder.

He waited to see if they would return, to see if there was any pain from them inside him, but there wasn't.

At first.

But then he felt them at the base of his neck, squirming, entering the back of his throat.

Gagging, Daniel rushed toward the bathroom, but didn't make it in time and he was in the hallway when he felt them curling and crawling on his tongue. He spat them out onto the floor.

Three dark, glistening worms dropped from his mouth.

He stomped on them as they wriggled across the carpet trying to get away, but when he lifted his foot they were gone.

Last fall when the blurs started, he'd been able to tell when he was going to have one because of the piercing headaches that came first—like earlier tonight with the blur of the girl in the nightgown. Now, however, he was losing touch with reality without any warning at all.

Not a good sign.

In his bedroom again, he picked up the notebook.

All the words were still there on the page.

Enough of this.

Rooting through his camping gear in the closet, he found a box of matches.

He ripped out the page with that weird handwriting on it and held it above his empty trash can, then lit a match and touched the flame to the bottom corner of the page.

As the paper caught fire, he thought of that girl again, the one wearing the white nightgown, the one who'd burned up before his eyes and then disintegrated into flecks of black embers that drifted away into the air.

Daniel discarded the paper in the trash can and watched it flicker and burn and turn to black ash.

He dug the *Psycho* DVD out of his school backpack and tossed it into the can on top of the ashes from the notebook page, which fluttered up around the DVD case, then settled back over it, as if it were a coffin that'd been dropped into a grave and they were the dirt that was being tossed down to cover it.

He opened his window briefly to air out the room so his dad wouldn't smell the smoke. Then, checking his phone, he took a few minutes to reply to a couple texts, including one from Nicole telling him goodnight again, and one from Kyle asking if his dad was mad that he'd gotten home late.

Just as he was finishing up replying, he received a new text: *Check the basement—M.*

M.

Madeline.

An unsettling thought came to him: *Is someone waiting for you down there? Is she here?*

Daniel felt a tight twist of discomfort in his chest.

He briefly thought about telling his dad what was going on, but then decided against it since he would've just asked who Madeline was and why on earth she would be inviting Daniel to look in their basement at this time of night. Besides, he'd seemed agitated earlier and Daniel didn't want to push things right now or have to get into explaining everything that was happening.

So, going alone, Daniel grabbed a baseball bat, went to the kitchen, opened the door to the basement, flicked on the lights.

And started down the steps.

CHAPTER ELEVEN

At the bottom of the stairs, in the rec room where he had his weights set up, he listened carefully for any sound, any indication that someone else might be here, but heard nothing.

He checked the bathroom, the spare bedroom, and the area around the fuse panel and the washer and dryer, but found no sign of anything out of the ordinary. Nothing out of place.

No one was there.

No one was waiting for him.

Only one place left to check—the storage space beneath the stairs.

There was probably just enough room for someone to stand in there between the shelves and the door.

He tightened his grip on the baseball bat.

And opened the door.

From the light that found its way past him, he could see that the space was empty, except for four cardboard boxes piled on the floor.

A thought: *It's here.*

What is?

What you're looking for.

He pulled on the drawstring to turn on the light bulb inside the closet-sized area.

Daniel wasn't sure which box to look in, or even what he was looking for, but he leaned the baseball bat against the wall and opened the top box.

Clothes that didn't fit anymore.

The second box held some old, well-worn baseball gloves and baseballs that he and his dad had put to good use before he started to focus on football and basketball a few years ago.

The third, Halloween and Thanksgiving decorations his mom used to hang up when she was living with them and the holidays rolled around.

The final box contained a pile of maps that he and his dad had collected over the years from hunting, camping, and fishing trips.

For some reason that he couldn't put his finger on, he felt like he needed to take a closer look, and he began to flip through them.

There were topos of the Wind River Range in Wyoming where they'd gone backpacking last summer; fishing maps of the flowage leading from Lake Algonquin, the biggest local lake; and even a nautical map that showed the location of shipwrecks on the Lake Superior shore about an hour away.

None of those caught his attention, but a topographical map of the nearby national forest did.

He studied it, evaluating the area, the places surrounding it, and comparing that to where the dead wolves had been found.

There was a research station—the Traybor Institute—that'd been built near the edge of the forest that surrounded Waunakee Lake. He wasn't certain what they did there. He'd heard something about fish population management studies.

The place was pretty new, just put up in the fall, and it wasn't on the map, but the location fit. It was right in the middle of the sites where the poached wolves had been found.

You're going to hang out with Nicole tomorrow. You can check it out with her.

Back in his bedroom, Daniel thought about the girl with the tears of blood, the one who'd told him that Madeline was waiting.

He wondered about the wolves and the map and the texts, and the man he'd never met before who just happened to drive into the snowbank in front of them.

What did it mean? What did any of it mean?

Did it have something to do with that research station?

It wasn't like math, where logic and clear reasoning led to the answers. This was more like unriddling a dream, with only hints and images, vague clues that didn't lead to anything concrete.

Not exactly his thing.

The blurs he'd had last fall had been about a girl who'd died.

No, not just died—a girl who'd been murdered.

Did someone else die? Was someone else murdered?

This time around, he didn't just need to figure out what the blurs meant, but what crime they might be helping him solve.

Eventually, after failing to come up with anything, Daniel changed for bed, lay down and, even though he suspected that he wouldn't be able to sleep very well with so much on his mind, he did fall asleep.

But when he woke up it wasn't morning. It was still the middle of the night.

And he was standing in his dad's bedroom, holding a hunting knife, staring down at his sleeping father.

CHAPTER TWELVE

Pale moonlight slanted through the window and landed on the foot of the bed, but lit his dad's room well enough for Daniel to see him lying on his side, turned toward the wall.

The knife's blade shone in the moonlight, sleek and hungry in the night.

Hungry for blood.

Blood.

No!

Yes, Daniel. Yes.

He stumbled backward and smacked into the dresser, bumping it hard enough to send a picture tumbling off the top.

As it hit the floor, the glass shattered.

His father woke with a start, sitting up, instantly alert; scrutinizing the room for what'd awakened him.

Daniel hid the knife behind his leg.

"Dan?" his dad gasped. "What are you doing in here?"

"Sleepwalking," he muttered. "I must have been sleepwalking."

It wasn't the first time he'd walked in his sleep. Besides doing it once when he was a kid, it'd happened last fall when everything was going on with Emily and the blurs. One night he'd gone outside in a storm and dug up the body of their pet dog who'd been hit by a car three months earlier. But later, when he woke up in bed, drenched and muddy, he'd had no memory of digging up Akira.

In fact, he hadn't found out what he'd done until the next morning when his dad discovered the dog's body on the hood of his car.

Daniel knew that his father kept a handgun beside his bed in the drawer of a small end table and right now he was just glad he hadn't gone for it. That would not have turned out well for either of them.

His dad flicked on his bedside light. Glass shards glinted up at Daniel from the floor all around his bare feet.

Keeping the knife hidden, he stared at the broken glass.

A knife. Why do you have a knife?

His heart was hammering and he felt overcome by a caustic kind of fear.

Typically, his dad kept the flip-flops that he wore around the house beside his bed, and now he slipped them on and stood. "Don't move. I don't want you stepping on any of that glass. I'll grab a broom and a dustpan."

He disappeared into the hallway and Daniel dropped the knife behind the dresser where his father wouldn't see it and where he could retrieve it in the morning.

What's going on?

You're starting to lose it.

You're—

His dad returned, swept up the broken glass, and emptied it in the bathroom trash can.

"So you're okay?" he asked.

"I'm good."

"Get some sleep." It didn't seem like a command. It sounded like the words were spoken more out of concern than anything else.

"Okay."

After climbing back into bed, Daniel closed his eyes but couldn't sleep. His mind just kept replaying what had happened.

It's getting worse.

You need to start taking that medication before it's too late. Before you do something you'll regret. Something that can't be undone.

Although he wasn't sure it would make much of a difference, he locked his bedroom door, located his backpacking tent in his closet, untied one of the ropes from the rainfly, looped one end around his ankle, and tied the other end to the bed frame.

He made sure the knot was secure enough so that he wouldn't be able to untie it in his sleep. That way, if he did sleepwalk again, the rope would stop him from going into his dad's room.

But in the end, none of that mattered because he hardly slept at all.

He just lay there thinking about waking up in his dad's bedroom holding that knife, and hearing that voice in his head telling him that the knife was hungry for blood.

CHAPTER THIRTEEN

After untying the rope from his ankle, Daniel stowed it with his camping gear.

He couldn't get the whole deal with the knife out of his head.

Why on earth would you have done that? What could have led you to get that knife, to go into your dad's room like that? What were you going to do with it in there?

He waited until he heard the shower start in the bathroom before slipping into his dad's bedroom, then he gently eased the dresser to the side and located the hunting knife.

The blade was designed specifically for cutting through muscle and flesh. It was the one he used to gut deer.

Nicole had never been too excited about him hunting, but without an adequate number of natural predators in the state, the deer population needed to be culled or problems with overpopulation—specifically disease—could decimate the herd.

She knew this, of course she did, and the last thing she wanted was for the deer to suffer, but still, she hadn't warmed up to the idea of anyone shooting them—let alone her boyfriend.

The running water in the bathroom's shower stopped.

Daniel slid the dresser back in place, returned to his bedroom, and replaced the knife in its sheath in his closet.

He was halfway through with breakfast when his dad joined him in the kitchen. "You're up early for a Saturday."

"I didn't sleep so well."

His dad went for some bagels and an apple. "Do you remember sleepwalking last night?"

"I remember waking up in your bedroom." He left it at that.

"You knocked over a picture. I was concerned you might step on the glass."

"No, I'm fine."

"I have to say, you startled me. You feeling alright?"

"Yeah. Sorry about that."

"No need to apologize. I'm just glad you're okay."

"I'm a little tired, but I'm good." After a few spoonfuls of cereal he said, "You told me once that I walked in my sleep after Grandpa died."

"Yes."

"You said that you asked me what I was doing and when I answered you, I told you that I was going to find him."

"That's right."

"What happened then?"

"We led you back to your room and put you to bed."

"Did I say anything else?"

"You said you were going to save him before they came."

"To save him? But it was too late for that."

"Yes. It was."

"And before who came?"

"I don't know. You were asleep, mumbling in your sleep. I'm not sure it meant anything at all."

Daniel couldn't figure out if that had anything to do with what was going on now or not. "Did you find out anything yesterday about the wolf poaching?"

"The ballistics came back. The same gun was used to fire all the shots that've killed the wolves so far. A .30 caliber; boat-tail hollow-point bullets." His dad took a seat at the table. "So what are your plans for today?"

"I'm meeting up with Nicole, and then later this afternoon we were thinking about checking out a movie in Superior with Kyle and Mia."

"Listen, I snapped at you last night. I'm sorry. It's just that there's a lot going on. I should've cut you some slack."

"Yeah, no. It's cool. It's fine. Did they find another wolf?"

"No. But I'd say four is plenty."

"Do you have to work today?"

He nodded. "I should be home by six."

After breakfast, Daniel took the bottle of meds that his dad had gotten for him yesterday and went into the bathroom.

He shook two pills into his hand.

They're going to help you, Daniel. They're going to make things better, get things back to normal.

But then another voice: *Things aren't ever going to get back to normal. Not after last fall. Everything has changed and there's no going back.*

He nudged the pills around his palm.

No going back.

Take them, Daniel.

No. Get rid of them.

Daniel was aware that everyone hears voices in their heads. We all carry on imaginary conversations, reframing what happened and thinking of clever comebacks after the fact. And it's not just that: our consciences dog us and afflict us and ghost-words from long dead insults and cheap shots haunt us. Sometimes for a lifetime.

But this was different. These weren't just words whispering through his mind. It was almost like one of the voices was coming from outside his head, as if he were hearing it spoken from another person altogether.

I'm real, Daniel. I am. You can listen to me and I'll tell you what you need to do.

Then the voice inside his head replied: *No, you're not. You're just an illusion, one that I hear.*

I'm just as real as your conscience, as your dreams, as your memories. Everyone hears voices, Daniel.

But you're not real. I know you're not.

You can hear me. You can talk to me. What makes me less real than someone you can see?

Because they're really there.

If I wasn't real, you wouldn't be able to hear me. If I wasn't real, why would you be arguing with me?

Conflicted, Daniel stared at the two pills.

His thoughts continued to go back and forth, shifting, tilting, turning into an argument with himself.

If it was going to be a week or two until the medication kicked in, even if he did take these now, it wasn't going to change things for a while.

He walked over to the toilet, just as he'd done so many times in the past couple months, to flush the two pills—always two at a time, never the whole bottle, just in case his dad happened to check his meds.

However, taking them would at least *start to* help. That was the thing. Everything had been getting weirder and weirder since yesterday morning and he needed to reverse that trend as soon as possible before something serious happened.

You need them. You need whatever help you can get.

He poured himself a glass of water, took a gulp, and swallowed the pills.

Daniel told himself that now things would be different, that the incident last night wasn't anything to be concerned about. But, as hard as he tried, he couldn't convince himself that he had carried that knife into his dad's room without any intention of using it.

He needed answers and he needed them before tonight when he would go to sleep again, and perhaps have another nightmare—or worse, go sleepwalking.

And maybe do more than just carry that knife around. Maybe use it.

He texted Nicole, asking her to give him a call when she got a chance and only a few minutes later his phone rang.

"Hey," she said. "What's going on?"

"You're up already?"

"Weird dreams. What about you?"

"I had trouble sleeping. Listen, there's something I want to check out. Can you meet at the parking lot to the trail-head for the Pine River Trail?"

"When?"

"This morning sometime. Ten or so?"

"Done."

"Dress for the weather."

"Are you going to tell me what we're doing?"

"It's a surprise, silly."

"You got that line from me." He could almost hear her smiling.

"That is possible."

Okay, so ten o'clock gave him a little over an hour to look into things before he needed to leave.

He'd been planning on searching for information about wolves to follow up on some ideas he'd had about the poaching, but right now, reading up on sleepwalking seemed like more of a priority.

Last summer he'd heard that there were people who had driven across town in their sleep, had even murdered people while sleeping, and, though it seemed unbelievable, it didn't take him long to find information online to confirm it.

He found himself reading account after account of people who'd done strange things while they were asleep: cooking meals, tweeting meaningful messages, swimming across a lake, and yes, even killing people.

Just the thought that it was *possible* to murder someone while you were asleep made him never want to go to sleep again.

How can you fight something like that? How can you control what you do while you're sleepwalking?

When he checked the time, he saw that it was already past nine forty and he needed to get moving if he was still going to make it to the Pine River trailhead by ten.

He texted Nicole that he was on his way, tugged on his winter boots, grabbed his coat, hat and gloves, and took off.

CHAPTER FOURTEEN

Though still covered with snow, the trail was flattened out and packed down by people cross-country skiing on it.

As they hiked, Daniel debated whether or not to tell Nicole about what he'd written in his notebook, or about the girl with the tears of blood, or especially about waking up in his dad's room holding that deer-gutting knife.

She already knew about the blurs he'd had last fall so it wasn't like any of this would be a complete shock to her. But still, the things that'd been happening to him over the past twenty-four hours were getting more and more disturbing and he didn't want to frighten her or make her worry about him.

In the end he decided that maybe she would be able to help him sort things out.

"Nicole, I walked in my sleep last night."

"Did you . . . I mean . . ."

"No. I didn't try to dig up any dead animals. I ended up in my dad's bedroom. He woke up while I was standing there. It freaked him out pretty bad."

"Yeah, no kidding."

She listened quietly as he summarized what'd been going on with the visions of the girl in the white nightgown, the one who'd burned up. For the time being he didn't mention the knife or the texts from Madeline.

"I think the blurs are trying to tell me something," he said. "Like part of my mind is working through things and then trying to . . . Well . . ."

"Reveal answers to you."

"Yes."

"Like with Emily last fall."

"Exactly."

"But answers to what?"

"That's the thing—I don't know."

He still wasn't sure he wanted to bring up that knife.

Move into the topic slowly.

"This morning I was doing research on homicidal sleepwalking—it's when someone who's sleepwalking kills another person."

"Why?"

"Why would they kill someone?"

"No, why were you researching it?"

"Because of . . . Well, because I wanted to find out if I might hurt someone while I was sleeping."

"But homicidal sleepwalking? That's crazy."

"I know, but it actually does happen, usually between family members. One time in England this guy strangled his wife in his sleep and when he woke up he had no memory of it. He was found not guilty of murder. Another guy threw his daughter out a window. Then this one woman—"

"Okay, I get it. I don't want to hear any more. It's kind of disturbing."

"Right."

"And so all this scares you? Is that it? I mean, considering that you've started sleepwalking again?"

"Yes. It does."

They both walked in silence for a little while, then Daniel finally said, "So the scariest thing is: How can you stop yourself from doing something terrible while you're sleeping? I mean, if you're not even conscious of it happening, you could climb out of bed, murder someone, crawl back into bed and wake up and not remember any of it."

"I don't think you need to worry about any of that happening."

Tell her about the knife.

No.

Yes. You can trust her.

No, she'll be afraid of you. You'll scare her.

When he didn't reply she reiterated. "Really, Daniel. You would never do anything terrible in your sleep."

You need to tell her. Go ahead.

"Nicole, last night when I woke up in my dad's bedroom I was holding a knife."

"What?"

"I was holding a knife. A hunting knife."

"So that's why you were looking up the stuff on homicidal sleepwalking."

"Yes."

"You would never hurt him, Daniel. You wouldn't hurt anyone. I just don't believe a person could do that, harm someone—or especially not kill 'em—unless that's part of you, unless there's something inside of you—I don't know, I mean without some hatred or anger or something like that motivating you to do it. And that's not you. Not you at all."

Two wolves inside.

Fighting.

Always fighting.

"I'm not so sure," he said. "But I know one thing."

"What's that?"

"We need to figure out why the blurs have started again. And we need to do it before tonight."

"When you go to bed again."

"Yes."

They had to leave the trail to get to where Daniel was planning to take her. After they did, he led her through the woods to the south, toward the Traybor Institute.

There were a few ponds nearby. The lakes and waterways in this part of the state would freeze, not always this early in winter, but it all depended on the weather. Right now, the ice was at that stage where you could probably walk across it safely, but taking a snowmobile or a car out there to go ice fishing would definitely not be a good idea.

"It's not too far," he told her as they bypassed the nearest pond.

They crossed a snowmobile trail that ended at an isolated road that led to a series of cabins encircling Waunakee Lake.

"So, are you going to tell me where we're going or is it still a surprise?" she asked.

At this point he couldn't think of any good reason to keep it from her. "It's that place they built last fall over on the edge of the forest, you know, that research station."

"Why are we going there?"

"I was looking through some maps last night and it got me thinking."

"Go on."

He still hadn't told her about the mysterious texts he'd been receiving. Everything else so far involved what he had been doing or thinking, but the messages involved someone else, because obviously someone was sending them to him.

The text last night led him to the basement.

It'll hurt her feelings if she finds out about the texts. She'll wonder who Madeline is. She'll wonder if there's something going on between you and another girl.

"It's kind of a long story," he said. "But this one map made me think of that institute. I'm wondering if it has something to do with the wolf poaching."

"Why would you think that?"

"After it was built, maybe a month or so later, the wolves started getting killed. Plus, it's located pretty much right in the middle of the area where the wolves are being shot."

They tramped through the snow until they could see the outline of the facility a few hundred feet away through the bare, leafless trees.

Going closer, they found a metal fence surrounding the property. It had a slanted top that was laced with razor wire.

"So, do you know what they do here?" Nicole asked.

"Fish management studies. That's what I heard."

"A fish management place that's surrounded with a razor wire fence?"

"Doesn't make a whole lot of sense, does it?"

"I'm thinking not."

While they stood there, a van from the Wisconsin Department of Corrections rounded the corner of a nearby county road and rumbled toward the building. The gate opened and the vehicle entered the property.

"Okay," Nicole said, "and why would a prison transport van be visiting a fish research facility?"

"I have no idea."

The two of them ducked behind a downed log, but leaned up just enough to watch what was going on.

Two officers—or they might have been prison guards, it was hard to tell—led another man out of the back of the van.

Nicole whispered, "Is that guy in handcuffs?"

"I think so."

"Okay, this is too weird. We should take off."

"They might see us if we do. We need to wait until they're inside."

Daniel recognized one of the cops as the man who'd driven into the snowbank last night, the one who'd congratulated him after the game.

When he and Kyle had gone to help him, Nicole hadn't gotten out of the car so Daniel doubted she would realize who it was. "That guard on the left," he said, "that's the man from last night, the one who went off the road."

"You're kidding."

"No. It's him."

Their conversation was interrupted by a series of deep, guttural growls coming from the other side of the property hemmed in by the fence.

Dark flashes of movement appeared between the trees as four guard dogs barreled toward them.

The officers who were leading their prisoner stopped and stared in Daniel and Nicole's direction, but the two of them quickly slipped behind the log again.

Daniel wasn't sure if they'd made it down fast enough to avoid being seen. He imagined the men coming closer, finding him and Nicole and questioning them, and he tried to think of a good reason why they would be out here hiding behind a log, something he could tell them that would satisfy them, but he couldn't come up with anything that sounded very reasonable.

He waited, waited, waited until he thought maybe the officers would've stopped checking in their direction. When he glanced at Nicole, he saw her staring at him, her eyes wide and nervous.

From the sound of it, the dogs were close.

Slowly, Daniel raised his head just high enough to have a look.

The guards and the prisoner were disappearing into the facility's front door, but the dogs had arrived and leapt at the fence, snapping and clawing at it.

"Okay. Time to go," he told Nicole. "Before someone comes to see what's up with those dogs."

They retraced their steps through the snow and were almost back to the Pine River Trail when a gunshot echoed through the air.

It didn't come from the facility, but rather from the other side of a hill just to their left.

CHAPTER FIFTEEN

Daniel scanned the forest to see if he could locate the person who'd fired the gun. Though he couldn't see anyone, to really get a good look he would need to climb the hill and search the woods nearby.

"Is it hunting season?" Nicole asked uneasily.

"Maybe for turkey and small game, but that sounded like a rifle, not a shotgun." If someone was rifle hunting, the shot could have been taken from a hundred or more yards away—depending on how good a shot the person was.

"And there aren't any shooting ranges around here," she said.

"Not even close."

"So. Poaching."

"Yeah. Maybe. Probably."

"What do you think we should do?"

"I guess we should check it out—at least take a quick look and see if we can catch sight of the shooter."

"Do you think that would be safe? Looking around, I mean?"

"As long as we're careful."

"But if the person who fired the gun really is poaching wolves, he certainly won't want to be caught."

"You're thinking he might fire at us?"

She was quiet.

If Daniel had been by himself he might have been a little more apt to poke around, but with Nicole here he realized he didn't want to take any chances. "Good point."

They skirted along the base of the hill. No one appeared; no more shots were fired.

They hadn't gone far before they found the trail of frothy blood in the snow.

It was still fresh and was paralleling a set of wolf tracks.

"Oh, no." Nicole's voice was ripe with sadness. "Please, no."

From Daniel's deer hunting trips with his dad, he knew that the frothy blood meant the animal had been hit in the lungs. Most likely a kill shot.

He studied the woods in front of them for any sign of the wolf, then looked back to see if the person who'd taken the shot might be following the blood trail. He didn't see the animal, and the forest behind them was empty.

Nicole looked at him. "We should follow the tracks to see if it's okay."

"I don't think it's going to be okay, Nicole." The tracks disappeared into a thick stand of pines that he couldn't see very far into. "That wolf is probably dying. We really don't want to be close to it right now. There's no telling how it might react."

"We'll keep our distance then. I need to see it, Daniel."

When she persisted he finally gave in. "Alright, I guess we can walk around those pines, see if it left the other side. But we're not going in there. I don't mind us keeping our distance—like you said—but I don't want to startle a dying wolf up close."

"Okay." She'd already started on her way. "Come on."

Silently, they traversed the pine grove, giving the shadow-riddled stretch of forest a wide berth.

They arrived at the other side just in time to see the wolf die.

CHAPTER
SIXTEEN

The wolf was lying at the edge of the pines and, based on the location of the smear of blood on her fur, Daniel could tell that he'd been right: she'd been shot in the chest.

She was breathing shallowly and it was clear that she wasn't in any state to attack them, so he and Nicole edged closer until they were about twenty feet away.

The wolf lifted her head slightly and stared in their direction, but she didn't growl.

It was unsettling how quietly she died.

One moment her eyes appeared keen and alert. And then, the next, as her head slumped back to the ground, they were simply staring blankly, unblinkingly at the forest around her.

Alive one moment.

Gone the next.

Just like that.

Daniel and Nicole waited for a few minutes in the still day, almost as a way of honoring the wolf's death, before going to her side.

Nicole took off her mitten and petted the dead wolf gently, stroking her fur, but being careful to keep her hand away from the blood.

"We're going to find out who did this," she vowed softly, but there was iron in her voice. "They're not going to get away with it."

Daniel eyed the area again for any sign that someone might be coming their way, perhaps following the wolf tracks to make sure the animal was dead. He didn't see anyone, but it was always possible the shooter might be coming through the stand of pines just as the wolf had.

He knelt beside Nicole. "We should get back to the car."

As he helped her to her feet, he noticed that the wolf's ear had been tagged, probably by the forest rangers so they could keep track of her and study her movement patterns.

He didn't know how many wolves in the area had been tagged like this, but from what he'd heard, the forest service was trying to tag as many as they could to monitor the wolves' numbers to see if the population was recovering.

"I wonder if the others were too." He didn't realize he'd spoken the words aloud instead of just thinking them until Nicole said, "The others were what?"

"Tagged." He pointed to the wolf's ear. "Like she was."

"You mean the other ones that were shot?"

"Yes."

"What are you thinking?"

"Just an idea." Using his phone, he took a photo of the tag on the wolf's ear. "I mean, I know there are more wolves around these days, but how many do you ever actually see?"

"I don't know. I don't think I've ever seen one in the wild before—but I don't spend as much time in the woods as you do."

"And I've only seen 'em a couple times. Wolves keep to themselves. So how is this person, whoever it is who's shooting them, finding so many in such a short period of time to poach?"

"You're thinking he's shooting ones that've been tagged?" They started back toward the car. "That he's locating them by using the tracking stuff, the GPS or whatever, on the tags?"

"It's a place to start. I think we should tell my dad about this tag."

His father wasn't really into texting, so Daniel went ahead and tried calling him. When he didn't pick up, he left a brief message that they'd found a dead wolf, then asked him to call him back. He sent him the photo of the wolf's tag.

Daniel and Nicole followed the path back to the trailhead. When they got there, he said, "We need to find out whatever we can about the wolf research tagging program."

He suggested that Nicole follow him home, but she explained that she'd forgotten to feed her cat that morning and her parents were gone.

"I need to take care of Harley," she said. "Swing by your place and grab your laptop. Let's meet at my house."

"Works for me. I'll see you in half an hour."

CHAPTER
SEVENTEEN

Nicole's bedroom walls were decorated with bird paintings and posters of ballet dancers. As a *Star Wars* geek she also had posters of Darth Vader and Han Solo, all from the original movies back in the seventies and eighties—not such a big fan of the more recent additions to the series.

On the wall, Darth Vader was inviting Daniel to the dark side of the Force.

Just like that wolf inside of him was doing.

Wolves fighting.

Killing—

—Dying, like the one in the forest today.

Nicole positioned herself on the bed with her back against the wall and propped her laptop on her legs. Her cinnamon-colored cat, Harley, now well fed and content, lounged on a pillow on the floor. Daniel sat on the edge of the bed with his computer on his lap.

"By the way," Nicole said, "I got you a Christmas present."

"I got you one too."

"Really? What is it? No, wait, don't tell me. I don't want to know—yes, I do. I hate surprises—well, not always; sometimes, yes, but—"

"I'm not going to tell you and you won't get it until Christmas. But you're gonna like it."

"I'm sure I will. Don't tell me."

"I won't."

"But I am sorta curious."

"Too bad."

"Good, because I don't want to know anything about it—but I kind of do."

"I know."

As Nicole nestled in among the stuffed animals and dolls that she still unashamedly kept piled beside her pillow, Daniel directed her attention to one of them. "I've never pointed this out to you before, and I don't mean to be Captain Obvious here, but your doll only has one arm."

"Yeah." She picked it up tenderly. "It sort of got loved off over the years. At first my mom tried to fix it—sew it back on, you know—but I just kept carrying her around by that one arm all the time and then it would tear off again. Finally, my mom told me there are people who only have one arm and that Rebecca wasn't any different. She said she was unique and special just like they are."

"That's cool."

"Yeah."

"But you said 'her' and 'she.'"

"Her and she?"

"Yeah, you said you kept carrying her around, that she was special. I would've said 'it.'"

"Her and she, sure, of course. Rebecca's a girl doll. All dolls are boys or girls. You probably had boy dolls."

"Sorry to disappoint you, but I never played with dolls."

"Oh really?"

"Nope. No dolls in the Byers home."

"And what about that Batman doll you have?"

"No, you see, that's not a doll."

"Oh? And what is it?"

"That's a vintage posable action figure toy."

"Uh-huh. A vintage doll."

"Posable action figure toy. Huge difference."

"Riiiiiight."

Okay, definitely time to change the subject. He pointed to a sketchbook sitting on Nicole's desk. "So, have you done any new ones?"

"A couple."

"Can I see them?"

"Um . . ."

From what he'd discovered in the past, Nicole didn't think she was very good at her line drawings and hadn't been all that forthcoming with showing them to him—in fact, he'd been going out with her for nearly six weeks before she finally let him see any of her sketches.

But she was wrong about them.

The drawings were amazing.

She did mostly landscapes, sometimes wildlife. She could visit a place once, or see a deer in the forest or a loon on a lake, and then come back and sketch it with details so intricate and precise that Daniel doubted he would've been able to notice them even if he were staring right at the animals out there in the wild.

"I promise I'll love them," he told her. "You know I will."

"You'll say you love them even if you don't just because you don't want to hurt my feelings."

"Okay, how about this—I promise to hurt your feelings if I need to."

"Oh. Well, that's much better."

"Anything I can do to encourage you."

"Aha."

He held out his hand expectantly and, after letting out a slight sigh, she leaned over, picked up the sketchbook, and handed it to him.

He paged past the drawings he'd seen before.

"You're almost done with this sketchbook."

"Just a few pages left."

He came to the new ones.

The first was a sketch of the Gateway Arch and the skyline of St. Louis. He knew Nicole had gone down there with her parents last June, but just the fact that she'd only recently sketched it astonished him.

"Nope. I can't hurt your feelings quite yet."

He flipped forward and saw a flock of geese flying over a marsh. "Still can't hurt 'em."

"Well, just wait. You think your blurs are disturbing. Wait 'til you see the last drawing."

He turned the page.

And paused.

She had sketched a man who was apparently asleep, lying on some sort of mat or cot. From what it looked like, a demon was hovering above him. It wasn't one of those cartoonish caricatures of a devil with horns and hoofed feet and a pointy tail and a pitchfork. No, this demon seemed like something straight out of a nightmare.

She'd captured wickedness and evil and horror in a simple line drawing that was disturbingly real looking. The demon's leathery flesh was stretched tightly across an outline of his skeleton and there was something about the way she'd drawn the creature that made it look like it was ready to lift off the page with its dark, bat-like wings, and fly straight into someone's thoughts or infest her soul.

"See?" she said. "I warned you."

"Is that just from your imagination?"

"Yeah, I mean, I was in a weird place when I drew it. I'd been reading the Bible and I came to the story of Job and, well, it kind of got to me."

Nicole wasn't afraid to talk about her faith so Daniel wasn't surprised now that she mentioned Bible reading. Some people didn't like to bring up anything about the supernatural, but Nicole had always been honest and forthcoming about what she believed, which was actually refreshing and one of the things that attracted him to her.

He wasn't super familiar with the Bible, but he at least knew enough from going to church with his mom when she was still living with them to know that Job was a guy who'd been rich and then lost everything. "Is the demon tempting him?"

"More like terrorizing him." Nicole typed on her laptop and pulled up an online Bible. "Job 7:13-15."

"What does it say?"

"It's Job and he's been having these frightening visions, and he writes, 'When I say, My bed shall comfort me, my couch shall ease my complaints; Then thou scarest me with dreams, and terrifiest me through visions: So that my soul chooseth strangling, and death rather than my life.'"

"So God sent him nightmares so horrifying that he would have preferred to be *strangled and killed*? Why would God send anyone nightmares like that?"

"Job thought they were coming from God, but, well, it's kind of complicated, but God was allowing Satan to basically torture him to see if he would turn away from his faith. But Job didn't know about any of that, so he assumed it was God sending him all these troubles."

"But ultimately, what's the difference? I mean . . ." Daniel wasn't trying to be argumentative; it just came out. "God either sent the nightmares or he allowed them, and either way he could have stopped them from happening."

"Yeah," she said somewhat uncertainly. "I guess so."

He closed up the sketchbook and put it back on the desk. "One time we talked about demons and you told me that you believed in them."

"I remember."

"How do you know if . . . well . . ."

"What?"

"If they're around you. Tempting you, torturing you, whatever they do?"

She looked at him with concern. "Is that what you think? That demons are torturing you?"

"Based on some of the things I've seen, I'm not sure what to think—although, I have to say, I've never wanted to be strangled and killed rather than see another blur. So at least there's that."

"Well, I'm no expert on demons, but I think people make a mistake when they either overestimate them or underestimate them."

"You mean they think demons are more powerful than they really are, or think they're, what—maybe not real at all?"

"Something like that. I mean, if you were a demon, the last thing you'd want people to know is the truth, right? You'd want them to be scared to death of you or believe you're not even there."

"And you're saying it's somewhere in the middle."

"Yeah, but I believe God's more powerful than they are and sometimes there's a bigger purpose at work than what we can see. Like with Job, and now with your blurs—there's more going on. We just need to figure out what it is."

Neither one of them seemed to know where to take the conversation from there.

"I guess we should get started, then," he said at last. "With the wolves, I mean."

"Good plan."

Two wolves.

Which one are you feeding?

When he glanced at his girlfriend's desk he saw the demon sitting on top of it, leering at him, its wings outstretched.

He blinked to make it go away, but that didn't help, and the demon flapped into the air until it was poised above the desk. Then it darted through the wall and was gone.

Letting out a soft breath to calm himself, Daniel shifted his attention away from that corner of the room and looked at Nicole, who was eyeing him somewhat cautiously.

"You okay?" she asked.

"Yeah."

"What is it?"

"Nothing."

"You saw something. I can tell. What did you see?"

"It doesn't matter."

"Daniel—"

"Let's just say that was a very realistic dragon you drew."

"You saw it."

"Yeah, but it flew away. So that's a good thing, right?"

"I'd say yes—but just seeing it at all is kind of disturbing."

"You're telling me."

Man, right now you do not need to be obsessing about demons.

Redirecting things back to the reason they were here, he said, "I think we should look into more than just the wolves being tagged."

"What do you mean?"

"That research facility, the Traybor Institute, we need to see how that place and the poaching might be tied together."

"I'll take the wolves," Nicole offered. "You take the fish research place with the razor wire fence."

"The one where they bring handcuffed prisoners."

"Exactly."

CHAPTER
EIGHTEEN

They researched things for about half an hour, then went to the kitchen to grab lunch and catch each other up on what they'd been able to figure out so far.

While they threw together some grilled cheese sandwiches, Nicole said, "There wasn't anything online about whether the other wolves that've been poached were tagged, but I did find out that a couple dozen were part of this joint research project between the Department of Natural Resources, the forest service, and a wildlife management program at UW-Superior."

"So it's at least possible that the other wolves were tagged too."

"Yeah. It's possible."

"I should tell my dad what we're thinking. Maybe he would know."

He still hadn't heard from his dad since leaving the voice-mail earlier, so he texted him to call when he had a chance.

Nicole flipped the sandwiches to brown the other side. "What do you have about the Traybor Institute?"

"Honestly, not much—which is sort of surprising. But since that van came from the Department of Corrections, I decided to see if there was any connection between the Traybor Institute and the Derthick State Penitentiary. I mean, since that's the closest prison, I figured I'd start there."

"Anything?"

"One thing that's kind of interesting. On the institute's website there's a list of their staff. I Googled the names and didn't come up with anything for most of them, but this one guy, Dr. Waxford, used to be in a private research program on how humans process time. I thought that was kind of weird, that he would end up counting trout and walleye for a living."

"How we process time?"

"Yeah. A chronobiologist. I guess there was this famous researcher back in the 1960s who spent two months living in a cave with no way of telling how much time was passing, how long he was sleeping, any of that. So Dr. Waxford did the same thing—only for four months. He wrote in a journal and eventually lost track of time so much that when they went in to find him he thought that only a few weeks had passed. He nearly went insane. Some people say he did."

"That he went insane?"

"That's what's out there, on some of the websites."

"But don't you think that time passes like that for everyone? Sometimes it drags, sometimes it seems to fly by."

"That's pretty much where his research was going. Anyway, eventually, Dr. Waxford started experimenting with testing the way darkness, sleep deprivation and different medications affect how people experience the passage of time."

"So what does that have to do with fish studies?"

"That is the question."

After lunch, they went back online but didn't really dig up anything earth-shattering. A few minutes after one o'clock Daniel got a text from Kyle that he was finished at work. He was wondering if they were still up for the movie.

Daniel figured that if he texted Kyle about what he and Nicole had found out, it was going to make for one really long text message. Instead he decided it'd be better to just explain it all in person when they met.

He replied that he wasn't sure about the movie, but could they still get together? Maybe at Nicole's?

Kyle texted back that he and Mia would be there as soon as they could.

After Daniel put away his phone, Nicole said, "I think you should tell them about the blurs, about the sleepwalking last night and the dream of the girl with the bloody tears."

When she reminded him about the girl, Daniel thought again of how the blurs he'd experienced in the autumn had revealed stuff to him to help solve the mystery of Emily Jackson's death.

So what was the girl in the nightgown trying to communicate to him? She'd told him that Madeline was waiting for him and that he needed to hurry before it happened again.

Before what?

The more he thought about it, the more he vaguely remembered that barn, not like something from a dream, but rather like a memory from real life, as if it were part of his past in the waking world, not just a fleeting image from a nightmare.

Maybe it has something to do with the facility or the wolves.

He couldn't shake the thought that the barn was real. "I'm thinking it might be best to bail on the movie," he said. "Remember I told you that the girl in the white nightgown led me to a barn?"

"Yes."

"I'm curious if I might have been there before. If it actually is a real place, I want to know if it has anything to do with everything else that's going on."

"How would you know if you've been there before?"

"If we can find it, hopefully that'll jar my memory."

When Kyle and Mia showed up, Daniel filled them in on his dream involving the girl and how he also saw a blur of her during the game.

Then he told them about what he and Nicole had witnessed at the Traybor Institute: "One of the officers, or prison guards or whoever, was the man from last night— the one who'd driven into the snowbank."

Kyle leaned forward. "You're kidding me."

"No. I don't know how it's all tied together, but one of the guys who works at the institute used to study ways to make it seem like time was passing faster or slower for people, using drugs, sensory deprivation, things like that." He explained about the chronobiology studies.

Mia said, "I heard Einstein once said something like, 'If you put your hand on a hot stove for a minute, it seems like an hour, but sit with a pretty girl for an hour, and it seems like a minute. That's relativity.'"

"Is that true, Daniel?" Nicole asked Daniel innocently. "The pretty girl part?"

"Absolutely."

"That was the right answer."

"That's my answer too." Kyle laid his hand on Mia's knee.

"Good for you, Cowboy."

He turned to Daniel. "But none of this chronobiology stuff has anything to do with fish management studies, does it?"

"No. At least I can't imagine how it would."

After a moment's deliberation, he went ahead and shared what'd happened last night when he'd sleepwalked.

His friends listened in silence when he mentioned the hunting knife.

Finally, he summarized how he and Nicole had been nearby when the poacher shot the wolf. "We were there when it died."

"Well," said Mia, "you guys had a memorable day."

"No kidding. Oh, and I've left a couple messages for my dad but he hasn't called back yet. He's usually pretty good about returning calls so I'm not sure what's up. Anyway, I'm hoping we can find out if the other wolves that were shot were tagged too. If they were, it might help narrow down who's killing them. In the meantime, I want to find out what that girl in the white nightgown wanted from me."

"How?" Kyle asked.

"In the dream I followed her to a barn that was at the end of a barbed wire fence. There was a field of dead corn beside it."

"I hate to tell you this, but you've just described half the state of Wisconsin in the fall."

"I know, but from what happened with Emily—the blurs—I don't think my mind is making these things up from nowhere. I'm wondering if sometime in my past I might've been there. There's this fuzzy memory I have of visiting the barn but I can't say for sure if my mind is just creating it based on the dream or if I'm remembering it actually happening."

"So what are you suggesting?"

"I want to go look for it. If I have been there before, that would be the most likely place to search for some answers about what's really going on here. I say we drive around a little, see if any of the farms I'm thinking of around here end up being the one from my dream. We can always go to that movie later on if we don't find anything."

Kyle nodded. "I'm game."

The girls were too.

Daniel pulled out his keys. "Then let's go. We only have a couple of hours before it gets dark."

PART III
A BLADE IN
THE NIGHT

CHAPTER
NINETEEN

While Daniel drove, Kyle helped with navigation and planning out the best route they should take for saving time so they could get their search done before dusk.

Although they passed a few farms that looked promising at first, when Daniel concentrated on the one he'd dreamt about, he realized that none of the barns were quite right.

Nicole had the idea that, if they found the property, they might be able to figure out who owned it by checking public access county courthouse land deeds. So, although cell coverage was spotty out here in the countryside, she and Mia went online with their phones and looked for a way to pull up the information.

As the afternoon slipped away, Daniel became less and less convinced that this search was going to pay off.

"Okay." His eyes were on the sun, low in the sky. "There's one other property out on County Highway N, over near where my grandma used to live. We can check it out and if it's nothing, we'll just head to Superior. It's on the way."

OLDHAM COUNTY PUBLIC LIBRARY

When they arrived, they found a strip of farmland that lay beside a sprawling frozen-over marsh that separated it from the national forest.

A desolate, partially dilapidated barn crouched at the far end of a snow-covered field. Sporadic dead stalks of corn poked through the snow, but other than that the field looked untouched.

The barn's wood was sun-bleached and weathered with the years. A section of the roof had collapsed. A crumbling silo stood nearby.

All that remained of the farmhouse beside it was the charred shell of a home that, based on the tangled and knotty thorn bushes that appeared to sprout from its remains, must have burned down years ago.

"You said your grandma used to live out here?" Kyle asked.

Daniel pointed. "Her house was maybe a quarter mile away, just on the other side of those woods. My parents sold it after she died back when I was nine."

"I remember when that farmhouse burned down," Mia said. "Or at least hearing about it. It was, like, five or six years ago. I don't think I've ever been out here, though."

Daniel wondered if the burning girl in his blurs and the burnt-down house had anything to do with each other.

Have you been here before? Think, Daniel.

He traced his memories back, following them through flickering images of the past, and found that some of them did lead to this place. It'd been years, and he hadn't thought of this barn in a long time, but he did recall it.

Yes.

He had been here.

Back when he and his parents visited his grandma.

Daniel parked the car. "This is the one."

"Are you sure?" Mia asked.

"Yeah. This is the one from my dream."

"So do we know whose property it is?" Kyle said.

Nicole checked the county records. "Someone named Hollister."

Daniel's hand was on the door handle but he paused. "Hollister?"

"Yeah. You heard of him?"

"There was a Hollister who used to hang out with Ty Bell back in the day—he killed someone, I think. Went to prison."

"Prison? Wouldn't he have been too young for that—I mean, if he was a friend of Ty's?"

"He was older. In his twenties, I think. Maybe his family owns the land." He pushed his door open and stepped outside. "Let's go. I want to know why I dreamt about this place."

As the sun dipped toward the top of the trees, the four of them started across the field.

CHAPTER
TWENTY

They followed the fencerow toward the barn.

The late afternoon was crisp, cold, and full of the stillness of winter.

Underfoot, the snow came halfway to their knees, but was piled deeper near trees and fence posts where the wind had swept it into drifts.

For as much as snow annoyed her, Mia did an admirable job of putting up with trudging through it without complaining.

The only sound came from the soft hush-crunch of their footsteps as they trekked toward the barn.

From being outdoors so much in the winter, Daniel had noticed it before—a quietness that's so stark it becomes like a companion to you. Then, as if he were reading his mind, Kyle said, "'Have you known The Great White Silence, not a snow-gemmed twig aquiver . . .'"

"What's that from?" Nicole asked.

"A poem by Robert Service: 'The Call of the Wild.' He was a balladeer who wrote a lot about the Yukon. Probably his most famous poem is 'The Cremation of Sam McGee.' The guy rocks."

"The Yukon has snow," Mia said. "Do not like snow. Remind me not to move to the Yukon."

When they were nearly to the barn, Nicole asked Daniel, "Do you have any idea what we're actually looking for here?"

"Something to do with my past. That's about all I can tell you."

The hinges on the barn's door creaked protestingly as Daniel and Kyle pushed it open.

Loosely strewn hay, along with narrow strips of wind-blown snow that had found its way in through the channels between the wallboards, covered the ground.

Where the roof had fallen in, the fading daylight made its way through the space high above them. A little light entered through the slits between the boards and, of course, through the open door, but most of the barn was held captive by a network of deep, cold shadows.

Daniel walked to a spot not far from the barn's entrance. "This is where the girl's nightgown burst into flames, where she . . . well . . . you know."

Thinking that the location might hold some significance, they searched the area but found nothing.

A rusted John Deere tractor that must have been thirty or forty years old sat long-abandoned in the middle of the barn. Near the collapsed part of the roof was a pegboard and a workbench with decades-old hand tools.

A hayloft with a rickety-looking wooden ladder had been built on the other end of the barn. Even from Daniel's vantage point he could see stacks of hay bales still on it.

The girl looked up there right before she burned up. She raised her arms toward that loft.

An old hay baler waited near the hayloft. It looked threatening with its spinning blades to chop up and draw in the hay before wrapping it into a bale.

"It doesn't look like anyone's been here in years," Nicole said. "I wonder why it was abandoned."

Mia gazed around the barn. "We'd better get looking if we're gonna have time to finish up and get back to the car before it gets dark."

Kyle and Mia offered to search the main part of the barn while Daniel and Nicole headed toward the hayloft.

He went up the ladder first to test the rungs and make sure they were safe.

As he climbed, he finally recalled the last time he'd been in this barn, or at least he thought it was the last time.

He'd been nine years old and the memory lingered right on the brink of his forgetfulness like so many memories from childhood do.

He'd walked over here from his grandmother's house. It was only sixty-four days before she died.

Math.

It was hard to turn it off.

Even when he wanted to.

Daniel reached the top and hefted himself into the loft.

Satisfied that everything was safe, he motioned for Nicole to join him, and when she had, he took her hand and helped her up.

The sweet smell of hay lingered in the air and Daniel realized he knew that smell, that and the dry, gritty taste of hay dust, from the days when he was a kid and he would jump from the loft into the bales that'd been stacked up beneath it.

Yes, he was sure of it: he'd been here more than once, but only now that he was here again did it come back to him.

Memories crowded in on the moment.

Memories of landing.

Tumbling.

Rolling.

Here, here in this place.

Yes. Up until that last day. And then he'd been afraid to come here, even to his grandma's house. Afraid that—

But if you spent that much time here as a kid, why didn't you remember it before now? Why did you block that out of your memory?

Yes, maybe the memories of being here were blocked, or maybe, like with so many things, he just needed a spark to bring the past back to him.

Really, memories were weird things. Sometimes the harder you tried to forget something, the more you remembered it. And then there were those things that you wanted to remember, but the harder you tried to, the less you were able to. It was all backward.

"Anything?" Nicole asked him.

"I used to come up here to play in the loft."

"With your friends?"

"By myself. It was a secret place. I'd sometimes sneak over when we visited Grandma. She was depressed a lot and it was kind of hard being around her. But I'm not sure what any of it means. It's like I can tell there's more, I just can't quite remember it."

Looking around, he took note of the birds' nests high in the rafters. The thick, braided rope that he would sometimes use to swing from the hayloft hung from one of the ceiling beams and dangled nearby.

The rope.

The hay baler.

Fuzzy memories. Nothing clear.

But something happened.

And it was not something good.

Over the years people had carved words and phrases into the side of the barn. There were names and initials of couples with plus signs between them and cupid hearts and dates, all scratched into the wood. Some people had written their name followed by "was here," and sometimes the year.

Some of the dates were from before Daniel had been born. He examined the carvings to see if any of them brought back anything specific and found himself calculating how many days ago those people had been here at the barn.

Seven of the names, even though they were different, looked like they'd been carved by the same person, like some guy had gotten carried away and done a bunch of them himself.

While Daniel looked them over, Nicole started working her way across the loft, brushing hay aside with her boot, looking for anything that might have been buried beneath it.

The longer Daniel was up here, the more memories came to the surface.

Summers.

Swinging down the rope.

But why did you stop coming here, Daniel?

Why would—

"Over here, Daniel."

Nicole was tapping a loose board on top of a small enclosed bench at the far end of the hayloft.

While he was on his way toward her, he saw that demon again, the one she'd drawn in her sketchbook.

He stopped dead in his tracks.

The demon lurked just to her left, and even though sunlight from the collapsed portion of the roof was landing on it, the light seemed to be swallowed in the taut coil of darkness that encircled it.

The creature grinned hungrily at him, its mouth widening like a snake's mouth, unhinging and opening larger than it ever should have been able to.

Then it swept forward, flying straight at him.

He instinctively ducked, but felt the rush of air as it passed. One of its wings scratched the back of his neck as it soared across the loft.

He turned to see where the demon would go from there, but it disappeared through the wall of the barn, through one of the phrases carved into the wood: Grady Planisek was here.

Wait . . . He knew that name.

"You're seeing things again, aren't you?" Nicole's voice was tight with concern. "What did you see?"

Isn't Grady that boy who disappeared when you were a kid?

"Nothing to worry about."

"Another blur?"

"Let's hope so."

He almost added, "At least then I'd know it wasn't a real demon," but held back.

Still wondering about Grady, he joined Nicole and worked at the board until he was able to pop it loose.

Inside, he found a wooden box about the size of a shoebox.

He picked it up and wiped off a thick, stubborn layer of dust.

The box's hasp had been padlocked shut. He tried to open it but the latch held. When he shook the box, it didn't sound like anything breakable was inside. Maybe a couple of books. Hard to tell.

"We found something," he called down to Kyle and Mia.

"Whatcha got?" Mia asked.

He walked to the edge of the hayloft and showed them the box. "It's locked. We'll need to pry it open."

Kyle went searching through the tools on the workbench and came up with a claw hammer.

Daniel was about to toss the box to the barn floor, but, realizing that it might possibly contain something fragile after all, he opted to carry it with him as he descended the ladder.

Nicole followed closely behind and when they reached the bottom, Daniel accepted the hammer from Kyle and positioned the claw end of it in between the clasp and the lock to see if he could wrench it loose.

It took a few tries, but finally the hasp cracked off from the wood and pulled free.

His friends gathered around as he tipped open the lid.

Inside were two aged leather-bound journals, a pile of yellowing papers, and a stack of black and white photographs.

He picked up the top journal and opened it. Nicole took the other one, while Mia went through the photographs and Kyle carefully unfolded the papers so he wouldn't damage them.

It only took a moment for Daniel to realize that he was holding a diary. The script was a little scratchy and hard to read, but he recognized the handwriting right away.

It was the same style he'd used when he wrote that phrase about the Lost Cove again and again in his notebook in English class.

CHAPTER TWENTY-ONE

He realized that he hadn't told his friends about what he'd written in class, so after filling them in, he concluded, "And this is the same handwriting."

"Okay, that's freaky." Nicole looked uneasy.

"How is that even possible?" Mia asked.

"I have no idea."

Kyle spoke up. "What about multiple personality disorder? It's this deal where people can have these completely different personalities—different names, habits, handwriting, all that."

Mia shook her head. "I heard that wasn't for real, that it was just other problems, or whatever, or people faking it."

Daniel thought about his visits to Dr. Fromke and figured that if the multiple personality deal was what was going on with him, it would have come up in one of their sessions. "Well, whether it's a real thing or not, let's assume for now that that's not what's going on with me."

"Have you ever seen that diary before?" Kyle asked.

"Maybe, I'm not sure." Daniel tried his best to remember. "I could have when I was here at this barn before. I'm just not sure."

"But you do know you were here?"

"I remember it, but it's not super clear and it's like I'm watching myself while it happens rather than seeing it through my own eyes."

Nicole nodded knowingly. "Observer memories."

"What are those?"

"I came across 'em when I was doing this research paper last year. It's when you remember something from another perspective, like you're watching yourself in a movie. Most people have them at some point."

"But how could that even be called a memory?" Mia asked. "I mean, if you're *watching yourself*, you're not *remembering* anything, right? If you're seeing something as if you were looking at it through someone else's eyes, your mind is obviously making things up. That's imagination, not memory."

"I know. It's really bizarre, but it's not that uncommon. Sometimes it's our mind's way of protecting us or of distancing us from something terrifying or traumatic. Sometimes we forget scary stuff altogether. I mean, think of children who are abused: they might block out those memories entirely. Or when a woman gets assaulted, sometimes she won't even recall the details—even right after it happens. It's sort of a defense mechanism, because the event is too terrible for them to process."

Daniel thought about it. "I'm not sure what any of that has to do with me."

"Unless something traumatic happened to you here, while you were in this barn."

They were silent.

Daniel shook his head. "That seems a little hard to believe—that I wouldn't remember what really happened here."

"But you did repress some stuff," Nicole pointed out. "I mean it's starting to come back to you, but that's only because we're here."

As he tried to climb back through his memories, he felt like there was a door there, one that he had his hand up against, but he couldn't quite open.

Or maybe you don't want to and you're holding back.

"I don't know," he told them. "Nothing's coming to me."

When Nicole asked if he knew who'd left that box up there, he said, "I'm not sure, but right now, I'm more concerned with what's in it and what that might have to do with what's been going on this week than with how it got there."

Mia shuffled through the photos. "Well, these are pictures of people near a shoreline—a beach, an ocean, something like that—this one looks like they're picnicking and playing lawn croquet. There's a lighthouse in the background."

Kyle was paging through the papers. "I've got some ledgers here, old records. I don't recognize all the towns listed—but I do know Bayfield. That's where Larry lives."

Larry Richter was Kyle's uncle and ran a sailing tour and boat rental place near the Apostle Islands, about an hour and a half from Beldon. In the past, he'd offered to let Kyle and his friends use some of the sea kayaks or skiffs whenever they wanted to, but Daniel had never made it up there.

"And this is a diary." Nicole was thumbing through the leather-bound journal. "It's from a lighthouse keeper back in the 1930s."

"Mine is too." Daniel looked at his friends. "Listen, it's almost dark. Let's get to the car. We can check out this lighthouse deal back at Nicole's house."

Stars were already piercing through the darkening sky by the time they climbed into Daniel's car.

No Northern Lights tonight, just a pale rising moon peering over the edge of the horizon.

The four of them agreed that they could see that movie anytime, but tonight, going through the contents of the box was definitely a bigger priority.

Back at Nicole's house, Daniel's phone rang while he was following her into the living room.

His dad's ringtone.

"Hey, sorry I didn't return your call earlier," he said after Daniel picked up. "I misplaced my phone. So you said in your message that you saw another wolf get killed?"

Daniel stepped into the hallway for some privacy. "Yeah, this morning out by the national forest. We heard a gunshot and found her tracks. She'd been shot in the chest. She died right in front of us."

A small pause. "And you didn't see who the shooter was?"

"No. But the wolf was tagged on its ear, you know, from the forest service for the pack studies. I sent you a photo. I was thinking: How is this person who's killing the wolves finding them? I wondered if he could be locating ones that've been tagged. Were the other wolves tagged?"

"I believe they were; however, a lot of the wolves in this part of the state are being monitored."

"But doesn't it seem strange that only wolves that've been tagged have been killed? Only someone with access to the database at the forest service could have found out exactly where those wolves were."

"So, you're suggesting that if someone could get in, hack in, whatever, they could get real-time GPS data on the wolves' locations?"

His dad knew that Daniel's blurs had led him to figure out who Emily's murderer was last fall. While he obviously hadn't been too excited that his son was seeing and hearing things, he had learned to trust Daniel's instincts.

"Right," Daniel said. "Maybe you could look into who accessed those files or when they were opened. If someone was viewing them around the time when the wolves were being killed, that would be something to at least check out, wouldn't it?"

Rather than answer him directly, his dad said, "Who else knows about this?"

"Just Nicole, Kyle and Mia."

"Let's keep it that way. I'll see what I can find out, but I don't want you sharing this with anyone. It might throw suspicion on someone who's not guilty of anything, and that's the last thing I want. Let me take care of it. You guys leave it alone."

"Sure."

Daniel described where they'd seen the wolf and told his dad that if he followed their boot prints from the trailhead toward the Traybor Institute, he would find it.

He expected that his dad might want to go out there in the morning since it was already dark, so he was surprised when he said, "I should really record that location as soon as possible. Are you in Superior?"

"No. We decided not to go see the movie. We're actually at Nicole's house."

Tell him about the box or not?

No. Find out what you can about it first. Go through the stuff that's in there, then you'll know what kinds of questions to ask him.

"I'll see you at the house, Dan."

"See you there."

After he'd joined his friends again, Nicole's parents suggested that they throw in some pizzas for supper.

No arguments with that.

They went to Nicole's room to wait for the pizzas to bake and Daniel told them what his dad had said on the phone. "I'm guessing that all this stuff is connected somehow—my blurs, the barn, the wolf poaching, the Traybor Institute."

"And the diaries too," Mia noted, "because of the phrase you wrote down in your notebook in that same handwriting."

Nicole took a seat on her bed next to her pile of stuffed animals. "So, what's our next step?"

Daniel held up two diaries. "We find out who wrote these puppies—who that lighthouse keeper was."

CHAPTER TWENTY-TWO

After splitting up the contents of the box the same way they had at the barn, the four of them got started.

Though Daniel and Nicole had their work cut out for them paging through the journals, it didn't take Kyle and Mia long to make their way through the papers and photos. When they finished, they shifted their attention to finding out what they could about lighthouses, using their phones to search online.

To save time, Daniel and Nicole decided to read the diaries in depth later. For now they scanned the entries, looking for the author's identity or anything unusual, especially anything that might have to do with Daniel's blurs or the events of the last couple days.

In a diary you don't necessarily list your own name, and that's what it was like in this case, so they still didn't know who the keeper was.

Nicole's mom called up that the pizzas were done and the four friends made their way to the kitchen. Nicole rounded up sodas, and after bringing some paper plates and pizza slices to her bedroom, Mia and Kyle spent a few minutes sharing what they'd discovered about lighthouses.

Mia said, "This doesn't really have anything to do with anything, but when you start talking about lighthouses, the idea of warning ships off the coast apparently goes back to ancient Greek times. They'd build fires on hills near the ocean in areas where there were rocks."

"And every lighthouse has a different signal," Kyle added, in between sizable bites of his crushed red pepper-covered slice. "They call it flash and dark times. One lighthouse's light might go on for two seconds and then off for three, while another has a steady pulse of flashing and going dark every four seconds. It happens when the lens spins. Some of the ones in the Apostle Islands also have different-colored lights—green, white, red. It's all so the guys on the boats can tell the difference, see where they are as they pass through the islands."

Mia took a sip of her root beer. "The more I think about it, the more I think I should maybe be doing my novel about a haunted lighthouse instead of a monastery. I mean, some of the stories out there are amazing. With all the shipwrecks and tragedy, the lonely hours and the lighthouse keepers going mad and . . ."

She caught herself, glanced at Daniel, and must have realized that the phrase "going mad" was not the best one to use around him. "I mean, they were probably mentally ill to begin with."

"Sure."

"That didn't really help a whole lot, did it?"

"Not necessarily, but you're good."

"I'll just shut up now."

"Let's look at some of these diary entries," Nicole suggested.

Daniel flipped open his diary. "The truth is, most of the ones I went through are pretty trivial."

He read a few:

May 12, 1936
Breakfast—oatmeal and jam on bread that I cooked yesterday. I am planning pancakes and muffins later this week.

May 15, 1936
I have planted onions, carrots, radishes and some lettuce and cabbage.

"Then in June the strawberries and raspberries ripen and he stores the preserves in the root cellar. It goes on like that. You get the picture—But they're not all that lame."

July 1, 1936
Tonight, on the edge of the wind, I thought I heard a woman scream.

I lit a lantern and searched the island, calling out for anyone who might have, by some stray chance, been there. All to no avail. For it is true—I am alone on this island and I know it was just my mind seeking either companionship or solace here in this place of rocks and gulls and cliffs that plummet into the fearsome depths.

"Okay, that's a little creepy," Nicole said. "Can you imagine being out on an island like that and you start hearing things?"

"And it's a totally different feel than the early entries," noted Mia. "More poetic."

"What happens then?" Kyle asked Daniel.

"From what I can tell the screaming woman isn't mentioned again—at least not in the entries I read. But check this out."

August 30, 1936
The storms have come now, the windiest season of the year.

Sometimes I stand in the tower and stare out across the lake into the night.

In the gales, I can hear the waves rage against the rocks below me and all I can think of is the souls who are out on the water and who are searching for a glimpse of my light.

Perhaps it is true of all light keepers, perhaps just true of me, but a thought crawls into my mind unbidden, unwelcome: a temptation to put out the light.

I do not know where this damnable idea comes from, be it a devil or a dark place in my own soul, but it is real and it raises its head when the strongest winds blow and the fiercest storms rage.

Oh, dear God, I must resist!

"So did he ever do that?" Kyle finished off his pizza and put his empty plate on Nicole's desk. "Turn off the light?"

"If he did, he didn't write about it. The last entry is at the end of October. Apparently, since there wouldn't be any ships coming through when there's ice on the lake, they didn't have the lighthouses running during the winter months. The last page is just about him leaving to go back to the mainland."

"So, okay." Nicole opened the diary she was holding. She'd dog-eared a few pages and now turned to the first one. "Mine picks up the next year when he went out there to work at the lighthouse again. The ones at the beginning of the summer are like the ones Daniel read—about gardening or things like that, but then it gets interesting."

June 12, 1937

And so it is.

> *Duty and routine.*
>
> *The light.*
>
> *I must keep her burning. I must!*
>
> *Thirty minutes before sunset I ascend the tower.*
>
> *Using a cotton cloth I wipe the lens and the mirrors, then trim the wick, light it and center it in the middle of the lens. I adjust the flame and place it in position, then release the brakes so the*

counterweights will continue to rotate the lens.

Six times a night I climb the spiral stairs and check on it.

You cannot let the light go out: That is what the constant voice in my head is telling me.

Mia, who'd been holding onto the photos, set them on the floor. "This guy is obsessed with keeping that light burning."

"Or *not* keeping it burning," Nicole added.

"Can you blame him?" Daniel said. "I mean he spends months out there by himself and he has only one job, one thing he has to do every day. It makes sense that it would become kind of an obsession for him."

Nicole shook her head. "He wasn't always alone."

"What do you mean?"

She flipped to the next dog-eared page.

June 22, 1937
There is a deep loneliness here.

The days stretch out long and hollow, running together in my mind. I climb the stairs, light the lamp, and check it throughout the night to make sure that it stays lit.

Perhaps all of this will change after July 4. Perhaps with companionship will come the end of tedium.

"Companionship?" Mia said. "So who's going to be his companion?"

Nicole paged forward in the diary.

July 4, 1937
My sister dropped off her daughter to spend two weeks with me. The girl just turned eleven yesterday.

I have promised to care for her as if she were my own child.

"An eleven-year-old girl?" Mia looked at her quizzically.

"Yeah. Why?"

"Hold on a sec." She sorted through the photos, then held one up for Daniel. "Is that the girl from your blur?"

Seeing her again sent ice running down his spine.

"Yes." He accepted the picture from Mia. "It is."

The girl was standing beside a rocky shoreline. Rather than the nightgown she'd worn in his blur, here in the photo, she had on a plain skirt that, although dated, Daniel imagined was probably in style back then. She was smiling and holding up a metal watering can.

Who are you? What do you want from me?

Nicole had paused while Daniel looked over the photograph, but now, as he set it down, she said, "That's as far as I got."

"Well, let's hear the next one," he said.

She turned the page.

July 9, 1937

Betty has been helping me check on the light. She enjoys going up the steps and staring out the window of the tower at the lake or standing on the narrow balcony encircling it.

She likes to carry the lantern for me, to lead the way up through the dark.

"Her nightgown caught fire in your blur, right?" Kyle asked Daniel softly.

"Yes."

He motioned for Nicole to go on, she thumbed to the next page, and shook her head. "It's just a description of a sunset."

She skipped past that.

July 12, 1937

She set the lantern down beside her. Oh dear God, she did.

It was not my fault, no, no, it was not—this is what I tell myself, but it was!

I was in the tower and saw her leave the house below. She called to me and waved, but then something, some movement in the night near the edge of the clearing, must have caught her attention because she looked that direction and then stepped to the side.

The lantern.

Oh, God!

The hem of her nightgown.

No, please!

I didn't make it down the tower in time.

No one spoke for a long time.

At last, Nicole read the next entry.

July 13, 1937

This morning I buried my niece here on the island. No one will find her. But now—oh! And what comes next?

Her mother will return in five days. And I don't know what I will tell her. What is there to say?

Perhaps that she went swimming in the surf and never returned?

But no—the truth.

God, not the truth! It is too terrible a way to die.

"There are some random words there, like he started to write something and then changed his mind. Nothing that makes sense. But then it goes on."

Seagulls hover and dive into the surf that is crashing up on the shore.

I see a specter.

The girl. Standing now in the twilight, now in the day, burning, her hands raised toward the tower but I cannot get to her in time.

Nicole went to the next page.

July 16, 1937

Every night now I see her and it cannot go on. I must end this. Yes!

Tonight, one last time I will go up the tower steps, and then never again.

I have found a rope that is long enough. They say that hell awaits those who take their own lives. And so, if I deserve the punishment of the eternal flames, I am ready for it, for what I allowed to happen to my niece and for what I will do tonight.

She slowly closed the journal. "That's the last entry."

They all sat there in silence.

Kyle pulled out the ledgers and sifted through them, then held the last one up for the others to see. "It looks like whoever wrote these out—maybe some sort of supervisor, I can't read the signature—he filled out the last one on July 18, 1937."

"What does it say?" Daniel asked.

"Just that there was a replacement, that there was a new keeper assigned to the lighthouse instead of Jarvis Delacroix."

"Delacroix? That was my grandma's maiden name."

"You think you're related to this guy?"

"It's not that common of a name. It would make sense."

Daniel was calculating dates, times, ages. "If Betty was related to Jarvis, then if I'm right about how all this works out, my grandma would have either been cousins with Betty, or maybe even her sister. Does the ledger say anything about the girl?"

"No."

"Jarvis Delacroix wrote that he found a rope that was long enough," Nicole said, "that those who take their own lives deserve to go to hell."

No one spoke. It was almost as if they were afraid that their words might have condemned Jarvis to the sentence he'd expected to suffer.

"If he hanged himself," she asked at last, "don't you think there'd be a record of it somewhere, something about this online? We should be able to find out what happened."

"I don't know," Mia said. "Something might have appeared in a newspaper article at the time, but who's to say that anyone ever went back and posted it on the web? If it was from some small regional paper from Bayfield or something, I'd say it's not very likely that anyone would have bothered uploading it to the Internet."

Nicole pulled out her phone. "It's worth a look."

As Daniel was about to get started searching online, he noticed a few texts and checked to see if any were from his dad, but it was only a couple of friends checking in.

Distracted by everything that was going on, he quickly typed in responses, then set his phone on the bed next to him and returned his attention to his laptop, but a moment later his phone vibrated and Nicole said, "You have a text."

Before he could reach for it, she picked it up to hand it to him and noticed the screen.

A strange look crossed her face.

"What is it?"

"Who's Madeline?"

"What?"

She turned the phone's screen toward him. "She's asking you to come by tomorrow. She wants to know when you're going to be there."

CHAPTER TWENTY-THREE

"Honestly, Nicole, I don't know who she is."

She didn't reply.

"I'm serious."

"Then why would she text that she wants to see you and ask when you're going to meet her?"

"I wasn't. I mean, I'm not going to."

"Well, she seems to think you are."

"I've been getting messages from her, but I don't even know who's sending them."

"Neither one of us does," Kyle cut in, trying to help.

Nicole looked from Kyle to Daniel and then back at Kyle. "So you knew about her too?"

"Nicole, calm down," Daniel said. "Let me—"

"I am calm. I'm calm. I just want to know what's going on. So you've been getting these texts from this girl: Where are they? I only see this one."

"They're archived." He showed her how to access them.

On the one hand, Daniel could understand why Nicole would be upset, but he just wanted her to give him a chance to explain. "For the last couple days I've been getting these weird texts from her—or him, whoever it is. No number comes up on my phone so I can't even reply to figure out who's sending the messages. I'm telling you the truth; I don't know who it—"

"So," she read the texts aloud, "'You need to come visit me. I have a surprise for you.' Okay, that's interesting. 'Be careful who you tell your secrets to.' Oh, and then there's this one: 'I'm here waiting for you, Daniel.' Huh. 'Check the basement—M.' Really? She was at your house?"

"No."

"But she left you something down there?"

"No. Nothing like that. That's where I found the maps. That's all."

Nicole was in the middle of scrolling through his phone's home screens when she suddenly paused.

"What is it?"

She didn't respond.

"Nicole?"

"Your recent downloads. So I was just seeing if there are any other chat or messaging apps . . . and . . ."

"And what?"

"And you have an app on here that lets you send anonymous texts."

"What are you talking about?"

"It's in your recent downloads. You downloaded it Wednesday afternoon."

That's right before you got the first text from Madeline.

"Are you saying the texts were sent from my phone?"

"I'm saying they could've been." She handed him the phone.

He stared disbelievingly at the screen, trying his best to remember either downloading the app or sending the messages, but couldn't recall doing either.

You're the one who's been sending the texts.

No.

Yes.

Then why don't you remember it?

There's a lot you're not remembering lately, Daniel.

"Did you send them?" Nicole asked.

"I honestly don't know. I don't even know who Madeline is or—"

"Hang on." Kyle was busy at his phone. "We were looking at lighthouses in the Apostle Islands, right? So there are twenty-one islands in the National Lakeshore, but there's one other island out there that's not part of the park. I saw it earlier when I was doing research, but I didn't make the . . ."

He tapped at the screen, then nodded. "Three guesses what its name is, and the first two don't count."

"Oh," Daniel said, "don't tell me it's Madeline."

"Look at that, first try: Madeline Island."

"And does it have a lighthouse?"

"It sure does." Kyle tilted his phone so everyone else could see the page he'd pulled up. "The Lost Cove Lighthouse."

"That's it, then. Let's see if there's any mention of a lighthouse keeper there committing suicide."

• • •

Sweeping his flashlight beam back and forth, Sheriff Byers scrutinized the dark forest.

He'd been able to follow his son's and Nicole's boot prints most of the way, but the wind was steadily erasing them and it was getting harder and harder to discern where their trail went.

He didn't see any sign of the wolf that Daniel had told him about.

The black wilderness lurked just on the boundary of the spear of light from his flashlight.

The sheriff decided to give it a few more minutes and then call it a night.

CHAPTER TWENTY-FOUR

Now that they were able to pinpoint their search to a specific time and place, it didn't take long for the four friends to find what they were looking for.

Kyle let out a slow breath.

"What is it?" Daniel asked.

"There was a newspaper back then, the *Northwoods Review*. There's a story about a shipwreck on July seventeenth that year. Twelve people died."

"Twelve people?" Nicole swallowed hard as she said the words.

"Yeah. The light had gone out. They hit the shoal in a storm." Kyle consulted the article he'd pulled up on his phone. "When the survivors went to the lighthouse later they found the keeper dead in the tower. Hanged himself. It was Jarvis Delacroix. They list his name."

"Send me the link," Daniel said.

He clicked to the site as his friend went on: "It looks like they couldn't confirm whether Jarvis killed himself before the shipwreck or after it. But the survivors said there was no light during that storm."

"So," Nicole muttered, thinking aloud, "either he gave in to that temptation to put out the light and then killed himself, or he committed suicide first because of his guilt about Betty's death and then he wasn't there to keep it lit during that storm."

"Does the article mention her at all?" asked Mia.

Kyle checked, then shook his head. "No. Nothing about anyone named Betty."

"But don't you think that's kind of weird, though? I mean, that next day—July eighteenth—was the day her mom was supposed to return to pick her up. Is it really possible that no one else connected Betty's disappearance with the suicide or the shipwreck?"

"I don't know. I guess it's possible. I mean, if there was that big of a tragedy—twelve people dying in a shipwreck— a missing girl might not really make it into the news."

"Or," Daniel suggested, "there might be another explanation."

"What's that?"

"That she never existed at all."

"Huh?"

"Maybe Jarvis had blurs too. Just like I do."

"But he mentioned her in his journal. And what about that photo of her?"

"Just because he mentioned her doesn't mean she was real. And we don't know who that's a picture of, just that it's the same girl I saw in my blur. If I saw the stuff in that box when I was a kid, maybe I somehow remembered it. Jarvis might have seen that photo too. We know he was lonely on that island. What if he made up someone visiting him to keep himself company?"

He turned to Mia. "Like you said earlier, lighthouse keepers sometimes go mad. Maybe that's what happened with him."

No one seemed to know what to say.

"But why now?" Kyle asked. "Why would you be remembering all this now?"

"That's what we need to figure out. Someone kept these diaries and hid them in that barn. The place is old, but I'm not sure it would have been there back in the 1930s, so that means someone stuck that box in the barn sometime later. But right now I'm wondering something else."

"What's that?"

"In my blur, the girl was crying tears of blood. Why? There's nothing in the diary to indicate that Betty—whether she was real or not—would have had bleeding eyes when she died."

"I'm not sure how literally you need to take everything from your blurs," Mia said. "I mean, even when Emily appeared to you a couple months ago, it wasn't like everything that happened in your blur was identical to what happened in real life."

"So what are you saying?"

"I don't know. Maybe Betty saw something horrible? The blood is metaphorical?"

Or maybe you did.

Maybe you saw something horrible.

There in the barn. Something to do with the loft, with the—

"If Jarvis really was from your mom's side of the family," Kyle interrupted his thoughts, "wouldn't she have told you about this?"

"It's not exactly the kind of thing you'd want to be sharing with your family members."

"Maybe she didn't know about him," Nicole offered.

"There's one way to find out."

"What's that?"

Daniel already had his phone out. "Ask her."

CHAPTER
TWENTY-FIVE

His mom was still up in Anchorage, Alaska, and he wasn't certain what time zone that was in, but he put the call through anyhow.

While he waited for her to pick up, he wondered how much he should tell her about everything that was going on.

Back in the fall when the blurs started, his dad hadn't felt like it was right to keep any of that from her and, honestly, Daniel had found himself agreeing. So even though he wasn't too excited about it, they'd filled her in and she knew about the blurs.

Naturally, she'd been worried about him and had emphasized that she wanted him to see a psychiatrist to talk things through.

However, once stuff was out in the open, neither she nor Daniel really brought up anything related to the blurs. Instead, they mostly talked about surface topics—what they'd been doing, Daniel's grades, if his team had won, things like that.

In a way, he wished they would talk more about stuff that really mattered, but on the other hand he was happy they didn't go there.

After all, once you start down that path with people, get to the emotional level, you end up in a place where you can get hurt.

There's really no in-between: either you can be close to someone and vulnerable, or distant and safe.

Sort of a catch-22.

The phone rang.

No answer.

Right when he thought it was about to go to voicemail, she answered and must have had caller ID because she spoke first. "Daniel?" It was clear by the way she said his name that she was surprised he was calling. "Is everything okay?"

The question itself said a lot about their relationship: when he called, she immediately assumed something was wrong.

"I'm fine."

"Oh. Well, okay. Good."

He felt a little stuck. How do you really get into the topic of talking about a relative who was responsible for the death of twelve people—fourteen, if you counted himself and the girl?

If Betty was even real.

You should have thought this through a little more.

His friends slipped away so he could speak to his mom in private.

"Dad said you're coming back for Christmas?" he said to her.

"I was planning to, but there's a big storm system moving in up here. If we get as much snow and ice as they're predicting, I might not make it back until after the holiday. But we'll just celebrate it then."

"Sure," he said. "That makes sense." But he was thinking, *And when were you going to tell us that?*

"How did it go last night?" she asked.

"Last night?"

"The game."

"Oh. We won."

"How'd you play?"

"Alright. I mean, I played okay."

"Well, then. That's good."

Silence stretched across the line.

"You're sure you're fine?" she asked.

Just ask her.

"Did your mom have any sisters?"

"What?"

"Did she have any sisters that you maybe just never told me about?"

"No."

"So, no one named Betty?"

"No." She almost made it sound like a question and Daniel could tell her curiosity was definitely piqued.

"Mom, what do you know about Jarvis Delacroix?"

"Jarvis Delacroix?"

"He was a lighthouse keeper back in the 1930s. Since Delacroix was your mom's maiden name I wondered if maybe they were related."

"Yes, they were." Her tone was impossible to read. "What is all this in regards to?"

"What do you know about him?"

"There was a Jarvis who was my grandfather's brother, but no one really talked about him much."

That's gotta be him.

So if Jarvis was Grandma's uncle, that means Betty would have been her cousin.

"And Betty?" he said.

"I don't know about any Bettys. Why do you ask? What's going on?"

"My friends and I came across Jarvis's diary."

"Where?"

"At a barn that's near where Grandma used to live."

"That farm out on County N?"

"Yeah. That's right. I used to go there sometimes."

"Yes."

"You knew?"

"I followed you one day but your grandmother assured us the neighbor wouldn't mind. So I let you play there. I know it was sometimes hard being in the house with her."

"Did something happen there at the barn?"

"What do you mean?"

"I don't know, just—anything weird?"

168

"Not that I know of. One day you just stopped going out on walks when we visited. You were hesitant even to go to her house. But I don't know why Jarvis's diary would have been there. A minute ago you were asking about Betty. Who's Betty?"

"Someone who's brought up in the diary," he said, somewhat vaguely.

"Why are you interested in all this?"

"Something's going on. My blurs. They started again."

"Oh, Daniel." It was amazing how much emotion she packed into those two words. "Have you told your father?"

"Not yet."

"What are the blurs of?"

"That doesn't matter."

"You must feel lonely."

That seemed like a curious thing to say, especially since she was the one who'd left him and his dad alone in the first place.

He switched gears, followed up on the loneliness deal. "Mom, why did you leave?"

He'd asked her this before and, honestly, he expected to get the same response he always got: that this wasn't the time to talk about it, that they would discuss it later.

Always later.

But tonight, to his surprise, she actually gave him an answer. "I wanted to protect you and your father."

"Protect us? From what?"

"I never told you how your grandmother died."

"Sure you did. She had a reaction to some pills she was taking."

"That was the best way to put it for you when you were younger. I just never corrected things. I guess it was easier to let that explanation stand."

"You lied to me?"

"No, I just didn't get into all of the details."

"So what happened? How did she die?"

A pause. "She took her own life, Daniel."

"What?"

"Pills. She overdosed on pills."

"How do you know it wasn't an accident?"

"She left a note."

Daniel tried to take all this in. "What did it say?"

"Daniel, I'm not sure we need to—"

"Mom, what did it say?"

"She wrote that she couldn't stand seeing them anymore."

"Seeing who?"

"We were never sure. She never told us."

"So she was seeing things, is that it?"

"We don't know that."

"But she could have been, I mean . . ."

"Like I said, we just don't know."

"So why didn't you—Wait a minute. It wasn't just Grandma, was it?"

"What do you mean?"

"You said you left to protect me and Dad, but you didn't say what you wanted to protect us from. It was you, wasn't it?

You've been seeing things? Or maybe hearing voices? Which is it?"

"This really isn't the best time to get into all this. It'd be better if we discussed this when I get back to—"

"Mom, I need to know."

She objected once more, then finally answered, "Yes, Daniel. Sometimes I see things that I can't explain."

"Do you sleepwalk?"

"Occasionally. Yes. I do."

"Did you ever hurt anyone while you were sleepwalking?"

"No."

"But you were afraid you might."

She didn't reply and he took that as a yes.

"So you didn't leave because you wanted to be with someone else other than Dad?"

"Of course not, no. I was just afraid of the things I was seeing. I tried visiting a psychiatrist a few times but it didn't help."

"Dr. Fromke?"

"Yes."

Daniel tried to process everything. There weren't that many psychiatrists in the area so if she was seeing one, it made sense that it would be him.

"I want you to come back, Mom."

"I'll be there as soon as I can."

"I don't mean just from Alaska. I mean come back. Come home."

"We'll talk more about this when I get down there, okay? And I need you to tell your father about these new blurs."

"I'll do it when I get home. You don't have to protect anyone, Mom. It'd be better if you were here."

"I love you, Daniel."

I love you, he thought, but he wasn't quite ready to say those words. "I'll talk to you soon," he said instead.

And with that, the call came to an end.

After he'd hung up, he joined his friends and summarized some of what his mom had said but he left out the part about her having hallucinations too. "Betty would have been Grandma's cousin, but my mom didn't know about her. We need to figure out what's going on: why my blurs have started again."

"How are we going to do that?" Kyle asked.

"Is the lighthouse still there?"

Kyle tapped at the screen of his phone. "Yeah. It's deserted, though. This page says the state has been trying to buy it, to preserve it as a historic landmark, but apparently that's all still in the works."

"Perfect. Tomorrow we head up there and take a look around."

"Are you serious?"

"Absolutely. My first blur led me to that barn. Now the diary we found there is leading us to the lighthouse. The girl in my blur told me that Madeline was waiting." He held up his phone. "And don't forget the text I just got tonight. Madeline wants me to come by tomorrow."

"She's not real, Daniel," Nicole said uneasily. "You sent that text to yourself."

"We don't know that yet, but even if I did, I wouldn't have sent it for no reason. Remember what I wrote in English class: 'Lost Cove is the key'? We need to visit Madeline Island and see what lies up there at the lighthouse."

• • •

Sheriff Byers returned to his cruiser and stowed his Maglite on the seat next to him.

As he drove home, he thought about his son's theory that someone with access to the Department of Natural Resource's wolf tagging GPS program might be the poacher.

He'd tried contacting Lancaster Bell earlier but hadn't been able to reach him. Now, he tried again and caught him at home.

Leaving out Daniel's name, he told Lancaster the theory about the wolf tags and asked if he could draw up a list of people who might have access to the files.

End call.

As he mulled things over, he recalled the missing gun, the .30-06 Browning Automatic Rifle, that the director of the Traybor Institute had reported stolen six weeks ago. It was the right caliber. It might be a stretch, but it could certainly be related.

No leads on that front.

Something to keep in mind, though.

So.

Get home.

Then find out from Daniel everything that happened when he and Nicole found that wolf.

. . .

As they tried to put together a plan for tomorrow, Nicole explained that she had church and then family obligations so she couldn't go along to the lighthouse.

Mia was babysitting her neighbor's kid all afternoon so she was out too, but Kyle and Daniel decided the two of them would cruise up to Bayfield.

"How are you going to get out to Madeline Island?" Nicole asked.

Sometimes, in really brutal winters, Lake Superior would freeze over, but this winter hadn't been that harsh yet, and besides, it was probably too early in the season for that anyway.

Daniel glanced at Kyle. "Your uncle Larry? You think he can help us?"

"Well, I mean, he's always told me I can use his boats, but I never really imagined I'd be asking him to use one in December."

Mia looked skeptical. "You really think you'll be able to make it all the way to the island?"

"I'm not sure. There's probably gonna be some ice on the lake, but it's at least worth a shot. We might not be able to get all the way to the lighthouse, but maybe seeing it in person will jar something loose in Mr. Ghost-Seeing Guy's memory."

"What do you think your mom'll say?"

"I should be able to convince her." Kyle looked in Daniel's direction. "What about your dad?"

"That may take a little work, but I think we should be fine."

"Alright, then. I'll call Larry first thing in the morning."

It was a little after eight and Kyle told them he needed to get home so he could tell his little sister a bedtime story, something he tried to do as often as he could. They agreed to touch base after he'd spoken with Larry tomorrow.

After saying goodnight to everyone, Daniel took the contents of the box with him so he could read through the diaries some more tonight.

As he drove home, he tried to think of how to convince his dad to let him investigate the lighthouse where his great-great-uncle went crazy and killed himself after a girl—who might have existed only in his imagination—burned to death.

• • •

When Sheriff Byers pulled into the driveway, he saw Daniel's car was already there but no lights were on in the house. There wasn't even a light coming out the window to the basement, where Daniel might have gone to lift weights.

Okay, that was a little strange. There was no way Dan would have headed to bed this early, not on a Saturday night.

Of course it was possible that one of his friends had picked him up, but he didn't really like depending on them for rides so he tended to be the one shuttling everyone else around.

The sheriff tapped the garage opener, pulled inside, then closed the door behind him.

Entering the kitchen, he tried the lights, but they didn't come on.

He clicked the switch up and down a couple times.

Still nothing.

Not even the microwave or the oven clocks showed the time.

All black.

A fuse?

Maybe.

But the garage door opener worked.

That might have been on a separate circuit.

Moonlight reflecting off the snow outside made its way through the window above the sink. Though it didn't provide a whole lot of light, it was enough for him to see the outline of someone standing at the far end of the kitchen.

"Daniel?"

No response.

"Are you alright?"

The figure came toward him and turned on a flashlight, directing the beam in front of him and making it impossible to tell who it was.

Sheriff Byers shielded his eyes and was about to pull out his own flashlight, but realized it was still in his cruiser.

"What's going on, Dan?"

The person came closer, but said nothing.

Law enforcement instinct told him to reach for his weapon, but his parental instincts stayed his hand.

When the figure was only a few feet away, he tipped the flashlight up, and just as the sheriff saw his face, he also saw the knife in his hand.

But by then it was too late.

The person swiped the blade forward, it slid into the sheriff's side, and, gasping for breath, he collapsed to the kitchen floor.

PART IV
THE ASYLUM

SUNDAY, DECEMBER 23

CHAPTER TWENTY-SIX

Daniel remembered only slivers and glimpses of what'd happened the night before and in the hours since.

Earlier, while he was half asleep, he'd asked a nurse why he was here. She'd been quiet at first, but finally told him that he'd hurt someone and that he was here for his own good.

"My own good? Who did I hurt?"

But then her response was lost in the fog of his dreams as he faded out again.

Now, he awoke with a doctor and a detective in the hospital room and they were asking him if he knew why he was here, if he knew what'd happened to his father. They pressed him, but he couldn't give them the answers they were looking for.

When he tried to sit up, he found that his arms and legs were strapped down to the bed.

One of the men said something about Madeline and the texts and about blood. Daniel tried to get him to explain more, but before he could, the doctor was jabbing a needle into his arm and giving him some sort of medication and he was feeling tired all over again.

Then, all the people were swallowed by the surge of all-consuming colors that swept over him.

And then they were gone.

Daniel dreamt.

Somehow you wake up but you're still asleep. The world is real and unreal at the same time. You're in your home and you rise from your bed and take a deep breath.

Awake.

Asleep.

It's all the same to you.

Your thoughts swirl through you. They flutter and twist before you. You try to grab one but it slips away and stares at you with a wide grin, with yellow-stained teeth sharpened to a point and you know that it is hungry.

You take a step forward. You're going to catch it.

Your feet move on their own, taking you into the hallway and then toward the kitchen.

And to the sink, where your thoughts hover.

They curl inward, creating a small dark whirlwind that traps the moonlight. Together, they descend and disappear into a point just above the drain that leads to the garbage disposal.

You reach out to grab the point of darkness that has swallowed your thoughts, tugged them into itself like a tiny black hole.

It drops into the garbage disposal, so you slide your hand into the drain. You can feel the blades, curved and sharp and patiently waiting for someone to turn them on.

You maneuver your hand farther into the sink's throat in search of your thoughts, your realizations, your hopes and dreams.

The blades are cool and smooth to the touch.

Cool.

And so, so smooth.

Above the counter, to the side of the sink, there are two switches next to each other—one for the light above the sink, the other for the garbage disposal.

In your dream you reach over to turn on the light.

And flick the switch.

But it's not the light switch after all.

You hit the wrong one.

In a whir of sound and spinning blades, the garbage disposal is alive and devouring your hand, drawing your wrist in. You hear the harsh grind of crushing bones, feel the wicked pain of tearing flesh, taste the fine spray of blood spurting from the sink.

You cry out in the night and jerk your arm out and stumble backward.

Your arm ends at the wrist in a blunt, ragged stump—shredded flesh hanging in gruesome strands, dripping dark blood onto the floor.

But then, before your eyes, your hand regrows. Four fingers and a thumb emerge from the meaty, raw end of your arm. They slide out, blood-covered, then the back of your hand forms and, as you turn it over, you see your palm appear.

The blood drips off as if it were being washed away by a stream of water.

Your hand has returned, reformed, regrown.

It's a dream, you know this, you tell yourself this. You know it's not real, but what is reality anymore? You're seeing and hearing and feeling things that could not possibly exist. But they do, they do. The real world is bowing to let them in.

The blood from your hand is pooling onto the floor, smearing out in a warm, wet circle.

Your eyes are drawn to that—to the way it glides into the grooved tiles and then eventually trails away in a neat, squared-off network of crimson on the linoleum.

You follow the line of blood with your gaze and see your father lying on the floor.

There's a knife in his side.

A kitchen knife.

Blood is pulsing from the wound. You rush over and kneel beside him to help him, but now you can't tell if this is really happening—maybe it did—or maybe it's going to?

A dream? A memory? Some sort of premonition?

You're not sure if you should remove the knife—if that would make it easier to stop the bleeding, or if it would just make it worse.

What have you done to your dad?

Voices in your head tell you to pull out the blade, to call 911, but you don't remember if you do or not.

The images fade into the cloudy, uncertain realm between unconsciousness and wakefulness as you reach for the handle of the knife.

Daniel opened his eyes.

He didn't know how long he'd been asleep, but they'd taken off the restraints and he sat up, somewhat groggy, then swung his feet out of bed.

Feeling a little nauseous, he hastily made his way to the tiny bathroom that was attached to his hospital room, then knelt in front of the toilet and emptied his stomach.

Maybe throwing up is a good thing since you might actually be getting rid of the drugs they gave you. Just get them out of your system, then you won't be so drowsy.

He rinsed the taste of vomit out of his mouth. As he did, he wondered what the staff might have given him and how long he'd been out since they'd drugged him.

The side of his head hurt. It felt like someone had smacked him with a two-by-four. When he rubbed the area he found a large tender welt.

He returned to the room to get his bearings.

First, he opened the shades.

Outside, a wooded park led to a shoreline. The far shore was out of sight so he assumed this would be Lake Superior since it was the closest body of water that large.

Based on the sun's location so low in the sky it was apparently either sunset or sunrise. By its orientation to the lake, he guessed it was almost dusk rather than dawn.

But what day?

Sunday?

The last thing he remembered clearly was leaving Nicole's house on Saturday evening and driving home.

You were supposed to go to the lighthouse on Sunday. Did you go and you just don't remember?

Could more days really have gone by?

There was no latch on the window, no way to open it. Four steel bars made it impossible to climb out, even if the glass hadn't been there.

Studying the room, he found no sign of his cell phone, car keys, or any personal belongings beyond the clothes he was wearing.

He went to the door that led to the hallway. A small slot at the bottom would allow someone to slide things into the room—maybe a meal tray, or a book, but nothing much larger than that.

A thick window with wire mesh running through it was located in the middle of the door to let doctors check on their patients from the hall.

No, this was not a normal hospital.

Daniel had never been in a psych ward before, but it didn't take a genius to figure out he was in one now.

An overweight cop sat in a chair on the other side of the hallway reading something on his phone.

You need to find out what happened to your dad.

Daniel tried the doorknob.

Locked.

No surprise there.

"Excuse me, sir," he called through the door. "Can you tell me what's going on?"

The man just looked up at him through the glass, rose stiffly, confirmed that Daniel's door was secure, then ambled down the hallway without answering him.

Daniel recalled that earlier a detective was in his room demanding that he tell him what he'd done with his father.

This guy's going to get the detective.

Daniel wracked his brain trying to remember what'd led him here, but could only bring to mind fragmentary images of the last couple days. It was as if he was sorting through a tabletop full of puzzle pieces, trying to slide them together, trying to solve a puzzle while having no clue what the final picture was supposed to look like.

Why? Is it the drugs they gave you? Why can't you remember what happened?

Here was a memory of breakfast with his dad.

There, one of him going to the barn with his friends.

One of the basketball game.

One of finding the DVD taped to his locker.

Nothing felt like it was in order.

Think, Daniel! What happened?

A party.

Calling his mom.

Seeing Ty Bell.

The blur of the girl.

Then leaning over his dad.

A knife was sticking out of his side.

This isn't right. You never would have hurt him. Never!

But the other night you did wake up standing beside his bed holding a hunting knife. What were you going to do with that if you weren't planning on using it?

He went to the window and tried to think things through, but was interrupted by the sound of someone at the door, unlocking it.

Turning around, he saw a hulking orderly standing there, blocking the doorway.

Okay, that guy spends some time in the weight room.

"There's someone here to see you, Daniel," he said gruffly.

"Who?"

Rather than answer, he just told him to follow him.

"What happened to my dad?"

The man was silent.

"Do you know?"

"No one does," he replied at last. "Except for you."

No, I don't. Not at all.

As they walked down the hallway Daniel tried to take everything in.

Yes, he was in a mental hospital.

He was just glad he wasn't in jail.

But what did it mean—being here instead? That they thought he was innocent? That they just didn't have enough evidence to arrest him yet?

It might mean they think you're crazy and you belong here rather than a prison cell.

Aren't you supposed to get a phone call or a chance to meet with a lawyer if you're suspected of a crime?

That's only if you're arrested. You're not under arrest here, Daniel. You're committed.

But who put you here? How did you get here, anyway?

Earlier, probably this morning—if it really was Sunday afternoon—his wrists and ankles had been strapped down. The hospital staff had given him some sort of drug to make him sleep.

But why would they do that if they wanted you to answer their questions about your dad?

Nothing made sense, and the more he tried to reason out the puzzle pieces, the more confusing and indecipherable the shape of the puzzle became.

Now, as they went down the hallway, Daniel could see that, just like the door to his room, the doors to the other patients' rooms also had reinforced glass windows and, as a result, he was able to get a look at some of the other people here.

And it was not encouraging.

One man was standing in the corner of his room smacking his head against the wall over and over. In his case, the wall was padded and it didn't look like he was hurting himself, but the sound of his head hitting that padding echoed dully, even into the hall.

The next room: A girl who looked a little older than Daniel sat on her bed with a long stream of drool oozing from her mouth. She was mumbling something to herself, although he couldn't hear what she was saying.

She must have noticed movement outside her door because she looked at him and smiled in a way that unsettled him, in a way that reminded him of the one the girl in his dream had offered him after she was consumed by the fire that started at the bottom of her nightgown and burned her to death.

Or the smile of that demon right before it flew toward you.

As they continued toward wherever they were going, an old man who was being led by a female orderly approached Daniel, stared directly at him and, as he was about to pass by, thrust himself forward and clutched Daniel's arm.

"You're the one!" the man cried.

His grip was tight and clawlike. The two orderlies struggled to pull him back and finally managed to get him separated from Daniel. But the old man didn't give up and kept trying to get to him. "You shouldn't have done that to your father!"

"What do you know about my father?"

Then the woman was leading him away, but he continued to call back to Daniel, accusing him of hurting his dad, and Daniel was shouting after him, "Tell me what you know about my dad!"

But there was no reply as they disappeared around the corner. Then Daniel's orderly was shuffling him past a maintenance closet farther down the hall.

Daniel had no idea who that old man was or how on earth he would've known anything about him or his dad.

This doesn't make any sense.

The orderly took Daniel into a visiting area near the main entrance.

Two male patients sat in the corner of the room across from each other at a checkers board, although only one of them was moving the checkers, as if he were playing against himself. The other man made indecipherable signs with his hands, doing his own private sign language to an invisible someone standing beside them.

Near the window, an old boxy television attached securely to the wall was playing cartoons with the sound muted. A woman who looked like she was in her fifties and wore a tattered, fuzzy housecoat was staring intently at the screen. Every so often she would laugh to herself, but her laughter didn't seem to have anything to do with what was happening on the television.

Why would they bring you here, to a place like this?

Then he saw who'd come to visit him.

No, it wasn't the detective as he'd suspected.

It was Nicole.

CHAPTER
TWENTY-SEVEN

She passed through a security checkpoint and was buzzed in to the room.

Daniel took a seat across from her at a hefty metal table that'd been bolted to the floor.

The orderly who'd led him here stepped a few feet away but Daniel imagined that he would still be able to hear his conversation with Nicole.

She reached across the table to take his hand but the man cleared his throat and shook his head to stop her.

After hesitating for a moment, she drew her hand back. "How are you?" she asked Daniel softly.

"I'm alright. Where are we?"

"Duluth."

"Duluth?" It was over an hour's drive from Beldon. He let that sink in. "Is it Sunday?"

"Yeah. Sunday afternoon."

"They said something happened to—"

"Yes. Something happened to Dad."

"To Dad?"

"Uh-huh." She tilted her head slightly so the orderly couldn't see her eyes, and then winked at Daniel, who caught on.

Maybe they only let family members visit.

But wouldn't they have checked her driver's license to verify who she was?

Maybe—but at least for now play this out like she's your sister.

"You really don't remember, do you?" she asked.

"He's missing."

Nicole was quiet.

"Tell me what's going on here."

She looked past him, then said, "They found you in the kitchen with a lot of blood all over everything. And he's gone."

"How could he just be gone?"

"I don't know. No one does. His car was still there. The blood on your hands, they had it tested. It was his. There was a knife on the floor. People are saying your fingerprints are on it."

"Who's saying that?"

"I don't know. It's just what I've heard."

"What kind of knife was it?"

"A kitchen knife."

"Not a hunting knife?"

"No. You don't remember any of this?"

He shook his head. "When I was asleep earlier, I dreamt about it—but I didn't think it was real—you know how dreams can be. Some of it was . . . Well, some of it couldn't have happened."

"What couldn't have happened?"

"I dreamt that I stuck my hand down the garbage disposal and that it got chewed up, that my fingers got torn off."

"Ew." She squinched up her face.

"Yeah." Though it probably wasn't necessary, he laid both hands on the table to prove that it'd only been a dream.

But if that part was just a dream, what about the part where you found your dad?

He thought about asking her how she'd heard where he was, but realized that if he did, it might give away that she wasn't his sister.

"Is there any word from Mom?" he asked. "They took my cell phone. There's no phone in my room. I don't have any way of contacting her."

"She's trying to get a flight out of Anchorage, but with the ice storm up there, it's not looking good—at least not for another day or two. But she knows what's going on."

He wasn't sure Nicole would have actually spoken with his mother, but it made sense that her mom would've been in touch.

"This is messed up," he said.

"Yes."

Daniel lowered his voice, hoping that the orderly who was still standing nearby wouldn't hear him. "Do we know any more about the lighthouse?"

She shook her head. "Kyle didn't go."

He leaned forward and whispered, "I need to get out of here."

"No kidding, but I'm just not sure how to—"

The man locked eyes on Nicole, then stepped toward them. "Sorry, visiting hours are over."

"I just got here," she objected.

"And now you're going to leave."

Daniel debated going toe-to-toe with this guy but couldn't see how, in the long run, that would work in his favor.

He stood and said to Nicole, "Tell Mom I'm fine. That I'll see her soon."

"I will."

He wanted to hug her, to reassure her, but when he took a step in her direction the orderly wedged himself between them.

Daniel felt the wolves fighting inside him, but decided the best way to see Nicole again soon was to let things be.

"It's going to be okay," he said.

"Yeah."

They said goodbye to each other and as Nicole left, he saw her touch away a tear.

On their way back to the room, Daniel took careful note of the location of the doors, where the security cameras were, the number of rooms in the hall, and the approximate distance between them, calculating, letting the math part of his brain take over, trying to create a mental picture of the building.

He had to find out where his dad was and that wasn't going to happen while he was locked up in a psychiatric hospital.

Yeah, he needed to get out of here and get back to Beldon as soon as possible.

But how he was going to accomplish that without a car was beyond him—even if he did manage to find a way out of the hospital.

The orderly led him to his room and, without a word, locked him inside.

Outside the window, the last few remnants of daylight were fading away, leaving only a black square in the middle of the wall, dotted with a scattering of lights from street lamps near the park.

They'll be looking for you in Beldon. The text from Madeline referred to meeting up with you. Somehow that lighthouse is at the center of all this.

You need to find out what's on that island.

While Daniel was considering that, he heard someone unlock the door to the hallway.

Turning to see who it was, he immediately recognized the man who stepped in and locked the door behind him.

Dr. Fromke.

His psychiatrist.

Well, good. Finally, someone who could give him some answers.

CHAPTER
TWENTY-EIGHT

"Is there any news on my dad?" Daniel asked urgently.

"Not yet. No."

"Dr. Fromke, you need to get me out of here."

"I'm working on that, Daniel. But first, we need to talk. You left your friend's house at just after eight last night. What were you doing there?"

"We were finding out whatever we could about the lighthouse."

"The lighthouse?"

"Yeah, where my great-great-uncle worked. The Lost Cove Lighthouse. He . . . Well, he killed himself and we were trying to figure out—look it doesn't matter. Right now we need to find my dad."

"Yes." He was still standing near the door as if he were guarding it from someone else coming in. "So, do you remember what happened at your house?"

Daniel had just been through all this with Nicole and he didn't really want to cover it again. However, he quickly filled in his doctor about what'd happened—at least as much as he could remember. He ended by telling him about the knife stuck in his dad's side, but explained that he'd only dreamt that part.

"So, he'd been stabbed, where? The ribcage?"

"Well, in my dream he was."

"Yes. Of course. Which side?"

"His right side—but none of that matters. We have to find him, not worry about where I dreamt he was stabbed."

"Indeed. And what's the next thing you remember?"

"Waking up here."

"And before you were there beside your father—do you recall what you were doing then?"

Daniel was getting irritated. "Just that I came back from Nicole's house. Before that we'd gone out to the barn on County N where I used to play when I was a kid. A blur led me there." He almost brought up the dead girl, but held back. "When do you think I'll be able to get out of here?"

"I'm working on it."

"You said that already."

"Yes," he replied. "I did."

"Why can't I remember what happened last night?"

"You had a nasty bump on your head. A little memory loss isn't uncommon for someone who gets a concussion. What do you know about the wolf being shot?"

"What?"

"A wolf was shot on Saturday. It was the last thing your father looked into before he went home. There was a picture of it on his phone along with a couple of messages from you about it."

"My girlfriend and I were out in the woods when someone shot it. What does this have to do with finding my dad? And how do you know about that, anyway?"

"We're just following up on everything we can."

"We? You're working with the cops?"

"I mean 'we' in general—all of us. We just want to find your dad and help him. You don't have any other information about where he might be?"

"No. How are you working on it?"

"Working on it?"

"On getting me out of here."

"I'm making the necessary arrangements. Don't worry. I'll take care of everything."

Based on how this little chat was going that didn't exactly reassure him.

Daniel said, "One of the patients here grabbed my arm when I was on my way to see Nicole in the visitors' room earlier. He said something about how I shouldn't have done that to my dad. How did he know anything about what happened?"

"I'm afraid word has gotten around."

They spoke for a few more minutes and then Dr. Fromke said he needed to get going.

"One more question," Daniel said.

"Yes?"

"We're in Duluth. You drove over here just to see me?"

"You are my patient, aren't you?"

"Yes, but I don't understand why you would come all this way on a Sunday afternoon."

"I thought it would be in your best interests if I did. I'm here to do what I can."

"I didn't do anything to my dad."

"Okay."

"Get me out of here, Dr. Fromke."

"I'm working on it."

After he left, Daniel ran through the conversation again in his head.

Weird.

And not very encouraging.

How did you end up in a psych ward sixty miles from home?

If they were suspicious that he might have been responsible for his dad's disappearance, why wasn't he in jail? Why did he wake up restrained in a mental hospital instead of handcuffed in a detention cell?

Then a thought came to him, and when it did, it seemed obvious, like something he should have realized right away: As his psychiatrist, Dr. Fromke could have had him committed. Besides his mom or dad, he was probably the only one who could have.

Maybe Dr. Fromke wasn't the one trying to get him out of this place.

Maybe he was the one trying to keep him in it.

For supper, rather than take Daniel to the cafeteria, the orderly who'd led him to the meeting room earlier slid a tray of food through the slot at the bottom of the door: cold soup, a turkey sandwich, a carton of skim milk and a stale oatmeal raisin cookie—nothing that you would need to use a fork or a knife to eat.

They didn't even give him a spoon for the soup. He had to drink it from the bowl.

No, it probably wouldn't be too smart to give crazy people in a mental ward knives and forks while they're locked up by themselves in their rooms. But no spoons. Seriously?

Without a clock, Daniel wasn't able to gauge time very well, but later, when he was getting ready for bed, he looked out the door's window and saw a cop sitting there.

It wasn't the guy who'd been there in the afternoon when Daniel first got out of bed; it was the man who'd been waiting for him after the game, the one who'd been leading the prisoner into the facility that supposedly did fish management studies, the man who'd driven into the snowbank.

He gave Daniel a look of recognition, then lifted a single finger to his lips as if to indicate to him not to make a sound.

CHAPTER
TWENTY-NINE

"Wake up, Daniel."

The voice sounded rushed, close to his ear.

At first he assumed he was hearing things or that it was just part of his dream.

He rolled to the side but heard it again, this time even more pressing: "Daniel. Wake up."

Eyes open now, he turned, but with only faint light from distant streetlights seeping through the window, the room was too black for him to see anyone. "Who's there?"

Someone gripped his arm and Daniel instinctively pulled away and tried to focus. The room was wrapped in shadows and he was still groggy.

The longer he had his eyes open, however, the more they started to become used to the darkness and now in the faint light he finally saw a man beside his bed.

"Ask questions later," he said, and finally Daniel realized he knew that voice: the cop—or at least the guy dressed as a cop—who'd been stationed outside his door. "Right now, we need to get moving."

"I'm not going anywhere until you tell me who you are."

"My name's Malcolm Zacharias." He put his hand on Daniel's arm again. "Come on. Let's move. I came to get you out of here. And believe me, right now that's what you want."

"Why are you helping me?"

"Because I need you to help me."

"How?"

"I'll explain later."

Daniel pulled his arm away. "Explain now."

"We have to go," Mr. Zacharias said emphatically. "You either come with me and find the answers you're looking for or you can stay here—and if you do, you won't be leaving any time soon."

"Why do you say that?"

"Because of what happened last night."

"With my father?"

"That's right, now—"

"Do you know where he is?"

"No, but I might know how to find him. Listen to me, the security guard on this floor is doing rounds on the other end of the wing but he's going to be coming this way any minute. After that it'll be too late."

Get out of here, Daniel. This is your chance.

Mr. Zacharias went to the doorway. He'd slipped something in between the frame and the door to keep it from closing all the way. Now he removed it, eased the door open, leaned into the hall, and whispered, "Now."

Daniel pinched his arm to make sure he wasn't still asleep.

He didn't wake up.

No, he was already awake.

None of the overhead fluorescents in the hallway were on. The only light came from the exit signs glowing at the ends of the hallway and a few dim emergency lights placed at regular intervals throughout the corridor.

The darkness around Daniel seemed to merge, regroup, combine and redouble heavier and thicker than before, as if it were alive.

He wondered if the shadows might shape themselves into the form of the demon he'd seen rise above Nicole's sketchbook or wing its way through the barn, but they didn't and he wasn't about to wait around for them to do so. He shifted his attention to Mr. Zacharias, who was motioning for him to come along.

Daniel went into the hallway, closed the door silently, and followed him.

But after a little ways, the movement of a flashlight beam cutting through the darkness at the far end of the hall caught his attention.

As the person appeared, even in the muted light Daniel could tell by the man's uniform that it was a guard, so he hurried in the opposite direction with Mr. Zacharias.

As he did, he recalled the logic problem Kyle had made up for him the other day at school: Guards in front of four doors. Two of the men always lie; two always tell the truth.

So now, Malcolm Zacharias—was he a truth-teller or a liar?

What benefit would he gain by lying to you? What benefit from telling the truth?

In the puzzle, logic led to the correct solution. Daniel tried to let it lead him now.

Who do you trust, Daniel?

He thought through what he knew—on Saturday Mr. Zacharias had been dressed as a prison guard and had led a prisoner into the Traybor Institute. It seemed a little unbelievable that he would show up now in another state dressed as a police officer, but Daniel had no reason to think that he was lying to him about trying to help him get out of the hospital.

And there's no reason to think he's telling you the truth either.

Except that he is helping you escape.

Or so it seems.

Daniel replayed his trip through the hospital earlier in the day as if it were a map unfolding in his mind. The layout, the distances, the locations of the security cameras were coming back to him.

He calculated that there wasn't enough time to get back to the room to hide from the guard, or enough time to get to the other end of the hallway.

"Are you coming?" Mr. Zacharias asked, his voice hushed and urgent. He was about ten feet farther down the hall.

Daniel remembered that the door just to his left was a maintenance closet.

It'll be locked.

At least try it.

He did.

Found it open.

Slipped inside.

Why is this unlocked? In a psych ward, why would they leave the maintenance closet with the chemicals inside it unlocked?

Questions with no answers—but right now that didn't matter. This night seemed to be governed by reasons all its own and he could sort them out later. First priority: get out of this place.

Mr. Zacharias stayed in the hallway.

This door didn't have a window so Daniel couldn't see into the hall, but he could hear the security guard's footsteps approaching.

His heart thumped so loudly in his chest that he imagined anyone nearby would be able to hear it, and that made him think of the Edgar Allan Poe story Teach had covered in class earlier that semester—"The Tell-Tale Heart."

It was another one of those stories where the protagonist was also the antagonist. The man who'd committed the murder heard his victim's heart continue to beat, continue to thrum in his conscience, driving him mad.

And what did Teach say on Friday? That the narrator might be unreliable. That he might not know the whole truth about what's going on yet.

Because he might be crazy, or delusional, or both.

The footsteps stopped just outside the maintenance closet.

So which is it for you?

Crazy?

Delusional?

Both?

"Stretching your legs?" an unfamiliar voice asked.

"Yeah," Mr. Zacharias replied. "It's a long time to sit outside that doorway."

"So they're going to transfer him out tomorrow?"

"That's what I heard. They don't want to take any chances. It's okay with me. This isn't the most exciting assignment."

That guard can hear your heart beating. He has to. He knows you're here.

No. That's impossible.

Daniel planned what he would do if the security guard opened the door. He couldn't allow himself to be locked up in that room again.

You can't let him grab you.

Push your way past him.

But then what?

Even if he made it to the visiting room where he'd spoken with Nicole earlier in the day, the main entrance would certainly be locked.

Daniel felt his hands tighten into fists as he waited in the closet. Fight or flight?

Well, both, if necessary.

"From what they're saying he slashed up his dad," the security guard said.

"That's what they're saying."

"Sick kid."

"Well, something's going on with him, that's for sure."

"They always bring the worst ones here. I wish I had your gig, just a temporary thing. You don't have to watch these nut jobs night after night."

"I'm thankful like you don't even know."

A pause.

"Alright," the guard replied finally. "Well, I guess I'll check the other wing."

"I'll see you on your way back through."

The sound of the guard's footsteps grew fainter and at last the door to the maintenance closet swung open and Mr. Zacharias gestured for Daniel to follow him.

The coast looked clear.

"How are we going to get out of here?" Daniel asked. "There are too many cameras near the entrance. They'll catch us before we even make it to the parking lot."

"How do you know about the cameras?"

"I saw them when I went to the visiting room this afternoon."

Depending on how good the cameras were, they might have already caught sight of him.

Daniel evaluated things. Most people coming into a hospital would enter and leave through the main doors, but not everyone. There might be a staff entrance, but even if there wasn't one, there would certainly be at least one other way out.

After all, what if there was a fire? With fire codes and that sort of thing there would need to be another way to exit the building.

Based on what he could make out about the size of the hospital from walking through it earlier, there was an even more obvious reason why there would be another door. "There's a loading area, right? A door out back where they make food deliveries?"

"So what they say about you is right."

"What's that?"

"That you're intuitive. That you're good at piecing things together."

"Who says that?"

Mr. Zacharias didn't answer, just said, "Come on," and he started to lead him down the hall in the opposite direction from the room where Nicole had been.

Soon, the hallway ended in an intersection. Mr. Zacharias made sure no other guards were in the hall, then whispered for Daniel to follow him.

They headed to the right, but they'd only made it a couple steps before they came to a patient's room with a man standing behind his door's wire-laced window, staring into the hall.

There was just enough light for Daniel to recognize the patient as the old man who'd grabbed his arm earlier and then told him, "You shouldn't have done that to your father."

The man flattened his palm against the glass as if he were trying to reach out and touch Daniel.

"What do you know about my dad?" Daniel asked.

"Come on," Mr. Zacharias said hurriedly. "We have to go."

"Hang on."

Daniel focused on the old man. "What do you know?"

"Time," he said. "You don't have time."

"Time for what?"

"He'll do it again."

"Who'll do what again? What are you talking about?"

Mr. Zacharias grabbed his arm. "Come on. We don't have time."

Daniel stared at him, then gave his attention back to the window in the door. No one was there.

The room appeared empty.

He just stepped to the side of the door. He's standing beside it.

Or, he might not have been there at all. You might have imagined him.

He tried the doorknob but it refused to turn.

"Can you open this?" he asked Mr. Zacharias.

"The only room key I have is yours."

"Did you see a man in there?"

"I wasn't looking. Now, let's go."

Daniel couldn't think of any way of confirming if the old man was real or not without getting the door open.

You need to keep going. You need to get out of here.

Sticking close behind Mr. Zacharias, Daniel entered the cafeteria.

Apart from being about half the size, it reminded him of the one at Beldon High.

They were on their way to the kitchen to find a delivery door when the alarm sounded.

CHAPTER THIRTY

A network of emergency lights flicked on as the alarm blared through the hospital.

Mr. Zacharias hurried toward the exit door with Daniel right behind him. "That alarm means we have twenty seconds before all the outer doors lock down," he exclaimed breathlessly.

"But you have a key, right?"

"Not to get past a lockdown."

Oh. Perfect.

With the time that had passed, Daniel guessed they had maybe fifteen seconds left.

As they rushed past the ovens and the dishwashing area, a clock ticked away in his head just like it did when he was on the free throw line during a basketball game.

Ten.

They reached the far end of the kitchen and Daniel heard the door from the hallway fly open and heavy footsteps charge into the room behind him.

Seven.

Mr. Zacharias fumbled with his keys to the exterior door.

Five.

Voices called out inside the cafeteria: "In here! In the kitchen!"

Mr. Zacharias threw open the door and they fled outside.

Two.

Daniel slammed it shut behind him.

One.

"Can they get out that door?" he asked urgently.

"They'll need to shut off the lockdown first, but that won't take long. Come on. I have a car waiting at the end of the block."

As they escaped into the shadows, Daniel heard people banging on the door as if they were trying to pound it open.

He and Mr. Zacharias made their way through the night to a nondescript black sedan waiting near a streetlight beside the park. It was a different car than the one with the Georgia plates, the one that'd gone into the snowbank on Friday night.

Lake Superior rippled nearby in the moonlight.

If they catch you, they're probably not going to just take you back to your room. They'll take you to jail this time to make sure you don't get away.

No, that didn't quite fit in with Daniel's plans of finding out what'd happened to his dad.

Mr. Zacharias clicked the unlock button on his key fob and slipped into the driver's seat.

The guards didn't see where you went. You're good for a minute or two. Figure this out.

Daniel climbed in beside him, and as soon as Mr. Zacharias reached around the steering wheel to slide the key into the ignition, Daniel grabbed his wrist with one hand, twisted it, and snatched the keys away from him with the other.

He'd been quick and had obviously surprised Mr. Zacharias, who now stared at him through the light cast down by the streetlamp.

"I want some answers," Daniel said, "and I want them now. We're not going anywhere until you tell me what's going on."

Honestly, he wasn't sure how Mr. Zacharias would react.

If he really was a police officer, or a prison guard, or whatever, he might threaten him or try to get the keys back, but Daniel had one hand on the door handle and was ready to take off if he needed to.

Kyle could certainly outrun this guy.

Can you?

Even though he wasn't as fast as his friend, based on how well he did on wind sprints for football and suicides for basketball, he was pretty sure he could get away.

Mr. Zacharias might have realized the same thing because he didn't go for the keys, but just said, "Despite what most people at that hospital think, you're not the dangerous one. The person who took your dad is."

"And who is that?"

"I'm not certain, but based on the amount of blood they found at the scene, your father was hurt very seriously and—"

"Who was it? Who attacked him?"

"I think it was a man we transferred from the Derthick State Penitentiary yesterday."

"The one you took to the Traybor Institute?"

Mr. Zacharias looked at him curiously. "How did you know that?"

"I was there."

"You were . . . Ah, so the dogs. You were the one they were after."

Daniel didn't mention that Nicole had been there too. "I saw you. The guy was handcuffed when you took him in. You're saying, that—what? He escaped?"

"Daniel, it won't be long before they find this car and when they do they're going to take you back into that hospital and this time around you won't be guarded by someone who's on your side—I can guarantee you that. But I *am* on your side. Believe me. Give me the keys. I'll tell you what I can on the way."

"On the way where?"

"Back to Beldon."

Whoever Mr. Zacharias was, he had helped Daniel out of the mental hospital and he was offering to drive him away from here. That much was true.

Though Daniel wasn't sure how much he should trust this guy, he did believe that the hospital security guards would be here any minute and if they managed to take him in, they certainly would be keeping a closer eye on him than before.

In the side-view mirror, he saw someone flare around the edge of the building, point at the car, and race in their direction.

Okay.

Time to go.

He handed over the keys. "Let's get out of here."

Mr. Zacharias started the engine and peeled away from the curb, keeping his lights off until he and Daniel were three blocks away.

"Alright," Daniel said. "Now tell me what's going on."

CHAPTER
THIRTY-ONE

"You said you were at the Traybor Institute." Mr. Zacharias continued picking his way through the city's back streets. "What do you know about it?"

"First of all, they don't study fish there."

"Why do you say that?"

"Lucky guess. It has something to do with chronobiology, doesn't it?"

"You really are starting to impress me. What else do you know?"

"Dr. Waxford isn't an expert on fish. He studies how humans relate to and process the passage of time. But I don't understand what that has to do with the prisoner you were leading into the facility."

Mr. Zacharias took a moment to gather his thoughts, then said, "Well, as you might know, the death penalty is becoming rarer these days. As a result, someone might be sentenced to several lifetime sentences in prison, or maybe even four or five hundred years for, say, being a serial killer. But they'll obviously never serve all that time because they'll die first. They might serve thirty or maybe forty or even sixty or seventy years—but that's still just a fraction of their actual sentence."

Daniel could see where this was going. "So, chronobiology. You're looking for a way to make it *seem* like hundreds of years have passed for someone. To make them experience, in their mind, that much passage of time."

"I'm not looking for a way to do it, I'm looking for a way to stop it—but yes, that's what the research is about."

"You're trying to stop it?"

"The group I work for is."

"What group is that?"

"I'm afraid that's something I can't tell you."

Why didn't that surprise him.

"You have a gift, Daniel. We know about what happened with Emily. With how you pieced things together after she was killed."

"How can you possibly know that? Even I don't know how I did that."

"Maybe I should've said we know *that* you did it, not *how*, because that's one of the things we're interested in talking with you about. We think you can help us locate people—missing people—maybe solve cold cases."

"How did you find out about me?"

"A source."

"A source."

"Yes. And we've been monitoring you."

"Monitoring me? What—my web searches?"

"And emails, status updates, instant messages, photos you've shared, texts. With technology the way it is today, do you really think there's such a thing as privacy anymore?"

"So you've been spying on me?"

"We've been collecting data."

That's a nice way to put it.

Daniel tried once more to get him to open up about who he was working for, but Mr. Zacharias remained evasive, so he let it drop. "You said before that I was intuitive. But I'm not. I'm not special. I'm just a normal guy who's starting to go crazy, to lose his grip on reality."

"Oh, you're special in ways you don't even realize."

"I still don't understand why you say that."

"Am I real? Right here? Right now?"

"Of course."

"How can you tell?"

"Because you're behind the wheel and I'm not. We wouldn't be going anywhere if you weren't really here, if you weren't really driving the car."

"But isn't it possible that you're still back in the hospital and you're imagining this, or dreaming it, or that it's all a blur?"

Daniel narrowed his eyes at Mr. Zacharias. "I never told you what I call them."

"What?"

"My visions, hallucinations, whatever. How do you know I call them blurs?"

"Research."

"Research."

"Yes. And for right now we'll have to leave it at that."

"And what about Nicole? How did she find out I was at the hospital?"

"I sent her a text."

"So she knows who you are?"

"It was sent anonymously."

There was an awful lot of that going around this week.

"Have you been sending me texts too? Signing them 'Madeline'?"

"No." He shook his head. "That wasn't me. You're going to need a place to stay tonight."

"What about you?"

"I'm set, but I need to take care of a few things. We have to find somewhere for you where you'll be safe."

At first Daniel thought that maybe staying at his own house would work, but then he realized that it would probably be one of the first places the cops would look for him when they found out he was missing from the mental hospital.

His two best options were Nicole's place or Kyle's house. Nicole had both parents at home, but at Kyle's there was just one parent to worry about.

"Let me use your phone," Daniel said. "I need to make a call."

PART V
GASOLINE

MONDAY, DECEMBER 24
CHRISTMAS EVE

CHAPTER THIRTY-TWO

Kyle answered right away and, after Daniel filled him in on what'd happened, said, "So, someone from a secret, shadowy organization was sent to help you escape from a mental institute and now wants to protect you because he's interested in your psychic crime-solving abilities?"

"Well, when you put it that way . . ."

"Bro, do you realize how crazy that sounds?"

"Let's avoid that term for now."

"Which one?"

"Crazy."

"I'm just saying—"

"I know, but trust me on this. We need to find my dad and the cops think I had something to do with his disappearance. If they catch me, they'll take me in—especially now that I snuck out of that psych ward. I need somewhere to stay tonight. Can I crash at your place?"

"Sure, no problem." It sounded like Kyle was shuffling his phone around, then he got back on the line and said, "Does this spy, or cop, or whoever it is, need a place to stay too?"

"He's real, Kyle."

"I didn't say he wasn't." But Daniel caught more than a hint of disbelief in his friend's voice.

"Here, I'll let you talk to him."

Daniel passed the phone over.

"My name is Malcolm Zacharias and Daniel is telling the truth. I'm here and I'm quite real; I can assure you of that." He gave the cell back to Daniel.

"Convinced?" Daniel asked Kyle.

He was slow in responding. "So it'll just be you?"

"Yes."

"How are you going to get over here?"

"Mr. Zacharias will drop me off."

"Well, um . . . Tell him to park down the street so Mom and Michelle don't wake up. I'll meet you at the front door."

• • •

THE TRAYBOR INSTITUTE
6 MILES EAST OF BELDON, WISCONSIN

In order to maintain the illusion that the facility was engaged in fish management studies, there were four large fish hatchery tanks for trout and walleye in the main section of the building.

However, the real research went on underground, in the rooms that did not appear on the blueprints.

Though in his midsixties, Dr. Waxford was not at all interested in retirement. He briskly entered the break room and, without putting any money into the snack machine, punched in D134 on the keypad and then took a step backward.

Instead of offering him a Snickers bar, the machine unhinged from the wall and swung forward automatically, revealing a set of stainless steel elevator doors behind it.

He leaned close to the retinal scanner beside them and after it positively identified him, the doors slid open and he stepped onto the elevator.

While the vending machine tracked back into place, he punched L3 in the elevator, then the doors closed and he began to descend.

As he passed the two subbasements L1 and L2, he thought of the importance of the work they were doing here.

Justice.

It was all in the name of justice.

Twenty-four years ago his younger brother had been murdered by a psychopathic killer who was responsible for the deaths of eight other people. He was sentenced to four hundred and fifty years in prison.

When he made his statement to the judge during the trial, he had mocked the pain of the victims and their families, claiming that he would never suffer as much as they had.

The man was fifty-two years old and a heavy smoker when he was caught. He died of lung cancer in prison less than five years later.

He served only one-ninetieth of his sentence.

That's what had gotten Dr. Waxford involved in this research in the first place.

If the United States of America was going to be a country governed by laws, if it was going to be a place where justice was truly served, then we needed to make certain we did all we could to ensure that the guilty served the sentences they were given.

Or at least that they *experienced* that many years of punishment.

That's all he was working toward.

True and lasting justice.

The elevator stopped.

No, of course there wasn't any way for someone to serve hundreds of years in prison. No one lived that long, at least not yet. Someday, through nanotechnology and bioengineering it might be possible, but that was still a few decades out.

In the meantime, through advances in chronobiology we had the capability to make it *seem* to someone like he was undergoing hundreds of years of imprisonment, or even solitary confinement, in much less time.

The doors parted.

It wasn't cruel and unusual punishment; it was simply the punishment that the courts had legally determined was just and fair. If the sentences weren't fair, why would they be handed down in the first place?

But not everyone was as forward-thinking as Dr. Waxford. And that's why his research was, for the time being, not open to public scrutiny.

He left the elevator and walked past the operating room.

It had a rolling gurney, medical equipment, computer monitoring feeds, and shelves containing the various instruments he used in his research.

And of course, the arrays of electrodes to stimulate the different parts of his subjects' brains that processed memory.

He was used to hearing screams come from that room.

He didn't mind them.

In fact, he'd come to expect them.

All in the name of justice.

Now, however, since no subjects were currently at the facility, the room was silent.

The inmate he'd been administering his treatments to on Saturday had escaped.

Dr. Waxford made his way to the security suite at the far end of the hall.

The four other subjects who'd been brought to the Traybor Institute since it had opened had been transferred to other prisons after the doctor was done with them, some still mentally intact.

Others, not so much.

He'd worked at two other facilities over the years and had been responsible for some of the major breakthroughs in the field of chronobiology.

That's what had caused the Department of Defense to take notice of his work.

Concerning the applications of chronobiology, the military had its own goals dealing with enhanced interrogations, but he didn't ask them about that. They were allowed to have their agenda and he was allowed to have his.

The Defense Department had an undisclosed agency that had been secretly experimenting for years to find ways to alter, implant, or erase people's memories and since they were helping fund his project, he was able to utilize their findings to augment his research.

Things had come a long way in the last decade.

He entered the institute's security center so he could review the video footage and try to figure out how inmate #176235 had escaped.

Here's what he did know: sometime between 4:20 p.m. and 6:25 p.m. on Saturday, the man had made it out of his holding cell on L2 before overpowering two guards and fleeing the property.

It was still unclear how he'd gotten out of that cell and how he'd taken out both guards so easily—and how he'd made it past the dogs outside—but somehow it'd happened and now he needed to be found before he did anything to compromise their research.

It was possible he'd received help once he was out. One of Dr. Waxford's hunting rifles—his .30-06 Browning Automatic—had been stolen out of his car a month and a half ago and he wondered if that security breach and this one might be related. He didn't want to write anything off as unrelated.

His staff hadn't been able to figure out what had happened on Saturday and now, tonight, he hadn't been able to sleep and had decided to come here himself to try his hand at getting to the bottom of things.

He sat down in front of the bank of computer monitors and pulled up the security footage to ascertain how the inmate had gotten free.

Maybe that would help determine where he was now.

The man was a loose end and he needed to be taken care of, whatever measures that required.

CHAPTER THIRTY-THREE

They arrived at Kyle's house and Mr. Zacharias parked down the block. "I'll be in touch with you tomorrow," he said to Daniel.

"I don't have a phone."

"Kyle does. I'll contact you through his number."

"And you're going to help me find my dad?"

"I'll do everything I can."

The phrase was nearly the same as the one Dr. Fromke had used when he'd promised Daniel that he was going to do all he could to help him get out of the hospital, so Daniel didn't find Mr. Zacharias's words as encouraging as he'd probably intended them to be.

"When are you going to text me, call me, whatever?"

"That'll depend. I have some things I need to take care of in the morning."

"We may be at the lighthouse."

"The lighthouse?"

"Up on Madeline Island. Long story. If you find out anything about my dad, text me right away."

"I will."

Daniel exited the car and watched Malcolm Zacharias drive off toward wherever he would be spending the night.

Just as Kyle had said, he was waiting at the front door and Daniel followed him quietly upstairs to his attic bedroom.

"Let me get this straight," Kyle said when they got there. "The guy we helped out of that snowbank, he's the one who got you out of the psych ward?"

"That's right."

"He's on our side?"

"He says he is, but honestly I'm not sure what to think. I just know he helped me escape from that hospital and then brought me here. On the way, he told me what they do at the Traybor Institute."

"Chronobiology research? Like we were thinking?"

"Yeah. It's to find ways to make prisoners serve their whole sentences, at least in their minds."

"Right . . . Okay . . . And . . . I don't even know what that means."

Daniel recapped what Mr. Zacharias had told him about Dr. Waxford and his research into making people perceive that they're spending hundreds of years in prison.

"But how's that justice?" Kyle asked. "Isn't that more like, well, torture?"

"I guess they would argue that it's not right for people to only serve part of their sentences." On the drive Daniel had taken some time to think about the whole deal. "What kind of justice is there in sentencing people to serve time you know they'll never serve? Just to make a statement? But to who? And don't you think it'd be a bigger deterrent if people who were about to commit crimes knew they actually would spend that much time experiencing solitary confinement if they were caught?"

"You sound like you believe in this stuff."

"I don't really, I just think . . . Well, I can at least see where they're coming from."

"And they're doing this on prisoners from the Derthick State Penitentiary?"

"Yes."

"How is that even legal?"

"I have no idea, but either way, Mr. Zacharias thinks the man they transferred from there to the Traybor Institute might have escaped and be the one who attacked my dad."

"What kind of crime landed him in prison in the first place?"

"Hmm . . . I didn't ask. I probably should have."

Kyle located a sleeping bag for Daniel and unrolled it on the floor of his bedroom, then went searching for an extra pillow.

You should've found out more from Mr. Zacharias about the prisoner—what he was in for, how dangerous he really is.

From past discussions with his dad, Daniel knew that in missing persons investigations the first twenty-four hours are the most important. After that, the odds are definitely not in your favor—at least not the odds of finding the person unharmed.

But Dad isn't unharmed anyway—remember? Nicole told you the tests proved it was his blood, that there was a lot of it.

Daniel was forced to just admit it: the odds weren't good for finding his dad *alive.*

Kyle returned with a pillow and gave him a T-shirt and a pair of shorts to sleep in. Daniel asked him, "Can you get away today?"

"My mom's spending the day with Glenn, shopping or something, I don't know. I'm supposed to watch Michelle while she's gone."

"Could Mia babysit for you?"

"No, she's going to Eau Claire with her family."

"Oh, that's right . . . What about Nicole? She's watched Michelle before."

"I'd need to clear it with Mom, but yeah, that should be okay. Why? What's up?"

"The lighthouse. We need to go up there like we were planning to do yesterday. Right now that's where everything's pointing. It's tied in with my dad's disappearance—I don't know how, but it is. We need to find him and our best chance is by starting up there."

"What about the Traybor Institute? You think we should check there first?"

Daniel shook his head. "If the person who attacked Dad did escape from there, then why would he go back? Plus, it didn't sound like Mr. Zacharias was working with them, so I'm not even sure how we would get in."

But then he decided that Kyle did have a point. "I guess we could anonymously call the police, maybe give them a tip to check out the institute. I mean, it couldn't hurt. Where's your phone?"

Although it was the middle of the night, if there was even a chance that his dad was there, the sooner law enforcement could search the place, the better.

Kyle dug through the stuff on his desk and came up with his cell. "But what if they trace the call? They'll find you, take you back, maybe arrest you."

"Download that app that disguises the sender's number."

Daniel wasn't sure it would stop a police dispatcher from tracing a call, but it was worth a shot.

Kyle tapped at his phone's screen, found the app and installed it. "Your dad's the sheriff. There's a good chance they'll recognize your voice at dispatch. Let me make the call."

He punched in 911, and as soon as the dispatcher picked up, Kyle said in a low, disguised voice, "The Traybor Institute. I think that's where Sheriff Byers was taken. Search it for him."

He hung up before the person on the other end could reply. They waited for a few moments just to make sure dispatch didn't call back. When the phone remained silent, Kyle asked, "What now?"

"We get some sleep."

"Okay. First thing in the morning I'll contact Nicole. I know she had some stuff going on, but if she can change her plans and babysit, then I'll clear things with my mom so I can go with you up to Madeline Island."

"They think I hurt my dad, maybe even killed him. You can't tell her that you're helping me."

"I'll think of something."

"I didn't stab him, Kyle."

"I know."

"I mean it."

A slight pause. "I know."

• • •

While he was reviewing the security tapes, Dr. Waxford got a call from the police that they were outside the institute and had an anonymous tip that the missing sheriff might be inside.

"I can guarantee you that no one else is here," he told him.

"You're here at the facility now?"

"Yes."

"Well, we need you to open the gate so we can have a look around."

He wasn't excited about the idea, but he was confident they wouldn't be able to find the research rooms and he didn't want to arouse their suspicion by arguing with them.

"Alright, I'm coming."

Who'd given them the tip to look here? His staff? No, that didn't make sense. Only a handful of people even knew about the true purpose of this place, and none of them would've had any good reason to call in the authorities. Then who?

The subject who escaped? Is he doing this to try to get law enforcement poking around?

Possibly.

That might explain things.

Still wondering what'd led them here, Dr. Waxford showed the sheriff's department deputies around and walked them through the main floor of the building. They studied things carefully but failed to find the elevator. Finally, when they were convinced that nothing suspicious was going on and that the place was clear, they thanked him for his time and left.

But he did not.

He'd committed himself to finding out what had happened with the missing inmate and he was going to stay here as long as it took to make that happen.

After returning to sublevel 3, he put on a pot of coffee, settled down in front of the computer monitors again, and went back to analyzing the footage.

CHAPTER THIRTY-FOUR

Daniel stood in front of the upstairs bathroom mirror at his friend's house.

On Friday night's bus ride to Coulee High, he'd looked out the window and noticed a faint reflection caused by the dim lights inside the bus. The image had overlapped with what he could see of the moonlit landscape outside and the two had merged, becoming one in that pane of glass.

Two realities filtering across each other.

Becoming one.

At the time, he'd reassured himself that he knew the difference between what was real and what wasn't, but since then he'd become less and less sure of that fact.

Despite himself, the wolves in Daniel's heart snapped at each other.

The protagonist can also be the antagonist.

We all play both roles in our lives.

A person can be his own worst enemy.

Dr. Jekyll and Mr. Hyde.

He stared at his reflection.

It was just a mirror. No way to see through it. No way to see another world.

But as he looked at himself and thought of Betty and the texts and the lighthouse and those words, "Lost Cove is the key," he saw a wound open up on his neck, an ugly slit about six inches long. It began seeping blood and should have hurt terribly, but he couldn't feel a thing.

However, when he drew his hand across it and looked at his fingers, there was a smear of blood on them.

Then the pain began.

And not just from the ragged incision, but also from inside it.

Something was moving around in there.

Daniel leaned forward and tilted his head so he could get a closer look at the cut.

As he did, a black worm emerged, thick and writhing and covered with a glaze of fresh blood.

It was the same kind of creature as the ones that'd crawled off the sheet of paper Friday night and burrowed into his arm.

This one started down toward the neckline of the T-shirt he was wearing, but he smacked at it and felt it squish to a juicy death beneath his fingers.

Immediately, half a dozen more came out.

He managed to brush them aside or crush them, but then a stream of others followed, teeming out of the cut, slithering across his neck and sliding down under the shirt. He gasped, ripped it off, and tried to knock them away, but others moved up the side of his head and across his chin toward his mouth.

There were too many.

"No," he cried as one of them went for his ear.

He snatched at it, but it broke in half and the part that was free wriggled in, disappearing into his ear.

"No!"

A knock at the door. "Daniel? Are you okay?"

Kyle's words sliced through the blur.

Shattered it. Sent images fleeting into midair.

The worms disappeared.

Daniel blinked.

Then again.

Nothing there.

He eyed himself in the glass. No bloody wound. No dark, squirming worms. Nothing out of the ordinary. The twitching, itchy sensations in his neck had gone away. He felt nothing in his ear canal.

"Daniel?" Kyle repeated.

"Yeah." He did his best to keep his voice calm. "I'm good."

"You sure?"

He was inspecting himself in the mirror as he ran his fingers across his healed, unscathed neck. "I'm sure."

Ever since his blurs had first occurred they'd seemed to be his subconscious's way of telling him something.

Okay, but what is that supposed to be telling you? A stream of black worms swarming out of your neck? Good luck deciphering that one, Daniel.

Well, he knew this much: the writing from English class that'd come to life and become those worms had been about the lighthouse.

So is this supposed to be your way of telling yourself to hurry up and go out there, or to stay away from the place for good?

He didn't know, but the weirder things got, the more he started to feel like he was just barely hanging on to the edge of a cliff, not sure how long he could hold on.

And not sure what it would mean for his sanity if he happened to let go.

When Daniel returned to the bedroom, Kyle informed him that Nicole had been able to rearrange her schedule and was set to babysit. "I told my mom I wanted to see you today. She heard you were in that hospital and she told me that it would be fine visiting you as long as Michelle was taken care of."

"At least you gave her the truth."

"Enough of it, anyway. She took off to meet with Glenn. Nicole should be here any minute. Oh, and I contacted my uncle—we're good to go in Bayfield. He's got a rowboat waiting for us. He said there's some ice surrounding the island, but he thinks we'll be able to get close enough to at least get a good look at the lighthouse, even if we can't actually make it to shore."

"That might not be enough."

"It might be all we can do. I doubt the ice will be thick enough to walk across."

A few minutes later, the ringing doorbell told them that Nicole had arrived.

CHAPTER THIRTY-FIVE

As soon as she was upstairs in Kyle's bedroom, she threw her arms around Daniel.

It felt so good to hold her, like an anchor back to what was real. He drew her close and, at least for the moment, stopped thinking of blurs and mental asylums and his missing father.

Here was something good, something right, and he didn't want to do anything that would make it slip away.

At last she stepped back and asked him breathlessly how he was feeling, how he'd gotten out of the hospital, if he'd heard anything about his dad, and how he'd managed to get back to Beldon.

Kyle went to the living room to watch Michelle while Daniel brought Nicole up to speed.

She listened intently as he told her about Mr. Zacharias and his theory that the man who'd been brought over from the prison had escaped and gone after his dad.

"So," she said, "this Zacharias guy transported that prisoner to the institute and now he's working against them? Does that make any sense to you?"

"I'm not sure how it all fits together, but I did get the feeling that he really does want to help me find my dad."

"He's going to be okay, right? Your dad, I mean?"

"Don't worry. We'll find him." Daniel wanted to say more, wanted to promise her that his dad was going to be fine, of course he was, but he couldn't quite bring himself to say it. In truth, he didn't even know that they were going to find him at all, but he felt like he needed to tell Nicole something, and reassuring her at least a little bit felt like the right thing to do.

"Yeah." She nodded. "Okay."

"Kyle and I should probably get going."

He waited at the top of the stairs behind the banister while Nicole went down to get set with Michelle.

The four-year-old knew Nicole from previous times when she'd babysat for Mrs. Goessel and now she went right up to her, took her hand, and asked if she wanted to see her new stuffed puppy named Penguin.

"Your puppy is named Penguin?"

"Uh-huh," Michelle said, as if it were the most natural thing in the world. "I named him myself."

After the two of them were in Michelle's bedroom and the door was closed, Kyle signaled for Daniel to join him.

"Anything you need before we go?"

The only clothes Daniel had with him were the ones he'd been wearing when he left the hospital. "If we're going to be out on Lake Superior, I'll need some warmer clothes."

As he and Kyle were about to head out the door, Daniel paused.

He hadn't spoken with his mom since his dad had disappeared and he felt like he should talk with her, fill her in—but when he brought it up, Kyle said, "What if she tells my mom that you called her? Don't contact her yet. Just let it be."

"If she hasn't found out yet, she'll hear soon enough that I broke out of that psych hospital. She's already got my dad to worry about. I don't want her to be freaked out when she hears I'm missing too."

"Dude, she took off. It's on her, not on you."

"She's just at her brother's house to celebrate Christmas."

"You know what I mean."

"She has a right to know what's going on. She *is* my mom."

"Well, she sure hasn't been acting like it."

Sharp words. And just a few days ago Daniel might have said them himself, but when he'd spoken with his mom on Saturday she'd told him that she had left in order to protect him and his dad.

She sees things too. She knows what it's like.

Daniel hadn't gone into all that with Kyle earlier and he didn't want to explain everything right now. "I hear what you're saying, but there's more going on here. I need to let her know I'm okay."

At last Kyle gave in.

In order to keep his mom from finding out he was with Kyle, when Daniel put the call through he used the app that disguises the sender's phone number.

She didn't pick up. When it went to voicemail, he left a quick message: "Mom, what they're saying I did to Dad—it's not true. I didn't hurt him. I'm okay and I'm going to find him. I promise."

As he hung up, he realized that in the last five minutes he'd promised two people that he was going to find his dad, and he had no idea how he was going to keep that promise to either one of them.

• • •

Sheriff Byers opened his eyes.

He couldn't see much, but with the light that slipped in beneath the door about twelve feet away he could make out that, apart from the bare metal cot he was lying on, he was in an empty, windowless room.

He tried to sit up, but pain shot through his right side and he ended up dropping back onto the cot again.

Looking down, he saw that his shirt was gone and his side had been bandaged, the place where he'd been stabbed covered with a fresh dressing.

Someone had handcuffed his left wrist to the cot's frame.

How did you get here?

He remembered being attacked, yes, but he didn't know how much time had passed since then. However, he had the sense that he'd been wavering in and out of consciousness for quite a while.

Maybe he'd been drugged.

Since his torso was bandaged, it meant that whoever had brought him here was trying to keep him alive, at least for the time being.

Interesting.

A ransom?

Possibly.

Where are you? What's going on? Get your bearings.

The room smelled of pine, with a touch of wood smoke from a fireplace or wood burning stove, and in the faint light he could tell that the walls were made of logs.

After working in law enforcement in this county for nearly twenty years, he knew a lot of the houses in the area. As far as he could tell, he'd never been in this residence before.

It might have been any one of the dozens of cabins that surrounded the lakes in the region.

Inspecting the cot, he saw that the legs had been nailed to the floor to keep him from moving it.

He listened.

Someone was in a nearby room. It sounded like he or she was going through a cupboard of pots and pans.

On Saturday night, in the instant before he'd been stabbed, he'd recognized the man who was attacking him, and now he wondered if it was the same guy in the other room.

Brandon Hollister: a killer he'd caught two years ago. He was in his twenties and had been one of the bad influences on Lancaster Bell's son, Ty.

But he was bright and had made it into medical school.

One night when he was back home for the weekend, he'd stabbed a neighbor in a bar fight after they'd both had too much to drink.

The victim had died, and Hollister's claim that it was self-defense didn't fly with the jury. He'd been sentenced to life plus fifty years for aggravated battery, first degree murder, and a slew of other charges related to fleeing and resisting arrest after the incident.

How he'd escaped from the Derthick State Penitentiary was a mystery to the sheriff—and so was the fact that no news had come through dispatch about it on Saturday afternoon or evening.

Why wouldn't the warden have released word to the law enforcement community?

Unless he didn't know the guy was missing.

But how would that have happened?

And if Hollister is acting out of revenge for you catching him, why would he have bandaged you up rather than just letting you die?

Sheriff Byers was tempted to call out to whoever was in the cabin with him, but realized that if it was Hollister, it might be better not to let him know he was conscious. Instead, he should probably spend some time assessing the situation and trying to find a way out of here.

His gun and radio were gone, as well as the keys to the handcuffs.

Okay.

Priorities: lie still to keep the stab wound from tearing open, and try to figure out a way to pick those cuffs.

CHAPTER THIRTY-SIX

Kyle and Daniel grabbed a quick lunch on the way, and arrived in Bayfield at quarter to twelve. They parked in front of the Apostle Islands Sailing Adventures & Boat Rentals office on the Lake Superior shore.

Just beyond the building, the lake stretched out dark and foreboding toward the islands. Daniel could see one of them a few miles offshore and even though he wasn't positive which one it was, from studying the maps online yesterday, he guessed it was probably the one they were looking for—Madeline Island.

Though most of the lake was still open water, there were some stray ice floes and it looked like a narrow strip of ice did encircle the island and also spread out from the shoreline near Larry's business. Some of it was missing near his dock, where he'd apparently cleared it away so he could get his boats onto the lake.

A skiff with an outboard motor waited for them.

"Okay," Daniel said as they approached the front door, "we can't tell him he's lending a boat to someone who just escaped from an insane asylum."

"Or someone who was found covered with blood at a crime scene where his dad went missing," Kyle added.

"That too."

Larry had joined the Peace Corps after graduating college with an agricultural degree. He'd volunteered in Africa for a couple of years before returning to the States and moving up here to work for the guy who owned this boat rental business. A year later, the man was killed in a snowmobile accident. He didn't have any family and had left the business to Larry, who'd been running it ever since.

Daniel had never met him, only heard about him, and now when Kyle's uncle opened the door, he had the sense that he would have fit in better on the beaches of Jamaica than a small town here in northern Wisconsin. Wearing a tie-dyed T-shirt, and with dreadlocks and scholarly glasses, he looked like a mixture of a hippie beach bum and tax accountant.

After a warm greeting, he invited them in.

Kyle simply introduced Daniel as his friend—not as someone who had hallucinations, heard dead people talk, or went sleepwalking carrying hunting knives around the house.

Better safe than sorry.

"Right on," Larry said amiably. "Well, there's no wind today so you should be okay. It's about two miles to Madeline Island. I checked the motor—she's working fine but there are oars in the boat in case you run into trouble. You know how cold it is out there, so don't do anything stupid. And life jackets: I want you both wearing them."

Kyle nodded. "Okay."

"Tell me again why you need to go to—no, wait, don't tell me. I probably don't want to know—or do I?"

"It has to do with one of my relatives," Daniel replied. "He used to be a keeper out there at the Lost Cove Lighthouse."

"Really?"

"Yes."

"That place hasn't been in service in years."

"This was back in the thirties."

"Huh." Daniel couldn't tell what Larry might have been thinking.

"No one really goes up there anymore," Larry noted.

"We just found out about him. We didn't want to have to wait until spring to see where he worked."

That was true enough.

"So, curiosity?"

Daniel and Kyle shared a look. "Right," Daniel replied.

Larry nodded toward Kyle. "And your mother? She's fine with this?"

He opened his mouth as if he were going to answer, then closed it again.

"Aha." Larry evaluated that. "Well, clearly there's more going on here, but I think I'll opt for plausible deniability—as long as you guys promise to be careful out there."

"We will," Daniel assured him.

• • •

On the dock, Larry handed them each a life jacket, then indicated the rowboat. "It's designed more for stability than for speed. Most people, they come up here and want to tool around the islands for a day or two. All I care about is them being safe."

"Right," Kyle said.

Larry dug a compass and a map of the islands out of his coat pocket. "If you're just going to Madeline you shouldn't need these, but there's a chance of snow and the visibility might be limited. You should be fine, but if it does start snowing it's pretty much a straight shot east. The lighthouse is on the northern tip of the island, on the other side of an inlet."

"Great." Daniel accepted the map and compass. "Thanks."

"I hope you find what you're looking for."

"So do I."

He and Kyle climbed into the boat.

Even though Daniel was familiar with how to run an outboard motor, he let Larry talk him through the steps.

Then they took off.

Just as the snow began to fall.

Nicole Marten was worried about her boyfriend.

It was a weird deal.

She cared so much about him, but she was also scared about the things that happened with him—the hallucinations; the sleepwalking; the bizarre, terrifying blurs.

She'd never been afraid of him, it wasn't like that. She trusted that there was a bigger reason behind everything that was happening, although she didn't know what that might be.

But right now, even more than being concerned about Daniel, she was worried about his dad.

Before leaving the Goessel's house, Daniel had assured her that they would find his father in time, but she realized there was no way he could guarantee that, no way anyone could.

Still, for some reason, hearing him say it had helped, at least a little.

Now, as she had a pretend tea party with Michelle, she prayed that Daniel would be safe going out on the lake, and she prayed for his dad—that he would be okay until someone could find him and help him.

In the back of her mind she was also thinking of her boyfriend's blurs and the research facility and the wolf poaching.

It seemed like, somehow, everything was tied together.

If Daniel was going to focus on finding his dad, and the wolf poaching was at all related to everything else, maybe she could help by trying to solve that.

She wasn't sure what she could do right now, but later, when she put Michelle down for a nap, maybe she could go online, search through the information they had on the wolf poaching locations, and see if she could uncover anything that they might have missed earlier.

CHAPTER THIRTY-SEVEN

The black, ominous-looking surface of the lake hungrily absorbed the snowflakes as soon as they landed.

As Daniel worked the motor, Kyle kept an eye out for ice floes.

Because of the noise of the outboard, neither of them spoke much, but Kyle pointed when he saw ice and Daniel navigated past it.

Being on the water reminded Daniel of fishing and canoeing trips he'd taken with his dad, and he found himself worrying once again about him.

Where is he? What really happened to him?

Questions about his dad's disappearance plagued him.

Who called 911 when he was attacked? Why can't you remember being there? If this escaped prisoner did stab him, where did he take him? Why?

The falling snow eventually made it impossible to see the island, but with the help of the compass, they soon found the ice-encased shoreline and followed it north toward the cove where Larry had told them the lighthouse was located.

Daniel throttled the outboard down so he and Kyle could talk.

"Hey, I have a question for you," he said. "It's something I've been curious about for a long time."

"What's that?"

"Why don't you go out for sports? I mean, I've seen you run. You could probably qualify for state in cross country—track too—if you wanted to."

"That came out of nowhere."

"I was just thinking about last night and how I might have needed some real speed. That brought it to mind."

"Last night?"

"I took Mr. Zacharias's keys when we were in the car. I thought I might need to outrun him and I realized you wouldn't have had any trouble doing it. Anyway, I was just wondering about track and cross country. If you don't want to talk about it, that's cool."

"I guess it's no big deal—telling you, I mean." But Kyle stared at the lake quietly for a long time before going on. "It has to do with something that happened back when I was a kid. At the time, I was playing baseball."

"I didn't know you ever played baseball."

"Well, I didn't for very long. Pretty much I sucked, and everyone knew it—including my dad. One game I was up to bat and we were behind. Bottom of the ninth inning. Two outs. Two guys on base, and we were two runs behind. It sounds like a cliché but it was true. My dad was in the stands when he got a page from the hospital. He must have figured I wouldn't get on base because he left to answer it. But I didn't know he'd gone anywhere."

Kyle's dad had been an emergency room doc and Daniel wondered how serious of a situation it had been. Maybe he needed to leave; maybe he just chose to because he knew his son would strike out.

Daniel maneuvered the boat around a slab of ice about the size of a car.

"So, anyway," Kyle went on, "like I said, I thought he was still there. So the first two pitches were strikes and, well, I didn't want to strike out without at least trying to hit one of the pitches with my dad watching. So I swung at the third one and actually hit it. I mean, I swung as hard as I could and it was just plain luck that I connected with the ball. But I did. It was the farthest I'd ever hit a baseball before in my life. It went over the fence—just barely, and I mean, you know, this was just a kid-sized park, but . . ."

"But it was a legit home run."

"Yeah. It was."

"And your dad didn't see it."

"Right. So the two other guys scored—obviously—and I was on my way toward home with the game-winning run and I glanced up to where my dad had been sitting and no one was there. I couldn't see him anywhere and I realized he'd missed seeing me hit the ball. I was so disappointed that I ended up staring at the ground when I crossed home plate."

Silently, he pointed out a six-foot ice wedge and Daniel took them past it.

"He apologized later when he found out he'd missed my homer," Kyle concluded. "I never told him about how I felt when I crossed the plate. I didn't want him to feel bad about what had happened, but I also didn't want him to be disappointed in me since I knew it was just a fluke and it wasn't gonna happen again. I didn't want to let him down so I just gave up on organized sports—all of 'em. After he died two years ago in that car crash I just, well, I just never got back into them."

"I think he'd be proud of you if you ran."

"Hard to say. But that's why I don't. There you go. Now you know."

The conversation ended somewhat awkwardly and abruptly.

As they rode in silence beside the ice surrounding the island, snow began to accumulate next to them on the seats of the boat.

Then they came around the corner of the inlet and got their first glimpse of the lighthouse.

CHAPTER
THIRTY-EIGHT

It was perched on a rocky point on the other side of the cove.

The lighthouse must have been painted white long ago, but over the years the paint had peeled and chipped away after being in the exposed sunlight and the unyielding wind coming in from across the lake.

From their research, Daniel knew that the tower rose one hundred and twelve feet above the rocks. The keeper's house was attached to its base and it looked like it was as long-abandoned as the lighthouse itself.

According to the journal entries, Betty had been standing in the field near the house when she bumped into the lantern and her nightgown caught on fire.

A chill sank down Daniel's spine.

Was she real?

Did she really die here?

He didn't know, but he was seriously starting to consider the possibility that Jarvis Delacroix had only imagined her, that she'd grown out of the insufferable loneliness that came from being stuck on this island by himself.

The field surrounding the house was covered with what appeared to be several feet of snow. It would make sense that the island would get battered with lake-effect snow and Daniel could only imagine how much would accumulate out there by winter's end.

A metal mesh fence skirted the property to keep trespassers out, but the lighthouse was accessible from shore—at least it would've been if it weren't for the thirty-foot-wide ring of ice that entrapped the island.

From where they were it wasn't possible to tell how thick it was.

Daniel stopped the boat's motor so he and Kyle could talk more easily and his friend pulled out the oars to row them up to the edge of the ice.

"Okay," Kyle said, "it looks like we're stuck out here, but at least we can get a look at the lighthouse. Does it make you remember anything?"

"Not really, except what we read in Jarvis Delacroix's journal about Betty dying out here. I think I need to go inside."

"How are you supposed to do that?"

"It's only about thirty feet to the rocks."

"Thirty feet is thirty feet, bro."

"We're going to have to cross the ice."

"When you say 'we,' do you mean 'we' as in 'you,' or 'we' as in 'both you and your not-exactly-thrilled-to-die-by-drowning-today friend'?"

"I've got an idea, but it would mean 'we' as in 'me.'"

"Seriously, I'm not thinking that ice is thick enough to walk on."

"I'm not going to walk on it."

"How do you plan to get across?"

"I need to spread out my weight."

"Yeah, well, it'd be ideal if we had some cross-country skis or something. Then you might make it, but . . ."

"Well, we have something close."

"What's that?"

"Hand me those oars."

CHAPTER THIRTY-NINE

"The oars?" Kyle said. "Are you kidding me?"

"If I kneel on the blades and hold on to the shafts, I should be able to slide them forward one at a time."

"And just, what—crawl across the ice with the blades distributing your weight?"

"Yup."

"That's crazy."

"We agreed not to use that word."

"Here it applies."

Daniel leaned over the rowboat's gunwale and felt the edge of the ice, but found that it was just an inch or so thick here, which he guessed was way too thin to support his weight, even if he were using the oars.

The water somehow felt even more frigid than the ice itself.

Despite himself, Daniel shivered as he shook the drops off his hand.

"What did I tell you?" Kyle said.

Daniel pointed farther down the inlet. "Let's check down there, see if it gets any thicker."

Though he still didn't appear excited about the idea, Kyle rowed while Daniel checked the ice at regular intervals and eventually, about thirty-five yards away, found a spot where a section of thinner ice had broken away and drifted off. The ice that remained was several inches thick.

"Hold on," he told Kyle. "This looks good."

From here, the ice stretched nearly forty feet to the rocky shoreline.

Daniel had heard that the average depth of this lake was more than four hundred feet, so even this close to shore he doubted that the anchor rope would be long enough. However, they needed to do something to keep the boat in place. He tried the anchor, and thankfully, after about fifty feet of rope had played out, it came to rest on the lake bottom.

He cranked up the slack to keep them in place.

"Okay," Kyle said, "let's assume for just one minute that you don't crash through the ice and drown."

"I'm good with that."

"What if you find something there at the lighthouse? How are you supposed to get it back here if you're crawling across the ice?"

"That'd be a good problem to have. I'll deal with that when the time comes."

After handing over the map and compass, Daniel placed one of the oars on the ice with the blade parallel to the boat.

He tried curling his hand around the shaft and found that, because of the way the oar had been cut, there was just enough room for his fingers to fit between the shaft and the ice.

It was a tight squeeze, but it would work.

All things being equal, water freezes first close to shore, where it's shallower and the current isn't as strong, so he figured he would need to be the most careful here, near this edge where the ice wouldn't be as thick.

Kyle shook his head. "There is no way this is a good idea."

"You're probably right." Daniel lined up the second oar. "I'll keep my life jacket on to avoid the drowning part."

"Somehow that doesn't exactly reassure me."

"Let me see your phone."

"For what?"

"I can use it as a flashlight if I need to look around inside the lighthouse."

"It's not waterproof. If you wreck it when you drown, I'm going to be very upset."

"I'll keep that in mind."

After pocketing the phone, Daniel gingerly climbed over the gunwale, and finessed himself so that he was kneeling on the oars.

Distributing his weight was tricky and getting back into the boat later was going to be even trickier, but he decided not to dwell on that right now.

Just don't fall through the ice or it's gonna be one long, cold trip back to Larry's.

As he eased forward, the ice let out a faint groaning sound.

Immediately, he stopped crawling. It seemed like his heart somehow paused midbeat and, at the same time, slammed out its rhythm even harder than before.

"It's not too late," Kyle said softly, as if he were afraid that the weight of his words might somehow crack the ice Daniel was kneeling on. "You can still get back to the boat."

"I'm good. I know how to swim and besides, you're a lifeguard, right?"

"Sorry, buddy, but I'm not diving in there for you."

"Not even for your phone?"

"Well . . . Maybe for the phone."

"Spoken like a true friend."

"Just take it easy, okay?"

"Yeah."

Daniel moved one oar then the other, using them to support him as he crawled toward the island. Occasionally, the ice would creak under his weight, but he was careful not to let either of his knees slide off the oars' blades.

At first it was slow going, but by the time he was about halfway across, he was able to get into a rhythm. From there, it went faster, and before long he'd covered the rest of the distance between himself and the shore.

Once he was on the bank, he called to Kyle, "See? No problem." He set the oars beside one of the boulders. "I'll be back in a couple minutes."

"Be careful."

"My middle name is Mr. Careful."

"That doesn't even make sense."

"I'll see you in a few."

Scrambling up the ice-covered boulders on shore was a little dicey, but he made it. Once he had his footing, he took off his life jacket and laid it on the rocks, then stepped onto the snowy field that he would need to cross in order to get to the lighthouse.

All was quiet on the island except for the splish-wash of waves against the ice as the wind began to pick up.

From here it was maybe twenty-five yards to the lighthouse.

Fresh deer tracks were the only thing that marred the otherwise pristine snowy field in front of him. With the woods beyond it and the snow continuing to fall, the day was tranquil and beautiful.

Then he reminded himself that this was the field where, supposedly, an eleven-year-old girl had burned to death.

You saw her in your dream. You saw her at the game. Are you going to see her again here?

Maybe she would appear to him standing in the snow, her blackened body sizzling as the snowflakes touched it, her arms outstretched toward the tower where her uncle was when her nightgown caught on fire.

Or maybe she would emerge from the top of the lighthouse and stand there, staring down at the island she would never leave.

Daniel peered up through the falling snow and could see the outline of the tower.

No girl.

No blur.

And she wasn't in the field either.

It was just a hushed, snowy day on an island in Lake Superior. Nothing out of the ordinary about it.

Was Betty real?

Did a girl actually die out here in this field?

He didn't know, but maybe the answer lay inside the lighthouse.

It looked like the only way into the tower was through the house.

The snow came up to his knees as he crossed the field and arrived at the front door of the keeper's home.

The windows were shuttered, but the door hung at an awkward angle on its rusted hinges.

It resisted, but Daniel muscled it open.

And stepped inside.

CHAPTER
FORTY

The entryway was littered with trash. Crude graffiti covered the walls. Stumps of candles and discarded beer cans lay in the corners.

It didn't really surprise him that this would end up being a place where people would come to party, but it did make him wonder if there would be anything helpful left here for him to find.

With the windows boarded up, the interior of the home was thick with shadows, so Daniel pulled out Kyle's phone and scrolled to a flashlight app.

Using it to guide his way, he entered the first room.

It must have served as some sort of central living space because it led to the kitchen and a short hallway with two attached rooms. One of them was only about eight feet long. With the shelves on one side, he guessed it might have been used for storage. The other was probably the keeper's bedroom.

Maybe Betty slept there in the storage room.

That is—if she was ever really here.

Turning to the left, he used the phone to illuminate the kitchen, which was still, inexplicably, stocked with a large pile of split logs to use in the potbellied stove.

Who knows—the wood might have been brought in by the people who come here to party.

Nothing appeared to be suspicious or out of place for an old abandoned lighthouse.

After searching through the storage room and the bedroom once again and coming up empty, he decided to investigate the tower itself.

The spiral staircase leading up into it appeared to have been designed for someone short, so Daniel nearly had to duck.

Kyle would have had a rough time being a keeper here.

There were no windows, making Daniel's ascent feel even more confined, but the door at the top must have been open because light was filtering in and windblown snow curled down around him.

These are the stairs that Jarvis Delacroix climbed six times every night when he came up to make sure the light was still burning.

Six times.

Every night.

Daniel wondered what it would've been like to do that, to know people were depending on your ability to stay awake—that they were betting their lives on the fact that you could keep the light in this tower burning.

He arrived at the top.

The glass from the light had been shattered and shards lay strewn across the floorboards. A narrow balcony hugged the tower. Cautiously, he stepped onto it.

The railing was gone, rotted away, so he was careful to stay close to the tower as he looked around.

From here he could see the barren shoreline stretching out in both directions, but with the snow cascading down on the lake he couldn't make out any of the other islands or the mainland.

He did, however, catch sight of Kyle in the rowboat. At the moment, he was looking toward the forest nearby rather than at the lighthouse.

Daniel tried calling to him, but his words were fighting the wind and Kyle apparently couldn't hear because he didn't face him. Thinking that if he yelled any louder it might make Kyle think something was wrong, Daniel turned his attention to the island instead.

Beyond the field, a wide swath of woods lined the rocky coast and, even though the deciduous trees had lost their leaves, the grove was dense enough so that, in the snowfall, Daniel couldn't see through it.

Jarvis Delacroix had written that he'd buried Betty on this island in a place where no one would ever find her.

Maybe that's why you're here. To find her body.

But no, there had to be something else, some other reason why he'd been drawn here, because there was no way he was going to find a hidden grave that'd been out here for nearly eighty years, especially not in frozen ground under two feet of snow.

Looking back at the boat, Daniel saw his friend staring in his direction and waving to him.

He waved back as Kyle called out something that he couldn't quite hear. He held one hand to his ear to indicate for Kyle to yell louder, but all he could make out was the word "Going."

Probably just telling him it was time to get moving.

There wasn't anything else to see up here.

After gazing one more time at the snowstorm blowing in across the lake, Daniel started down the stairs.

He'd descended twenty-nine steps when he felt something in the empty stairwell bump against his leg.

CHAPTER
FORTY-ONE

He stared around uneasily.

Nothing was there.

You weren't imagining that, Daniel. Something touched you.

However, he was most definitely alone on the stairs.

Spurred on now to get out of the tower, he took the next few steps more quickly, but then felt it again. This time something banged even more solidly against his shoulder.

When he looked up, he saw what had touched him.

Boots.

A body was hanging there, swaying slightly, perhaps from the force of Daniel knocking against its feet.

From where he stood, he could see the dead man's face, lifeless and bloated and pale. There was a noose around his neck, at the end of a long rope leading up into the tower.

Daniel closed his eyes and told himself that he was just seeing things, that this was a blur, just like the other ones, that there wasn't really a body hanging right above him.

After a long moment he slowly opened his eyes again.

The body was still there, coming to a rest now, still and grim in the air.

A blur.

But it looked so real hanging there in the center of the spiraling stairwell.

Make sure.

Make sure it's not there.

Hesitantly, Daniel reached out to touch one of the boots to see if this was just a blur, just his imagination.

The leather felt rough and worn, just like real leather might.

But no, it can't be real. There's no way this is actually happening.

As he was lowering his hand, the dead man tilted his head and peered down at him. When the corpse spoke, its lips barely moved, but its voice was clear and obviously not just a trick of acoustics from the wind channeling down the stairwell.

"Daniel."

No, this isn't real!

"Two thousand six hundred and seventy-five days, Daniel. Remember what happened on August twenty-eighth."

Then the man's mouth stopped moving and he simply hung there and stared at Daniel with his vacant, dead eyes.

Without looking back, Daniel descended the remaining stairs, taking them two at a time.

What happened on August twenty-eighth?

What does "two thousand six hundred and seventy-five days" refer to?

Just get out of here. Get back to the boat. Figure it out there.

But when he came to the kitchen, he recalled what Jarvis had written in his diary about storing strawberries and raspberries in his root cellar.

Wait.

What root cellar?

To get to a cellar in bad weather, it would've made sense that it would be located under the house. However, Daniel hadn't seen any access doors on his way up to the building—which meant that, if there really was a root cellar, there might very well be a stairway down to it located somewhere here in the keeper's home.

But he hadn't come across one.

Get going, Daniel. There's nothing here.

But maybe there is, just do a quick check, then you can get on your way.

Though he was intent on leaving, he was also here to get answers and at this point all he had were more questions.

Avoiding the stairway up the tower so he wouldn't see the all-too-real blur of Jarvis Delacroix again, he went back through the house room by room and didn't find any doors that might lead to a cellar.

Curious, he returned to the kitchen, and his gaze landed on the three-foot-tall pile of split logs lining the west wall.

CHAPTER
FORTY-TWO

Daniel began to move the wood aside.

As he made his way through the stack, he noticed that a couple of the floorboards beneath it had a different grain than the rest of the floor.

He kept going, removing logs.

And that's when he saw the hinges.

Yes.

A trapdoor.

He had no idea how long this pile of wood had been here, and frankly he didn't care, but he did care about what it was covering up.

Both more motivated and more nervous about what he might find, he set to work uncovering the rest of the trapdoor to the cellar.

• • •

A few minutes ago Kyle Goessel had watched Daniel disappear into the tower.

Since the wind had starting whipping up whitecaps on the lake, he'd tried calling to his friend, encouraging him to hurry, but with the distance he wasn't sure Daniel had heard him.

From the start, Kyle hadn't been thrilled about Daniel exploring the lighthouse by himself. Despite his own apprehension about the ice, he would have gladly gone across if there were some way they could've both made it safely to land.

But there was only one set of oars and once Daniel was onshore there was no way to get them back to Kyle in the boat, except perhaps trying to throw them, but the distance was too far to guarantee that they'd make it to him.

Now, the storm was picking up and the gusts coming in across the lake had a sharp edge to them.

Kyle loved creative writing and a phrase came to him: the teeth of the wind gnawing at the shore.

And you're caught in their path.

He was waiting for Daniel to come out the front door of the keeper's house when he caught sight of a glimmer of movement on the edge of the forest.

He'd thought he might have noticed something earlier, right before Daniel appeared at the top of the tower, but now he was nearly certain that something was there.

Using one hand to shield his eyes from the snow, Kyle stared at the trees, scrutinizing the woods, but couldn't make out anything unusual.

But you did see something just now.
You did.

He studied the periphery of the forest: only bare trees in a strengthening storm.

It was probably just your eyes playing tricks on you.

Probably just—

No, wait.

There.

Yes.

A deer?

No.

Someone was standing behind one of the leafless oaks. It was only because of the way the person was turned that Kyle was able to pick him out.

A dark blue coat. That was about all Kyle could see.

Then the man emerged and entered the field, heading toward the keeper's house.

Black jeans. A black ski mask covering his face.

He was carrying something.

It looked like—

Yes.

A gasoline can.

CHAPTER
FORTY-THREE

Kyle yelled for him to stop, but the wind overwhelmed his words and the man continued to cross the snow-covered field.

• • •

Finishing with the logs, Daniel tipped the trapdoor open, then started down the rough-hewn wooden steps that led into the root cellar.

• • •

Kyle shouted louder, and finally the man looked his way, but his face was hidden behind that ski mask.

For a moment he stood there stock-still, a dark, faceless form outlined against the snow, then he turned once more to the keeper's home and strode toward it.

• • •

Daniel arrived at the bottom of the steps and began to look around.

Using the cell phone as a flashlight in one hand, he used his other hand to sweep aside the thick cobwebs that laced the air in front of him.

The earthen walls were supported by stout timbers that'd been fitted in place against the floorboards of the kitchen.

Underfoot, a smattering of small rocks covered the dirt floor.

The air felt cool, but not bitterly cold—low fifties, maybe. The root cellar smelled of dust and mildew.

There were two dozen jars of preserves piled on the ground and a stack of dried herbs near the wall.

Other than that, the place appeared empty.

But something didn't feel right.

He turned in a slow circle, taking everything in, and his math mind noted that though there were six support beams on the left side, there were only five on the right.

Not a huge deal, but everything else about the house, about the tower, was symmetrical. Why hadn't the root cellar been dug out in a square to match the floor plan of the kitchen above it?

The Edgar Allan Poe tale that Teach had mentioned in class on Friday, "The Cask of Amontillado," came to mind.

In the story, the protagonist, who was also the antagonist, had buried another man alive, sealing him up in the catacombs.

He did it in a place where no one ever found the corpse.

Daniel set down the phone with the light angled toward the wall, and began to inspect the pile of dirt in the corner where the sixth timber should have been visible.

Kyle eyed the ice that stretched between him and shore.

You need to stop that guy. He's going to burn down the lighthouse. You need to warn Daniel!

Although the rowboat was still anchored, it'd drifted slightly. So, after guiding it up to the edge of the ice, Kyle killed the motor and seated himself somewhat precariously on the gunwale with his feet hanging over the ice.

Taking a deep breath, he lowered his left foot.

The ice held.

Good.

He transferred more weight onto it.

It held.

Alright. This was going to work.

He swung his other leg into place and was steadying himself, ready to let go of the boat, when the ice underfoot cracked and splashed away. Losing his balance, he almost went in—as it was, his boots dipped into the ice-cold water—but he managed, just barely, to hold onto the gunwale.

The boat rocked wildly as he scrambled back inside it, his heart jackhammering in his chest.

That was close.

Okay, so walking across the ice was not going to happen.

But you need to do something!

Hoping to make enough noise to alert Daniel that something was up, he clambered to the back of the boat and fired up the outboard.

• • •

The ground wasn't frozen and Daniel was able to scoop out handfuls of the loose, rocky soil.

He'd gone in about eighteen inches when his hand found something hard and round and about the size of a melon. A rock probably.

But, no. It felt too smooth to be a rock.

Carefully, Daniel brushed the soil aside.

CHAPTER FORTY-FOUR

It was a skull: blackened and charred.

He stumbled backward.

Betty.

This is where Jarvis buried her after she died.

This is where—

He heard footsteps on the floorboards above him.

At first he thought it might be Kyle, but then he realized how ridiculous that was: there was no way for him to have gotten to shore.

But if it wasn't him—

You left the trapdoor open. Whoever's there will know you're down here.

Daniel started for the steps, but had only made it halfway there when someone slammed the trapdoor shut.

Hurrying up the stairs, he pressed against the door to open it, but whoever was up there must have been standing on it because it wouldn't budge.

"Hey," he called. "Step back!"

No one replied.

A moment later, though, Daniel smelled gasoline and felt some of it slosh through the floorboards above him.

He ducked his head to the side so the gas wouldn't spill onto his face.

"Hey!"

He heard wood being moved around and guessed that whoever was up there was piling the split logs over the trap-door again, or at least bracing one in place against the wall to keep him from opening the door.

Then, the person in the kitchen ignited the gasoline and a few more drops of it fell, burning this time, in and around Daniel in the root cellar.

He thrust his shoulder against the door but it held fast.

You need to pry it open or wedge something in and break the clasp.

It would've been ideal if he had a knife or even a set of keys to jam in there, but all he had was Kyle's cell phone.

Scanning the cellar, he tried to see if there was anything he'd missed, anything else he could use, but there was nothing.

No.

Wait.

There was one other thing down here that he might be able to use.

Not the dried plants or canned preserves.

From anatomy class, he knew that the femur is the strongest bone in the human body.

It won't be sharpened on the end, but if you can find a way to snap it in half . . .

No, Daniel, do you even realize what you're thinking?

What choice do you have? You have to do it.

No!

You're going to die down here unless you can get that trapdoor open.

He directed his attention to the wall where he'd been digging, then rushed down the steps to see if he could locate one of the skeleton's upper leg bones.

● ● ●

Kyle saw curls of black smoke slither out of the spaces between the boards covering the windows of the keeper's home.

No!

The person who'd carried the gasoline can into the house exited the front door and then traversed the snowy field toward the oars that Daniel had used to cross the ice.

● ● ●

Digging through the bones was sickening and heartrending, and Daniel prayed that he wouldn't be cursed or haunted somehow for disturbing them, but right now he didn't feel like he had much of a choice.

He found the pelvis and tunneled in deeper, cupping away handfuls of dirt and various bones that he thought were probably from Betty's spine.

At last his fingers closed around a bone that felt large and sturdy.

He drew it out of the soil.

Yes.

The femur.

But just as he'd expected, the ends of it were rounded, so he propped it against one of the support beams, angling it in place so it wouldn't slip to the side when he kicked it in the middle.

Honestly, he didn't know if this was going to work—if the bone would be brittle enough to break.

But if it is brittle, will it help you get out of here?

Try it.

You have to.

It's your best shot.

After lining up his foot, he stomped against the center of the bone like he might've done if he were breaking a stick for a campfire.

It shattered into three pieces. He snatched up the longest one and tried to pry open the trapdoor, but it didn't give him enough leverage.

Quickly returning to the skeleton, he dug desperately through the rock-infested soil for the other femur.

Flames flicked down and around the floorboards above him.

It took a minute, but he found the bone.

Tugged it out.

Hurry.

He jammed the femur in place against the beam and brought his boot down.

This one broke in half. He grabbed the longer piece, drove the sharpened end into the space between the boards along the edge of the trapdoor, and tried to crack the hasp from the wood to pop it open.

CHAPTER
FORTY-FIVE

As Kyle frantically tried to think of a way to help his friend, a channel of flames burst out of the top of the lighthouse and flared into the sky, devouring the sheets of snowflakes slashing against it.

In this wind it wasn't going to take long for the wooden lighthouse—and the keeper's home along with it—to be totally consumed.

● ● ●

Crying out from the effort, Daniel cranked on the femur, heard the clasp snap, and threw open the trapdoor.

Half a dozen split logs tumbled down as a rush of stifling heat enveloped him.

The floorboards above the root cellar were blazing and, even if he could've tried running across them, at this point he wasn't sure they would've supported his weight. The last thing he needed right now was to end up plummeting back into that cellar.

The only clear path to the front door was along an adjoining wall where the flames weren't as intense.

Thick smoke and fumes choked him and the searing heat from the fire blasted against his face and bare hands where his coat didn't protect him. Drawing the top of his shirt up over his mouth so he could breathe through the smoke, Daniel rushed toward the door.

Because of the heat, he had to shield his face with one arm. Flames radiated across the floor in front of him, but he was able to leap over them and pivot past a column of fire that was flaring up the wall.

The front doorway was engulfed, but Daniel rushed it, pounded it open, and stumbled out of the building, dropping and rolling in the snow.

The cold air and wet snow felt good on his face and hands, immediately cooling his exposed skin.

Yes, yes.

He tugged his shirt back down past his mouth and struggled forward through the knee-deep snow to get away from the burning building.

After he'd made it about forty feet, he paused and glanced back.

Even with the snow blowing in his face, he could feel the raging heat of the fire.

A spectacular but also unnerving sight.

As he watched the lighthouse burn, he thought of what Mia had told him on Saturday—in the early days, fires on hills were used to serve as warnings to ships.

They didn't set the lighthouses on fire, though.

The truth of what'd just happened slammed into him: *Someone tried to kill you.*

And a second revelation: *You need to get off this island.*

He hurried toward the boat, and when he got to the rocks that he'd crawled over when he first arrived, he found that his life jacket was gone.

So were the oars.

Kyle shut off the motor and shouted, "Are you alright?"

"Yeah. Did you see who did this?"

Kyle shook his head. "He was wearing a ski mask. He took off toward the other side of the island."

"And he took the oars and the life jacket?"

"I don't know why, but he did."

Daniel eased onto the ice.

"You don't have a life jacket," Kyle said unnecessarily.

"Then I better not fall through."

"You're not really gonna walk across?"

"Do I have a choice?"

"I don't know, I—"

"There's someone on this island who wants me dead. He knew I was in there when he started that fire. If he sees me here alive, who knows what he'll do."

Kyle gave in. "Alright. But be careful."

Here, close to the shoreline, the ice would be thicker, but still, Daniel was tentative as he took his first few steps.

"Steady," Kyle urged him.

Concerned that the ice might break if he moved too quickly, Daniel continued to take it slowly as he gently flattened his foot with each step to spread out his weight.

The farther he went, the more confident he became that he was actually going to make it.

Just get to the boat and get out of here.

But when he was about three quarters of the way to the skiff, withering cracks began to spiderweb out from beneath his feet and he heard the crinkle of splintering ice.

He froze, afraid to make the slightest movement.

But it didn't help.

All at once the ice beneath his feet split open with a crack that sounded like a gunshot echoing across the water.

• • •

"No!" Kyle watched helplessly as Daniel dropped into the inky black water ten feet away from him.

And didn't come back up.

CHAPTER FORTY-SIX

Knives.

Hundreds of knives stabbing into him, all over him.

That's what it felt like.

Daniel tried to remain calm, tried not to panic, but he hadn't gotten a good breath before he went under, and now as he sank into the freezing lake, it felt like he had no air in his lungs.

Though faint light filtered through the ice above him, the water below him was impossibly dark.

He scissors-kicked toward the surface, but didn't see the opening he'd fallen through.

You need to swim toward open water.

You can make it.

Relax.

But the heavy winter clothes and boots were dragging him down. He gave up on the idea of trying to get the boots off, but managed to untangle himself from the bulky winter coat that was making it nearly impossible to swim.

He stroked upward and kicked fiercely against the incoming tide, which seemed intent on taking him closer to shore where he would never be able to break through the ice above him.

He searched desperately, but couldn't locate the fractured ice that'd broken away and plunged him into the lake.

Battling the stiff current, he went for the ice sheet's edge, but what little air he had was quickly running out and, despite himself, he let out a gasp of bubbles that burst into the water and then rose, gurgling around his face.

Still ten feet to go, but it might just as well have been ten miles.

He wasn't going to make it.

You have to!

More bubbles escaped, and he had to fight the terrible urge to breathe in because if he did, if he took even the smallest gulp, it would all be over.

Swimming as hard as he could, Daniel aimed for the surface, but it felt like something had wrapped around his leg and was pulling him down.

A quick glance down: he saw the demon that Nicole had drawn, its bone-white grin gleaming in the eternal darkness, its claws clenching his foot.

A blur.

Reality.

All the same.

He kicked at it violently and as it swirled away into the angry, churning depths, he focused on getting to the open water above him.

You can do it. You can make it. For your dad. You need to save your dad!

The final dribble of air floated from his mouth.

He stroked once more and reached for the edge of the ice. Caught it.

There.

Yes.

But he could barely hold on.

He was too tired, too fatigued.

When he kicked forward with what little strength he had left, he wasn't able to pull himself up or hook his other hand around the ice's edge.

He couldn't get his face to the surface.

It's over.

His grip was weakening, and just as he felt like it was going to slip away for good, a dark form moved toward him—

The boat?

But—

Something snagged his wrist as the fathomless lake tugged at him, trying to claim him for good.

Daniel felt himself being drawn upward.

But then he felt nothing but a cold, clutching darkness, and even the feeling of the knives piercing into him was gone.

CHAPTER FORTY-SEVEN

Kyle clasped Daniel's wrist as tightly as he could and leaned back in the boat to bring his friend's head to the surface.

The waves were washing against the other side of the boat, threatening to move it closer to the ice and crush Daniel or break Kyle's grip on him.

Come on, man, pull. You've got this!

He repositioned his hand and heaved again, this time managing to get Daniel's head above the surface. It didn't look like he was breathing. His skin was drained of color.

You need to get him in the boat.

Now!

He hauled up his friend, managing to get his armpits to the gunwale.

The rowboat wobbled perilously but kept from capsizing.

Bracing his leg under one of the seats for leverage, Kyle reached down, grabbed the back of Daniel's belt, and lifted. As the skiff tilted to the side again, nearly taking on water, he hefted Daniel up and swung him into the rowboat.

His body dropped heavily to the bottom of the boat, his head lolling to the side.

From being a lifeguard, Kyle realized he needed to get air into Daniel's lungs immediately.

With the boat's seats in the way, positioning his friend on his back was tricky, but once he managed, he tilted Daniel's head to open up his airway, and gave him two rescue breaths.

His chest rose.

Nothing's blocking his airway.

He found a pulse on Daniel's neck.

Good. That's good.

Kyle knew that sometimes when a person falls into ice-cold water, an instinct kicks in—he didn't know what it was called, but he knew it was there—closing off their throat so that, even though they might drown, their lungs won't necessarily fill with water.

If that's what'd happened with Daniel, it might actually work in his favor.

He gave Daniel another breath.

Come on, buddy. You're okay. You're gonna be okay.

But Daniel didn't come to.

Kyle tried again, then shook him and slapped his face, hoping to revive him.

Nothing.

Another breath.

Then another.

Come on!

Kyle was leaning down to give him one more breath when his friend's body lurched and he coughed up a mouthful of water, then gasped for air.

Hurriedly, Kyle rolled him onto his side so he wouldn't swallow any water again and so he could clear out his mouth.

Daniel coughed twice, spitting out more water as he did, then drew in a long hoarse breath as deep shivers began to wrack his body.

Shivers are good. They're the body's way of trying to stay warm.

Kyle held him. "You're alright, man. Just breathe."

Daniel nodded.

"I'm gonna get you to shore." Kyle was still supporting Daniel's back. "You okay on your own?"

•   •   •

"Yeah." Daniel wasn't exactly sure that was true, but he didn't want his friend to worry about him. "I'm good."

It took a lot of effort, but he was finally able to scooch over so his back was against the middle seat of the rowboat.

Kyle offered him his coat, and he accepted. He sloughed off his wet shirt and slipped on the warm, dry jacket while his friend hoisted the anchor, revved up the motor, and aimed the skiff's bow toward the mainland.

•   •   •

Nicole watched as Michelle fell asleep.

The girl hadn't wanted to take a nap, but while she was reading her a story—something about a moonbeam becoming friends with a unicorn—Michelle had ended up nodding off beside her on the bed.

Gently easing herself to her feet so she wouldn't wake her up, Nicole went to get her cell phone from where she'd left it in the kitchen.

She'd just started looking up online news articles about the wolf shootings when there was a knock at the front door.

Going to the living room, she peered out the window beside the Christmas tree. Two police officers stood on the porch. From their uniforms it looked like they were troopers with the state patrol.

Another knock.

A bit apprehensively, she opened the door. "Yes?"

"Hello, ma'am," the taller of the two men said. He was holding out his badge. "Is this the Goessel residence?"

"Yes."

"And you are?"

"I'm Nicole. I'm the babysitter."

"Nicole." He put the badge away. "We're looking for Daniel Byers."

"Okay."

"He disappeared from a hospital in Duluth early this morning. We understand that Kyle Goessel is one of his friends and we're following up on . . . Wait—" He appraised her. "You said your name is Nicole. Are you Nicole Marten?"

"Yes."

"Your name was favorited on Daniel's cell phone as well."

"He's my boyfriend." *Say what they'd expect you to say. Don't act weird.* "What do you mean you're looking for him? Is he okay?"

"Well, that's what we're trying to ascertain. We don't know his current location. He's not here?"

"No."

The other officer cut in. "And do you know where he is?"

Sure, she had an *idea* of where he was, but Daniel and Kyle might be anywhere between here and Bayfield, so, officially, she didn't know.

She went with that and shook her head. "Uh-uh. I saw him at the hospital yesterday, but I couldn't tell you where he is now."

"Do you mind if we come in and take a little look around?" the first cop said.

"I don't think you better. Mrs. Goessel's not here."

"She's not?"

"No. Like I said, I'm the babysitter."

"We'll be quick. I promise we'll—"

"No. Daniel's not here. And you can't come in."

The officer eyed her coolly. Finally, his partner handed her an official-looking business card. "If you hear of anything, please call us. My cell number's on there."

"Thanks," she said noncommittally.

She watched them return to their patrol car and when they were pulling away she tried Kyle's number.

No answer.

She texted him to call her right away. If the cops were out searching for Daniel, he needed to be on the lookout for them.

Then, distracted by her thoughts about him, she went back to finding out what she could about the wolf poaching.

Who would have been able to access those wolf tags? Who would even think of killing those wolves?

Of all the people she knew, Ty Bell was the first one to come to mind: not only was he the kind of guy who might actually do something like this, he might have been able to access the tagged wolf locations from his dad's office.

He'd also been the person who found the second wolf.

How convenient.

She thought of ways to narrow things down and had an idea.

Tapping at her phone's screen, she did a search to see if there was any evidence that the wolves had been shot after or before school hours and if there were any more details about Ty's discovery of that second poached wolf.

CHAPTER
FORTY-EIGHT

Daniel stood in Larry's shower with one hand against the wall to keep his balance and stay on his feet. He'd stripped down to his underwear and now blasted the hot water.

At first, the heat didn't seem to do any good, but as the tiny bathroom steamed up, the shivers began to subside and he started to regain his strength.

Both Larry and Kyle had crowded into the bathroom to make sure he didn't collapse. The shower curtain was yanked to the side and water was pooling on the floor, but Larry didn't seem to care and simply tossed some towels down to sop it up.

"So, you feeling any better?" he asked Daniel concernedly.

"Starting to. Yeah."

Daniel tried to let the hot water rinse away the dark residue of fear that had lodged in his mind when he was under the ice, but it didn't work. He guessed it would stay with him for a long time, probably forever—especially the image of that demon grinning at him, trying to drag him down into a nothingness that would never end.

On Saturday, Nicole had said that Job had been so haunted by his nightmares that he wished he could be strangled and killed.

The way things were going, Daniel could start to understand how the guy might have gotten to that point.

You're holding on to the edge of the cliff.

Don't.

Let.

Go.

When he was finally warmed up, he stepped out of the shower and toweled off.

Before leaving for the kitchen to round up something hot for him to eat, Larry lent Daniel a set of clothes. Since he was almost as tall as Kyle, the clothes didn't fit much better than Kyle's had—long arms but tight across the shoulders—but Daniel didn't mind. He was just glad to be here.

To be alive.

To be out of the clutches of that lake.

Kyle joined Larry in the kitchen while Daniel changed.

Outside the window, Daniel could see that it was still snowing and it was nearly dark.

Man, he'd been out of it, hadn't even noticed how much time was slipping away. Larry and Kyle must have been working on warming him up for longer than he'd thought.

Once he was dressed, he followed the smell of stew down the hall.

As Daniel took a seat at the table, Larry asked him again if he was okay and he reiterated that he was fine.

"You were not looking good, amigo," Kyle said. "Blue is not your color."

"Good to know. Listen, thanks for pulling me out."

"No problem, but I gotta say, when you're dead, you're heavier than you look."

"I'll try to lose some weight before drowning again."

"A few weeks of Zumba should do it."

"Only if you join me."

"I'll have my people get back to you."

Larry went to the stove and ladled out three bowls of stew. "Do you want some coffee or tea or anything?" he said to Daniel. "Something hot to drink?"

"No thanks. I'm not really thirsty."

"I can't imagine why not."

Larry found three spoons, dipped them into the bowls and delivered them to the table, carrying all three at the same time to save himself a trip across the kitchen—which wasn't really that big anyway.

Daniel accepted the stew. "Thanks."

"Yeah."

After Larry took a seat, silence settled over the table. As they ate, Daniel tried to relax, but failed.

The blur of Jarvis Delacroix's corpse hanging in the lighthouse tower had been troubling enough, but then digging up Betty's corpse and using one of her leg bones to pry open the trapdoor was even worse.

And then there was the little excursion under the ice with that demon pulling him down.

Man, what a day.

He couldn't stop thinking about Jarvis Delacroix speaking to him in that raspy, long-dead voice: "Two thousand six hundred and seventy-five days. Remember what happened on August twenty-eighth."

When he'd first heard the words, he'd wondered what they referred to, but now that he had a chance to think things through, the answer came to him almost immediately.

Two thousand six hundred and seventy-five days ago was August twenty-eighth.

And that was the last day he'd been in the barn when he was a kid.

Just sixty-four days before Grandma died.

But he couldn't remember what happened that day in August, or why he'd never gone back to the barn again.

"So," Larry said gravely, "Kyle told me someone burned down the lighthouse while you were inside it."

"Yes."

"And neither of you have any idea who it might've been?"

They both shook their heads.

"Sorry about those oars and that life jacket," Daniel told him. "I'm guessing they might be gone for good."

Larry waved that off, then set his spoon next to his nearly-empty bowl. "Listen, I need you boys to be straight with me. On the one hand I'm wondering why on earth you would have chanced crossing that ice in the first place just to get to a deserted lighthouse, but on the other hand, I'm much more curious why someone would have lit it on fire while you were inside. I need to know what's really going on here."

Daniel and Kyle exchanged a glance.

"So?"

Daniel set down his spoon. "It's going to sound nuts if I tell you."

"Try me."

Well.

Okay.

He decided that since Larry had helped them out as much as he had, he did have a right to know, so he told him about the blurs of the girl in the white nightgown, the strange handwriting in English class, Jarvis's diaries, and his father's disappearance.

He even shared about the psych ward and getting out of there with the help of someone who apparently worked for some sort of clandestine government agency.

Larry listened in silence.

"I told you it was going to sound nuts."

"Well, you nailed that one."

"My mom's stuck in Alaska and I need to find my dad. That's why I crossed the ice. I thought the answer to what'd happened to him might somehow lie inside that lighthouse."

"And did it?"

"No."

Admitting that was hard.

Daniel considered bringing up seeing the demon in the lake or Jarvis's corpse in the tower or finding Betty's skeleton in the root cellar, but decided that Larry probably didn't need to know everything. He could tell Kyle all that stuff later.

"This person on the island"—Larry had finished his stew and was getting a beer out of the fridge—"the one who started the fire, you don't know where he went or how he got out there?"

"No," Kyle answered. "It was a man, though. I could tell that much by his size, by how he walked."

"Well, there is a dock around the other side of the island."

"I didn't see it from the tower," Daniel said.

"Doesn't surprise me, not with the snow falling. It's not that big, but locals would know where it is. I can make some calls, see if anyone else had a boat out on the lake today. It's a small town and there aren't that many people who would've been running rentals. In fact, if anyone else was, I'd be surprised."

"How did the person who set the fire even know we would be there?" Daniel wondered aloud. "How could that be?"

"It does seem pretty suspicious. I mean, there's no way it was just a fluke that he ended up there while you were there. Who knew you were going to that island this morning?"

"Just Mr. Zacharias and Nicole."

"Nicole?"

"My girlfriend."

"Ah." Larry nodded. "Okay. So here's where I'm at: If someone tried to kill you, can you give me one good reason why I shouldn't call the state patrol or our local sheriff's office and tell them everything?"

"Because the authorities think I had something to do with my dad's disappearance. They'll take me in and we won't be any closer to finding him."

"Even after everything that's happened—I mean, a guy burning down that lighthouse—you still think they'll suspect you?"

"They'll at least take me in for questioning. Right now we can't afford that. It's already way later than I thought it would be before we were gonna head back, and we're not any closer to finding my dad."

"So what do you think is the best thing we can do right now to move forward on locating him?"

"Kyle and I need to get back to Beldon. That's where Mr. Zacharias dropped me off. He said he'd contact me through Kyle's cell phone, but—" He caught himself. "Oh."

"What?" Kyle asked.

"I left it in the root cellar. Sorry about that."

"Root cellar?"

"Under the keeper's house. I was down there when the guy started the fire. I guess I owe you a phone."

"Yeah, well." He brushed it off as no big deal. "It was time for an upgrade anyway."

Larry appeared to be deep in thought. "Honestly, I'm not really sure where to take things from here. I have the sense that we should call your mom, Daniel, and tell her about your near-drowning, but I guess right now that would just make her more worried. And if I called your mother, Kyle—I'm not even sure what I would tell her."

"I'll explain everything to her. Just let me do it in person."

"When you get back tonight?"

"I was thinking more along the lines of next month sometime."

Daniel couldn't tell if his friend was being serious or not.

"Tonight," Larry emphasized.

"Okay."

"And I have your word on that?"

"Yeah."

"Good. And this Mr. Zacharias you mentioned, Daniel—how are you going to get in touch with him?"

"I'm pretty sure he'll find a way to get in touch with us."

Larry pulled out his cell phone. "Take this along. With the snowstorm I'm not excited about you two driving back without a phone. I can get it back in the next day or two. Maybe I'll swing down your way and see my sister for Christmas. In any case, I have a landline for the business so you two can still call me if you need to."

"Okay." Kyle accepted the phone. "Thanks."

"Be safe out there. I don't like the condition of those roads, and they're not going to get any better."

After Daniel and Kyle had assured Larry that they would be fine driving home through the storm, they said goodbye, and left for Beldon in Kyle's car.

PART VI
CARVED NAMES

CHAPTER FORTY-NINE

Nicole Marten was back at her house.

About half an hour ago, Mrs. Goessel had returned home. The guy who was with her reached out to shake her hand. "I'm Glenn Kramer. I don't think we've met."

"Nicole. Nice to meet you."

"You too."

"I'm a gun collector."

"Um. So I've heard."

Okay, this is awkward.

They shook hands, he told everyone Merry Christmas, and when he was gone, Mrs. Goessel asked Nicole if she'd heard from Kyle.

"No. Not since he left this morning."

"Huh. I haven't been able to reach him either. That's a little strange, don't you think?"

"Maybe. I don't know. Any word on Daniel's dad?"

"I haven't heard any news." Michelle came to her mom's side and Mrs. Goessel picked her up. "So, anything exciting happen while I was gone?"

Nicole wasn't sure if she should mention the state troopers stopping by, but decided that if she did bring it up, Mrs. Goessel would realize Daniel had escaped from the hospital and might wonder what was going on.

"Pretty quiet," Nicole said.

"And was Michelle a good girl?"

"She was okay, I guuuuuess," Nicole told Mrs. Goessel with a wink.

"How long till Santa comes?" Michelle asked impatiently.

"Not until morning, dear."

"That's not fair." She climbed down and resignedly went off to play with Penguin in the other room.

After paying Nicole for babysitting—and giving her way more than she expected, actually—Mrs. Goessel thanked her. "Michelle always loves to see you. I'm glad you could come over. I just wish I knew why Kyle wasn't answering his phone."

"If he texts me, I'll let him know you want him to check in."

"Thanks."

"Merry Christmas.

"You too."

On the kitchen table back home, Nicole found a note that her parents had left for her: they'd gone to a Christmas Eve party at the Newtons' house and would be back around eight.

She'd forgotten about that. The Newtons. Totally spaced on that one.

She was frying up a falafel burger when her phone rang.

Though she didn't recognize the incoming number, she still hadn't heard from Kyle or Daniel and thought it might possibly be one of them using someone else's phone. She picked up. "Hello?"

"Nicole. It's me."

"Daniel? Where are you guys?"

"We're on our way back. The trip up here was, well . . . interesting."

"Define 'interesting.'"

"It has to do with a little sightseeing in Lake Superior."

"Did you say *in* Lake Superior?"

"Yeah, but things are good. We should be back in just over an hour, so I'm thinking six thirty or so. Can we meet and regroup at your place?"

"Sure, I'm here now. Why didn't you reply earlier? I texted Kyle a bunch of times—and whose phone are you calling from anyway?"

"Kyle's was lost in the fire. This is Larry's."

"Wait—fire?"

"Yeah, when the guy tried to kill me in the lighthouse."

"Kill you!"

"Didn't quite succeed though."

"Yeah, well, I think I caught hold of that much. Who tried to kill you?"

"Don't know. We're still trying to figure that out."

"Was this before or after the sightseeing in the lake?"

"Before."

She listened as Daniel recounted barely making it out of the lighthouse in time and then falling through the ice on his way back to the rowboat. When he was done she said, "That's insane. Did you learn anything about where your dad might be?"

"I had a blur of Jarvis Delacroix. He told me 'two thousand six hundred and seventy-five days.' That's the last time I was in the barn, that many days ago, back when I was nine. I'm still trying to figure out how that ties in with all this. Oh, and as far as Betty goes—let's just say, I'm pretty sure she was buried out on Madeline Island. I'll explain when we get there. See you soon."

"Two state troopers stopped by at Kyle's house looking for you. Keep an eye out."

"Thanks."

"Oh, and tell Kyle his mom is worried about him. She wants him to call her."

"I'll let him know."

Hearing Daniel's voice was reassuring to Nicole, but also a little stressful, especially when she heard what he'd been through.

Man, a lot had happened since Friday when his blurs started coming back.

She thought back to finding that dying wolf with him. She'd knelt beside its body, had promised to find out who was doing this, had vowed to stop him.

A lot of progress you've made there—

She checked the time.

5:26 p.m.

Okay, Daniel had said six thirty, so that gave her just over an hour to look into things, maybe see if she could pull up anything that would help lead to the poacher, or to finding Daniel's dad, which was by far the bigger priority anyway.

The two things are tied together.

Maybe.

Maybe not.

As long as she was moving forward on one front, that was at least something.

Carrying her purse in one hand, she brought a plate with her falafel burger, some sour cream potato chips, and apple slices up to her room with the other. She laid her purse beside her bed and set the food on her desk.

During the afternoon she'd only found out when the wolves had been discovered, not when they'd been shot.

But Ty had found that second one, and she couldn't ignore that. Of all the people who might have stumbled across the wolf, it seemed like an awfully big coincidence that it just happened to be him.

Going online, she checked to see if the Bells lived anywhere near the Traybor Institute, where the majority of the wolves had been killed, but found that they lived on the other side of town.

She reconsidered things.

After shooting the wolf on Saturday, the poacher had made it through the forest without being seen, even though she and Daniel had been close by. Logically, he'd either walked through those woods or had a snowmobile or car waiting to get out of the area. But there weren't that many roads around there.

You and Daniel would have seen a car—or at least heard one. Same with a snowmobile.

Maybe he had a place nearby within walking distance where he could hide, or keep his gun, or whatever.

Or, he could have been cross-country skiing.

Hmm. That was true.

With a gun?

Sure on a sling, carry it across your back. No problem. There's even an Olympic sport where they do that.

When she and Daniel were out near the institute they'd passed a snowmobile trail to a lake with some cabins surrounding it.

So, one of those cabins out there?

That would make sense.

Or somewhere along the network of cross-country ski trails. You need to find out who lives out there.

While she ate, she used her laptop to pull up the county courthouse land deeds at the website she'd been looking into on Saturday, and began to scroll through them.

• • •

After Daniel had finished talking with Nicole, he'd handed the phone to his friend and Kyle called his mom and told her that he was fine and was on his way home.

Faintly, Daniel could hear Mrs. Goessel on the other end of the line: "I thought you were going to be home hours ago to take over watching Michelle."

"It's complicated."

"My phone says this call is from my brother—but Bayfield is the opposite direction from Duluth. What's going on here, Kyle?"

"I'll explain it all when I get home. I promise."

Daniel couldn't imagine what his friend was going to say.

It was going to take some major explaining.

After the call, Daniel tried to make sense of what had happened during the day, but he just kept coming back to one simple, undeniable fact: someone had tried to kill him.

And he had no idea who it was or why they would want him dead.

CHAPTER FIFTY

Sheriff Byers heard a key in the lock of the door to his room.

Closing his eyes, he lay still and pretended to be unconscious, but even with his eyes shut he could sense light from the other room sweep in and surround him as the door opened.

Footsteps approached the cot and stopped when they were right beside him.

He doesn't know you're awake. You have the element of surprise.

But you're cuffed to this cot. How are you supposed to take him out?

The sheriff still had his right hand free. If the guy came close enough, he could go for his throat—either a strike with the edge of his hand or maybe grab his neck to try to choke him out.

He could hear the man's coarse breathing.

What is he doing? What is he waiting for?

He didn't want to assume too much, but if this was the same man who'd attacked him at his house, then it was Hollister, and he was not going to be an easy guy to take down.

He was a medical student. He bandaged your side. He doesn't want you dead.

But then why did he stab you?

The breathing got closer.

Yeah, the guy was definitely leaning down toward him.

Deciding to take advantage of the moment, the sheriff snapped his eyes open while at the same time cocking his arm back.

A look of surprise shot across the man's face.

Yes.

It was him.

Brandon Hollister.

And he was close enough.

Sheriff Byers slashed his hand forward, driving the side of it into the front of Hollister's throat.

It was a solid hit, but a little too low, and it only stunned him for a moment. As he clutched his throat, the sheriff grabbed his shirt, yanked him close and, while Hollister was still catching his breath, threw his arm around his neck, hoping to choke him out.

Cut off oxygen to the brain, give it ten seconds, maybe fifteen, and he would go unconscious.

That's what you need.

Just a few more seconds.

Then you can search him for the handcuff key and—

Wrestling against the sheriff's grasp, Hollister punched him in his wounded side.

A crippling wave of pain rocked him and his grip loosened.

Hollister pulled free.

Grimacing deeply, the sheriff collapsed back onto the cot.

"You shouldn't have done that." Hollister's voice was forced and harsh. He'd moved backward, out of reach, and was rubbing his throat. Sheriff Byers saw he had a syringe case and fresh bandages with him.

Maybe he came to change the dressing—that or drug you. Or both.

"You don't even understand what's going on," Hollister said.

"Tell me what's going on."

But instead of answering, Hollister just stared at the fresh blood soaking through the bandages on the sheriff's side. "Put some pressure on that. I can't have you dying on me before he comes back."

"Before who comes back?"

He coughed and rubbed his neck again, but didn't reply.

"My son's car was at the house when you attacked me Saturday night. Is he okay? I swear to God, if you hurt him—"

"He's fine. Maybe a little bump on the head, but that's all."

"What is it you want?"

"I want the world to know what happens at that institute and I want you to help me get the word out."

What?

He went to the door and closed it.

The sheriff did not hear it lock.

Once he was alone, Sheriff Byers let out a long, painful breath.

Institute? What institute?

The only one he could think of in the area was the Traybor Institute, but they did fish management studies there and what that might have to do with Hollister was beyond him.

But he knew one thing he hadn't known before: Hollister was not working alone.

No.

He'd mentioned someone was coming back.

And the sheriff didn't like that prospect.

Despite the nearly debilitating pain, he managed to press his right hand against the stab wound to quell the bleeding. If Hollister's partner was on his way, he really needed to get out of here and get to a hospital as quickly as possible.

As he repositioned himself, trying to get more comfortable, one of the springs from the cot dug into his back. He slid to the left so it wouldn't jab him.

But then he had a thought, and turned to study the spring.

Yes. The tip looked narrow enough. If he could just uncoil it he could use it to pick the handcuffs.

Or at least, try to.

After a quick glance at the door to make sure Hollister wasn't on his way back in, Sheriff Byers began working on removing the spring from the cot's frame.

CHAPTER FIFTY-ONE

Kyle hit a patch of ice and the car skidded briefly before the tires gripped the road again.

"You okay?" Daniel said.

"I'm good."

"Listen, we really need to figure out who tried to kill me back there on that island."

"No kidding, but no one knew about the lighthouse or where we were going."

"Could it have been the escaped prisoner Mr. Zacharias mentioned? Maybe the wolf poacher? What about—"

"Larry," Kyle interrupted him.

"What?"

"Larry knew we were going out there. He also had other boats available that he could've used and he knew where the landing was on the other side of the island."

"That doesn't make any sense. He wouldn't have burned down the lighthouse. Besides, why would your Uncle Larry have tried to kill me?"

"I don't know, but who else . . . Wait, what about Mr. Zacharias? Earlier, you said he knew we were going there too."

"Yeah, I mentioned it to him when he was dropping me off at your place, but he wouldn't have tried to kill me either. He's on our side."

Kyle drove in silence.

"Or at least I think he is," Daniel muttered, suddenly unsure about anything.

"Either way," Kyle said, "we need to find a way to get in touch with him. Maybe then we'll finally be able to figure out what's going on here."

"Back up for a minute. On Saturday, Nicole asked me how the box got up there in the hayloft."

"That's backing up more than a minute."

"Track with me. I looked through it when I was younger— at least we can assume I did, based on what I knew: the handwriting style I used in English class, everything."

"You're thinking that you're the one who put it up there?"

"That would make the most sense. We know that the farm belongs to the Hollisters, right?"

"Sure. I mean—at least it does now."

"Now?"

"It could have changed hands over the years."

"Huh . . . good point."

What matters most isn't who owns the barn now, but who owned it back when the box was left up there.

"I think," Daniel said, "we need to find out who owned that land back then, when I was nine, two thousand six hundred and seventy-five days ago."

"Because of that blur of Jarvis Delacroix?"

"Yeah."

"My mom's a real estate agent. She could probably figure it out, maybe look up the records, find out the last time the land changed hands."

Kyle was busy battling the icy roads so Daniel put the call through. When it rang, he handed the phone to Kyle, who spent a minute trying to explain what he needed without giving away everything that was going on, which was not easy.

When he hung up, he shook his head. "She said she would need to be at her office to check the files. Dead end."

Daniel closed his eyes and searched through his memories, attempting to decipher the message that the blurs seemed to be trying to tell him: what had happened in that barn when he was nine years old on August twenty-eighth.

Why were you in the barn?

What did you see?

And why did you block out those memories?

• • •

Dr. Waxford had spent all day at the facility.

He still had no answers about how the subject had gotten away and no idea who would've called the police to report that the missing sheriff was there at the facility.

No, he hadn't found anything in the security camera footage concerning inmate #176235's escape, even after reviewing it dozens of times—which meant that somehow the subject had evaded all the cameras.

And that was virtually impossible.

The only other explanation Dr. Waxford could come up with: someone had hacked into their system, and either altered the footage or found a way to loop the video preceding the escape, which, with their security measures and military-grade encrypted firewalls, seemed just as inconceivable.

But *something* had happened here and he needed to get to the bottom of it.

Though it was Christmas Eve, he had the private cell number he needed. He got on the phone with his contact at the Department of Defense to see what she could tell him about individuals or agencies that would have the capability of pulling something like that off.

CHAPTER FIFTY-TWO

Nicole found what she was looking for.

It didn't answer all of her questions, but it was definitely something worth looking into.

A piece of property on Waunakee Lake, near the institute, belonged to the Bells. She called the forest service's tip line about the poaching, but no one picked up.

Not surprising. It is Christmas Eve.

She was about to hang up when a recording invited her to leave a message and she decided she might as well—who knows? Maybe someone would be checking them later tonight or tomorrow.

"Um . . . My name is Nicole Marten. I think I might have information about who's poaching those wolves." She left her number and hung up.

You're assuming a lot here, Nicole.

True.

But three things were also true: (1) Ty had found one of the wolves, (2) his family owned property right in the middle of the wolf poaching sites, and (3) he could have accessed the wolf locations through his dad's office.

No, of course, Ty's involvement wasn't certain, but there was enough here to make her think something was going on.

She tried texting Daniel at the number he'd called from earlier, but the text didn't go through.

There were a lot of dead spots out there near the national forest where you couldn't get a cell signal, so it didn't surprise her.

Resend it in a few minutes.

But for some reason she suddenly didn't like the idea of being home alone and she hoped Daniel and Kyle would make it to her house before their six-thirty ETA.

• • •

Getting the spring off the cot was proving to be harder than Sheriff Byers had expected it would be.

The way the cot was designed, while his weight was on it, there was too much pressure on the spring, making it impossible to untwist it.

To get it off, he would need to sit up and lean off the edge of the cot.

And that was not going to feel good on his wounded side.

Steeling himself, he took a deep breath, swung his legs over, and slowly sat up.

Pain shot through him, but he did his best to block it out as he edged forward to get his weight off the spring, and then started uncurling it from the cot's frame.

CHAPTER FIFTY-THREE

The vibrating phone interrupted Daniel's thoughts about the barn.

A text from Nicole. It included an address, 1594 West Creek Drive, and a note that it was the Bell's property. *Could Ty b the poacher? b safe, c u soon,* she typed.

He told Kyle about the text and while they were discussing it, the phone rang.

Daniel picked up.

"Hello. It's Malcolm."

"How did you get this number?"

"I've been monitoring Nicole's calls and she spoke to someone on this line before calling the forest service."

"The forest service?"

"Yes. She also texted you a few minutes ago."

"Yeah, I got it, but she could have been talking with anyone at this number. How'd you know it was me?"

"I'm good at what I do, Daniel. I connected the dots. I've been trying to reach you."

"Through Kyle's phone?"

"Yes."

"Out of commission. We were looking into the Lost Cove Lighthouse. Someone tried to kill me."

"What?"

"He lit the lighthouse on fire while I was inside it."

"Do you know who it was?"

"No."

Go ahead. Just ask him.

"Was it you?"

"No, of course not." He paused as if he were waiting for Daniel to respond, but when that didn't happen, he continued, "If I wanted you dead, I never would have helped you escape from the hospital. I'm on your side."

"Yeah, that's what you keep saying."

"Trust me on this."

"What've you been doing all day?"

"I was looking for your dad."

"And?"

"I have a few ideas on where Brandon might have taken him."

"Brandon?"

"Brandon Hollister. The inmate who escaped."

"That's the family who owns the barn," Daniel muttered.

"What barn?" Mr. Zacharias asked.

"The one where we found the diary—but that doesn't matter. You said you have ideas where my dad might be. Tell me."

"In person. Meet me at the front gate outside the institute."

"Why?"

"I don't trust phones—it's too easy to listen in on someone else's calls. Meeting in person is always best."

"But why there?"

"Dr. Waxford's car is at the facility. He's inside. We need to talk to him."

Daniel weighed his options. Meeting with Mr. Zacharias might help, talking with Dr. Waxford might too, but it would mean canceling his plans with Nicole, which might not be that big of a deal, but—

"Here's what I don't get," Daniel said. "You two have opposite goals? You're trying to stop his research? Is Dr. Waxford working for the government too?"

"I never said I worked for the government."

That caught Daniel off guard. "But you were wearing a Wisconsin state prison guard's uniform, and then later, one from a Minnesota police officer."

"Yes, that's right."

"But you don't work for the government and Dr. Waxford does?"

"Yes."

"Who do you work for then?"

"That's something I can't—"

"Who do you work for, Mr. Zacharias?"

"I'll explain everything when we meet."

"No. Enough of this. I want you to tell me what's going on. Why were you waiting for me after the game on Friday night? And how did you just happen to go off the road into that snowbank right in front of our car after we left the party?"

"I wanted to meet you myself. To see if it was real."

"If what was real?"

"What I heard about you."

"About me being intuitive and good at piecing things together," Daniel said, repeating what Mr. Zacharias had told him in the hospital in Duluth.

"That's right."

"Who told you that?"

"A source."

Daniel was getting exasperated. "And I suppose you can't share that name with me either?"

"Not over the phone, no."

Of course not.

"Alright," Daniel said, "one more thing: you told me you were trying to stop the chronobiology research. How?"

"How?"

"How are you trying to stop it? I mean, I saw you transport that prisoner to the Traybor Institute. If you're trying to stop what they're doing, then why were you a part of it?"

"I needed to get inside, have a look around, see if the intel my agency had about it was correct. Now, listen, I—"

"But . . ." Then it hit him. One of the puzzle pieces locked into place. "Oh."

"What?"

Daniel hoped it wasn't the case, but the more he thought about it, the more it made sense, even though he didn't want to believe that it could possibly be true. "You helped him."

"Who?"

"The guy who escaped—Hollister. You helped him get out of the institute."

"Why would I—?"

"But you did, didn't you? And then when he was free he went after my dad."

"Right now isn't the time to—"

"You didn't answer my question. Are you responsible for Brandon Hollister getting out of that research center?"

Daniel waited him out and finally Mr. Zacharias replied, "I didn't know he would go after your father."

He felt his hand tighten around the phone. "I can't believe this. What happened to my dad—it's your fault."

"When I found out what they were doing there, when I saw it for myself, I couldn't just leave Hollister inside. Listen, we can talk more in person."

"Where's my dad?"

"I don't know. That's all I can tell you right now. Meet me at the institute. We need to discuss Hollister's known associates and who might have driven him to your house on the night he attacked your father."

The line went dead.

"Mr. Zacharias?"

Nothing.

"Are you there?"

No reply.

Daniel smacked the car door.

"So," Kyle said, catching the gist of the phone call, "Mr. Zacharias is the one who helped the guy escape from the institute? Seriously?"

"Yeah. Brandon Hollister. But it sounds like someone else drove him to our house Saturday night. Did you hear the call?"

"Just your side of it."

"Mr. Zacharias wants me to meet him at the institute, to talk to Dr. Waxford . . ." Daniel noticed where they were on the road. "Listen, my house isn't too far. Swing by there so I can pick up my car."

"You think there'll be cops watching your place? I mean, considering you escaped from the hospital and they're looking for you?"

"There aren't a lot of extra deputies in this county so I doubt it—I'm sure they're busy enough looking for my dad. And with the roads this bad, I'm guessing the state troopers are spread pretty thin with helping people who've gone into ditches. But drive past my house and we'll see. If there are any patrol cars around, we'll just keep going."

"So, then, split up: You meet with Mr. Zacharias and I head over to Nicole's?"

"Yeah, that way if we figure out where my dad is, at least one of us will be able to follow up on it. Also, I need to untangle what happened on Saturday night and I'm thinking that if I walk through our kitchen maybe it'll help jog my memory, like being in the barn did."

"Makes sense."

"Turn left up ahead," he said. "We'll take the shortcut."

CHAPTER FIFTY-FOUR

Dr. Waxford learned that in addition to a few international terror groups, there were several government agencies here in the States and a few private firms who might have the technological capabilities to get past the Traybor Institute's firewalls.

That didn't really narrow things down as much as he'd hoped.

However, the NSA had intel that a freelance operative named Malcolm Zacharias who specialized in asset recovery had been seen in the Twin Cities area recently.

That was just a couple of hours from Beldon.

According to Dr. Waxford's contact, Zacharias was the most likely actor.

He could've helped Hollister escape, might have doctored up the footage.

Find him.

He can lead you to Hollister.

It wasn't clear to Dr. Waxford how he might locate Zacharias, but he might as well utilize all the resources available to him.

He called his Department of Defense contact again and asked her to gather whatever she could on Zacharias. "And alert the local authorities," he said. "Get them looking for him."

"Under what pretense?"

"Tell them that you suspect him of abducting Sheriff Byers. That'll get their attention."

In the meantime, he needed to take measures to ensure the integrity of his research. He hadn't wanted to do so before, but if Zacharias was involved, he might've been the one who called law enforcement earlier and told them to look for the sheriff here at the facility.

If it is him, if he really did help Hollister escape, he knows more than he should. He might know enough to bring this research to a halt.

With that in mind, Dr. Waxford realized that if he couldn't find Hollister or Zacharias, he might have to take other, more extreme measures to make sure no one would discover that any of his research had ever happened here.

There were systems in place for this eventuality.

The explosives were already wired into the walls. It would look like a gas leak explosion when it was over and it would seal up and cover the underground research rooms.

His staff would be relocated.

A clean start.

He took out his laptop and started to download the files he would need to take with him so he could carry on his research elsewhere if he did need to destroy the facility.

• • •

No one was staking out the house, but Daniel told Kyle to stay in the car and keep an eye out as he went into the kitchen.

It's not law enforcement's job to clean up after crimes occur, so there was still dried blood on the floor.

It was in the exact spot where, back when he was at the psych ward, Daniel had envisioned his dad being attacked. So apparently that part of his dream had been true, even if the part about his hand getting chewed up in the garbage disposal hadn't been.

Seeing the bloodstains here, now, for real, was tough.

Man, he could not believe Mr. Zacharias was the one who'd helped Hollister escape.

But where does that leave you?

What happened to your dad?

He knelt beside the blood, placed his hand on the cool linoleum and then let his thoughts take him back to Saturday night.

And found that he'd been right.

Being here did jar his memory.

He closed his eyes as one image after another wisped through his mind, each becoming clearer, each nudging him back closer to the truth.

You go to your room, planning to read through the diaries, but then decide to grab a soda from the kitchen, so you put the box containing the journals on your desk beside your phone and head down the hall.

Halfway to the living room, the lights cut off.

Your dad's not home and there's no storm outside, so you figure it must be a fuse.

You know where the fuse box is, over by the washing machine in the basement. You find a flashlight in the junk drawer in the kitchen and descend the stairs.

You're on your way to the panel when the garage door opens.

A moment later, your dad calls out to you and you think that's odd because, with things as dark as they are, he wouldn't have any idea that you're down here. Besides, it doesn't sound like he's trying to be heard down the steps, but instead like he's speaking to someone in the kitchen: "Daniel? Are you alright?"

And then: "What's going on, Dan?"

All at once there's a pained cry and a thud.

Silence.

You shout to him, asking if he's okay, but there's no reply.

Hurrying up the stairs into the kitchen, you swipe your flashlight's beam across the room and see him lying on the floor near the fridge.

"Dad!"

He isn't moving.

You rush to him.

A knife is sticking out of his side and it quivers slightly with each labored breath that he takes.

You try to decide whether to go for your phone to call for help or to stay here and try to stop the bleeding, but then realize that if you don't get an ambulance here soon, your dad is going to die.

But whoever did this is probably still—

You scan the kitchen, see no one.

Quickly returning to your bedroom, you find your cell and punch in 911 as you hurry back to help your dad.

You set down the flashlight and try to control the bleeding, but there's a lot of blood.

So much blood.

On your hands.

All over.

As you wait for dispatch to pick up, you hear movement behind you—the slight creak in the floor that tells you someone is there.

Whipping around, you see a figure emerge. He swings something toward your head.

There's a splinter of stars and then you see nothing, feel nothing, except for the weight of a wide, sweeping darkness that's quickly overtaking you.

But right before you pass out, you hear someone calling from the basement steps. "That's Daniel," the person says. "This changes everything."

Daniel blinked, then stared at the door to the basement.

His heart was racing.

There were two people here, not just one.

Whose voice did you hear?

He closed his eyes again and concentrated, but he wasn't able to recall any more details about who might have knocked him out or who'd been in the stairwell. However, even though he couldn't identify the voice, he had the sense that he'd heard it before.

So.

Was it one of Hollister's past associates?

Mr. Zacharias helped Hollister escape. Could it have been him?

Now there was a thought.

Go. Get moving. Meet with him. See what he has to say.

While Kyle left for Nicole's house, Daniel kept Larry's phone with him and, after tracking down a set of keys, he took off in his own car to meet up with the man who might very well have been there at the house when his dad was stabbed.

CHAPTER FIFTY-FIVE

Sheriff Byers managed to pull the spring free, but as it popped off the cot, it shot across the room and ricocheted off the wall.

Rolling.

Rolling.

And finally stopping, out of reach.

But it might just be close enough for you to get with your heel.

With the cot's legs fastened to the floor, he couldn't scoot it closer, so instead, he swung his leg out and stretched out as far as the handcuffs would allow him.

After two tries, he was able to nudge the spring back toward him with his foot.

A little more work, and he managed to roll it close enough to grab.

Then, spring in hand, he slipped the tip into the lock mechanism of the handcuffs, trying to free himself.

• • •

Daniel wasn't far from the institute. As he drove toward it, he let his mind flip through the facts, the blurs.

What he knew.

What he didn't.

Malcolm Zacharias wanted to talk to him about past associates that Hollister had who might've helped him, and one of those people was certainly Ty Bell, who used to party with him before his arrest.

Was it him?

Could Ty be working with Hollister?

Is he the one who attacked your dad? Or, could he have been the person you heard coming up from the basement right before you blacked out?

Nicole had sent him the address of the property the Bells owned: 1594 West Creek Drive.

It was on Waunakee Lake, near the institute, and right in the center of the sites where the poached wolves had been found.

Could Ty be the one who tried to kill you at the island? He's pulled a knife on you before. He's capable of—

Larry's cell phone rang, jarring Daniel out of his thoughts.

The caller ID simply said "business" and Daniel anticipated that it was probably Larry calling from his landline. Talking on the phone while driving in a snowstorm wasn't easy or smart, but Daniel wasn't about to take the time to pull over to take the call.

He answered. "Larry?"

"Yeah, I found out something. Remember how I was looking into if anyone might have rented a boat from another company? Well, one guy, a friend of mine from across town, he did rent a boat to someone."

"Who'd he rent it to?"

"Grady Planisek."

"Planisek?"

"Yeah. He arrived after you did, must've gone around the south side of the island and that's why you didn't see the boat. Or it might have been the snow and the limited visibility—in any case, does the name ring any bells?"

"Actually, it does. There was a boy from this area who disappeared back when I was a kid. That was his name: Grady Planisek."

And that's what the demon flew through at the barn— the carved words, the phrase "Grady Planisek was here."

Daniel thanked Larry and hung up.

Who would have used that name to rent the boat?

Grady went missing seven years ago.

As far as Daniel could remember, the boy was ten when he disappeared.

An idea came to him out of nowhere and it reshuffled all the puzzle pieces that he'd assumed were already in place.

Could Grady Planisek still be alive?

Is that possible? Could—

A strip of ice and a momentary skid toward the snowbank jolted Daniel's attention back to navigating along the worsening roads, but after regaining control of the car, he thought about Grady.

You have the address of the Bell's property.

It's on the way to the institute.

It's close.

Could whoever attacked your dad be there?

Would Malcolm Zacharias be in the area, at the institute, because of that?

Is he behind all this?

Or is it Grady?

Or Ty?

You could check it out.

Mr. Zacharias wants to meet to talk about people Hollister knew before going to prison. Ty Bell is one of them.

So: Meet with Mr. Zacharias or go and investigate the property on the lake?

The intersection was just up ahead.

You never told Mr. Zacharias when you were going to meet with him. You can get to West Creek Drive if you take the turnoff up ahead. Check it out. If there's nothing there, you can go see him afterwards.

Daniel came to the road, made the turn, and headed for 1594 West Creek Drive.

• • •

Nicole was checking her messages to see if Daniel had texted her back when she saw the sweep of headlights cut briefly through the window as a car entered their driveway.

Huh, Daniel and Kyle made a lot better time than they thought they would.

A few moments later the doorbell rang.

After setting her phone on the coffee table next to the couch, she went to the front door, flicked on the porch light and glanced out the window.

No one was on the porch.

Okay. That was weird.

Who rang the doorbell?

After a short internal debate, she went ahead and eased the door open. "Hello? Daniel? Kyle? Where are you guys?"

She peered into the snowy night and saw no movement, nothing.

However, as she was about to close the door and lock it, someone leapt out of the shadows around the side of the house and rushed her. Stumbling backward, she tried shutting the door, but he wedged his foot in the way.

She moved back, her heart pounding tightly in her chest.

Ty Bell entered the living room.

"Hello, Nicole."

And closed the door behind him.

CHAPTER
FIFTY-SIX

Last September, Nicole had been driving through the country at night with Daniel after both of their dates failed to show up for the Homecoming dance.

As it turned out, Ty and his three buddies were waiting for them on the road. Daniel had faced them down when they were about to break into the car and get to her—she didn't even want to think of what they might've done to her if they'd been able to get in—and they left. That's what'd led her to carry pepper spray in her purse ever since.

And now she was alone with him, and her parents weren't supposed to be back until eight.

Okay, but Daniel and Kyle are on their way. Daniel said six thirty. You just need to hold out, keep him talking, until then.

"How did you—" she began, but then anticipated what'd happened. "Oh, you were at your dad's office, is that it? You heard the voicemail I left on the tip line."

"I was doing a little research."

"On where the wolves are."

He smiled and tilted his head slightly to the side. "Look at you. Threading things together."

Anger rose inside her.

"How many have there been, Ty?"

"How many?"

"Wolves. How many have you shot that haven't been found?"

"They've found all of them except for one. It's been a good run."

She stepped forward and slapped him.

Hard.

He's bigger than you are. He's stronger. You shouldn't have—

Screw it.

She was glad she had.

She backed up. "What are you doing here?"

He rubbed some fresh blood off his split lip. "I thought you and I could have a little chat."

"Daniel and Kyle are going to be here any minute."

"Then we better not waste any time."

Stall.

No, you need to call someone. Get help.

She'd left her phone beside the couch and, as she slowly backed up toward it, Ty must have guessed what she was after, because he pounced forward, shoved her out of the way, and nabbed the phone.

"I'll take that." He slid it into his pocket. "This way we can have a little privacy."

Oh, not good.

Not good.

You need to get out of here.

But he took a step so that he was standing between her and the front door. "I know where your boyfriend's dad is."

"What?" she exclaimed.

"If you go online right now and confess to shooting those wolves, I'll tell you where he is."

"You attacked Daniel's dad? It was *you*?"

"No." He shook his head. "It wasn't me. But I do know where he is. And I'll tell you." He waved his phone at her. He had a video app pulled up. "You just need to admit to the world what you've been up to."

"That's crazy. Who would ever believe I'm the one who killed those wolves?"

"They will because of the gun they're gonna find in your garage."

"That's not enough. Daniel was with me when we found the wolf you shot on Saturday. He knows it wasn't me. He'll vouch for me."

"Psycho boy?" He scoffed. "He's not the most stable guy around. Besides, everyone would expect him to cover for you." He patted the pocket he'd slipped her phone into. "They're also going to find the tagged wolf locations on your cell."

"Oh. I see. After you download them."

Another smug grin.

"You can't possibly think that I would agree to that."

"Well." He put his phone away. "At least I tried."

She didn't like the look on his face.

Just go ahead and do it, Nicole. No one will buy it anyway and maybe he'll tell you where Daniel's dad is.

"Okay," she said. "I'll say I shot them. Let me have your phone."

"Just the fact that you believed me tells me how naïve you really are."

The wicked glint in his eyes frightened her and she thought again of the time when he'd pulled the knife on Daniel and tried to get to her in the locked car.

He carries an automatic knife.

He probably has it with him tonight.

He—

Without waiting another moment, she spun and bolted up the stairs to her bedroom. Slammed the door. Locked it.

Slid her dresser over against it.

But then she heard Ty stalking up the stairs.

"We have some unfinished business, Nicole. But we can take care of it in your bedroom, if that's how you want this to go."

CHAPTER FIFTY-SEVEN

Sheriff Byers heard the mechanism in the handcuff's lock click.

The cuffs popped open.

He unsnapped the link from around his wrist and pushed himself unsteadily to his feet, then crossed the room.

He hadn't heard Hollister lock the door earlier, but he was ready to kick it down if necessary.

He tried it.

Unlocked.

Good.

Quietly, he swung it open.

Jacked up on adrenaline and ready for a fight, he entered the cabin's living room and took it in: rustic wood furniture. A couch. Two chairs. A fireplace. Three mounted white-tailed deer heads on the wall near a pendulum clock.

An open doorway to the kitchen. Glass French doors on the far wall.

Suturing thread, needles, bloody dressings, and some empty syringes and medicine bottles sat on one of the counters.

He didn't recognize the place. Hadn't been in here before.

No sign of Hollister.

Where is he?

He glanced around the room for a phone, but found none.

Get out of here. You're in no shape to fight anyone. Just get moving.

He was on his way toward the front door when a photo on the mantel above the fireplace caught his attention.

It was a picture of Ty Bell sitting beside a dead whitetail, a gun laid across its antlers.

The sheriff paused.

Who would have put that picture up in his cabin?

Most likely someone from his family. Most likely—

Is this Lancaster Bell's hunting cabin?

Is he involved?

Hollister mentioned someone else, said someone was coming. Is Lancaster the one who—

"Stop right there, Sheriff." Brandon Hollister emerged from the kitchen, holding a long serrated survival knife. "Sit down. On the couch."

Sheriff Byers let his hands form into fists. "Think I'll stand."

· · ·

Nicole tried to calm her breathing and figure out what to do as Ty wrenched at her locked doorknob.

"Don't be like this, Nicole. We can come to another arrangement."

Think, Nicole, Think!

He has your phone.

She desperately searched her room for—

Yes.

He did have her phone.

But she had her laptop.

· · ·

Daniel crossed the bridge spanning Pine River, and then turned onto West Creek Drive.

He'd only driven on this road a couple times, but based on how close he was to the lake, he figured he was less than a mile from the property.

· · ·

Sheriff Byers watched Hollister carefully, waiting for him to let his guard down long enough to move in and disarm him.

"Put down the knife, Brandon."

"No."

"Put it—"

"No! Sit down." He checked the clock on the wall and fidgeted with a small case on his belt, about the size of a cell phone case. "Now."

"You said before that you wanted my help, but I'm not going to help you with anything while you're threatening me with that knife."

Hollister didn't move.

They both stood their ground.

The sheriff tried a different tack. "Why did you stab me if you want me to help you?"

"I wanted to kill you at first, but he told me not to."

"Who told you not to?"

"He's coming and . . . you don't know what it's like. Time becomes . . ." His voice broke with what sounded like a tremor of fear. "I want the world to know the truth about what they're doing there."

"Where? At the prison? Were you mistreated?"

"Not the prison. The institute!" Hollister tapped the blade against the side of his own head. "In your brain. They do things up there. Make it seem like . . ."

"Brandon, you need to set that knife down."

Hollister aimed it at him. "You're the one who arrested me! It's your fault I ended up there!"

"Okay. What institute are you talking about? The Traybor Institute?"

"They were asking for volunteers, said it would shorten our sentences, but . . . in the room." His hand was quivering. "They strap you down. Can you imagine solitary confinement? But without a break, without any relief. That's what it felt like—weeks—even though I was . . ." Hollister shook his head violently. "They won't believe me." He waved the knife back and forth as if to accentuate his point. "But they will believe you."

Careful. This guy is losing it. Keep him talking, but don't push things.

"Alright, I'm listening. Tell me what's going on."

CHAPTER FIFTY-EIGHT

Daniel parked.

Exited the car.

There weren't any other vehicles in the driveway, but the lights inside the cabin were on, so it appeared someone was there.

Check it out, then go meet with Mr. Zacharias.

He approached the front window to see if he could peer inside, but the shades were tightly drawn.

Going around the side of the cabin, he found some French doors on the deck.

Through the glass he could see two men standing at the other end of the room in the main living area.

One of them was his dad.

He's alive!

Thank God, he's alive!

The other guy was about ten feet away from him, holding a knife.

Daniel recognized him as the prisoner he'd seen at the Traybor Institute.

It's Brandon Hollister. He went to prison for murder. He's going after your dad!

Daniel tried opening the French doors but they were locked. With the wind already rattling the glass, neither man noticed him.

You need to get in there. You need to help your dad.

But how?

He returned to the front of the cabin, but that door was locked as well.

Alright, then.

Find another way in.

• • •

Nicole set her laptop on the dresser beside the door so the microphone would pick up Ty's voice from the hallway.

Having someone admit to the wolf poaching was a good idea, but it wasn't going to be her who was confessing to the world.

"So does your dad know what you've been doing?" she asked.

There are tons of ways to call for help online, and as she worked, she sent out texts and emails to at least half a dozen of her friends that she needed the cops at her house *now*.

Ty didn't reply so she went on. "Or, what about those three guys you always hang out with?"

"No one else knows. It's our little secret."

She checked the levels, made sure that his voice was coming through.

Yes.

Good.

He tried the doorknob again. "Open the door, Nicole."

"So you shot all the wolves yourself?"

She waited. He said nothing.

"Why'd you kill the wolves, Ty?"

"Target practice."

She felt another surge of anger because of what he'd done. "Even if you put the gun in my garage, it'd get tracked back to you. Even you must know that much."

"You think I'd use my own rifle?"

"What? Whose did you use?"

"There's this research center. There's a certain guy who works there. I borrowed his Browning Automatic. Now—"

"You mean you stole it."

He cranked on the doorknob one more time. "I'm not here to hurt you, Nicole. I just want us to come to an understanding."

"What kind of understanding?"

C'mon, Daniel. Hurry!

"One that—"

As she was uploading the audio she accidentally tapped 'Play' and it started replaying, aloud.

"What was that?" Ty shouted. "You recorded me?"

Oh, no!

She scrambled to post the audio, but Ty slammed his fist against the door and she retreated across the room.

He pounded it again, trying to break it open.

Nicole dropped her computer onto her bed.

And went for her purse.

• • •

Moments ago at his car, Daniel had used Larry's phone to punch in 911 to get some officers and an ambulance here for his dad. Dispatch told him that with the roads as bad as they were and with him being that far out of town it might be up to eight or ten minutes before any help could arrive.

No.

That was way too long.

He needed to do something himself to help his dad.

Opening the trunk, Daniel retrieved the shovel that he kept to dig out of snowbanks if necessary, then headed for the deck of the cabin.

• • •

The sheriff listened as Brandon Hollister explained what he'd gone through at the Traybor Institute.

He kept checking the clock. "When he gets here we'll take care of everything."

"When who gets here?"

"You'll see."

"After I help you, what are you going to do with me? Are you going to let me go?"

"You get your name on the wall."

"What?"

• • •

Daniel didn't know for sure if this was going to work, but he did know that if he sat around doing nothing waiting for help to arrive and Hollister killed his dad, he would never forgive himself.

Positioning himself close to the glass French doors, he gripped the shovel's handle, as if it were a baseball bat, then brought it back behind his shoulder and swung it forward as hard as he could, smashing the blade through the door, which shattered, spraying glass across the inside of the cabin.

Avoiding the jagged teeth of glass that were still embedded at the bottom of the doorframe, Daniel stepped through it, raised the shovel, and started toward Hollister. "Drop the knife."

While the guy was distracted, Daniel's dad made his move, springing at him.

They struggled for a moment and Daniel dropped the shovel and went to help his father, but by the time he'd crossed the room, his dad had already torqued Hollister's arm back, forcing him to drop the blade.

"No!" Hollister struggled fiercely, but couldn't get away. "You don't understand!"

"Quiet, Brandon." Daniel's dad kicked the knife across the floor toward the front door. "Dan, are you okay?"

"Yeah. You?"

"I'm good." But he was obviously in pain as he led Hollister, who was trying his best to break free, to a nearby room. "Come here, Dan, I need your help."

His dad maneuvered Hollister to a cot and had Daniel clamp the open handcuff around the man's wrist, shackling him to the frame.

Once he was restrained, his dad searched Hollister's pockets and came up with the handcuff key. However, as he was stepping back, Hollister suddenly whipped a syringe out of a case on his belt with his free hand and stabbed it into Daniel's dad's leg, depressing the plunger as he did.

"There," he said. "Let's see where that takes us."

• • •

Sheriff Byers yanked the empty syringe out of his leg and threw it across the room. "What was that?" he demanded. "What'd you give me?"

Hollister just smirked. "You're about to get very sleepy, Sheriff."

CHAPTER
FIFTY-NINE

Kyle turned onto Nicole's street. At the edge of his head-lights' beams, he could see that neither of her parents' cars was in the driveway.

But Ty Bell's SUV was.

• • •

Daniel's dad couldn't get an answer from Hollister, so he went into the other room and began flipping through the empty syringes and medicine bottles on the counter, trying to identify what he might've been drugged with.

"I called 911 a few minutes ago," Daniel told him. "They're on their way."

• • •

Nicole watched in alarm as the lock broke apart and the door flew open.

Knocking over the dresser, Ty barreled toward her.

When he was about to reach out and grab her, she brought her hand forward and emptied the pepper spray into his face.

He cried out and threw his hands up, rubbing frantically at his eyes.

• • •

"Dad, sit down," Daniel said. "An ambulance is coming."

His father, who was looking weaker by the second, stumbled over to the couch. "Hollister said you had a bump on the head?"

"I'm fine." He didn't mention the fire or the near-drowning. "Just rest until the paramedics get here."

• • •

The front door to Nicole's house was unlocked and Kyle burst inside. "Nicole? Are you okay?"

She shouted to him from the upstairs bedroom.

Sprinting up the steps, he found Ty Bell drawing his fist back to punch her.

Kyle grabbed him by the shoulders and manhandled him to the floor.

His eyes were puffy and swollen.

He was crying out in pain and anger.

Nicole was still holding the can of pepper spray. "He has my phone," she told Kyle.

Despite Ty's best efforts to fight him off, Kyle didn't waste any time recovering it from his pocket.

While Nicole put a call through to the police, Kyle said, "We need to make sure he doesn't go anywhere."

"There's some duct tape in the kitchen in the drawer beside the fridge."

"That'll work."

CHAPTER SIXTY

As Daniel's dad positioned himself on the couch, he cringed in pain.

Keep him talking.

"Dad, do you remember Grady Planisek?"

"What?"

"Grady Planisek. He was a kid who disappeared back when I was nine."

"Okay," he answered, half out of it.

"Listen: He has something to do with what's going on here. Someone used Grady's name today to . . ."

Who did you hear calling from the stairs Saturday night right before you passed out?

Mr. Bell?

Ty?

Grady Planisek?

"Something's not right here, Dad. Something doesn't follow."

Daniel's thoughts shot forward, circled back around. Looked for a place to land.

In that blur, Betty warned you to be careful who you told your secrets to. "You have to stop him before it happens again," she said. "You can't let him get away with it."

Then there was the old man in the hospital. He'd warned Daniel, "You don't have time. He'll do it again."

Who was he talking about?

Who'll do it again?

But you might have been imagining him. You don't know if he was really there.

"Did you see someone else on Saturday night?" Daniel asked his dad.

"What?" By the way he spoke Daniel could tell he was fading fast.

Dispatch said eight or ten minutes.

That's too long.

Going into the other room, Daniel tried to get Hollister to tell him what the drug was, but the man just jangled his handcuffed wrist. "Let me go and I'll tell you."

Daniel listened for sirens, but only heard the sound of the wind in the night. Snow was blowing in through the splintered glass of the French door, and even here on this side of the cabin, he could feel the gusts of cold air.

"Well?" Hollister asked. "Are you going to save your father? You just have to uncuff me and I'll help you. I promise."

"That's not gonna happen."

Daniel returned to his dad. "We need to get you to the hospital." He reached out a hand to help him to his feet. "Come on, I'll drive you myself."

"We can't just leave Hollister here."

"He's cuffed. He's not going anywhere. There are officers on their way."

"Just give me a moment." His dad closed his eyes and didn't take Daniel's hand. "I need to catch my breath."

But as the seconds passed, his father didn't move.

"Dad?"

Don't let him fall asleep.

"Dad!"

Daniel shook his shoulder to keep him awake.

He stirred. "Yeah. I'm good."

"We're leaving. Now. C'mon. We need to go."

This time his dad didn't object and he let Daniel help him to his feet; however, Daniel found that he needed to support most of his weight.

As he wrapped his arm around his father's side and carefully avoided putting pressure on the bandages, the blood on them made him think of the dream of seeing him in the kitchen, and also of his own hand getting ground up in the sink, when the blades of the garbage disposal chewed through his skin, his bones, his—

Why did you block out what happened at the barn when you were a kid?

Because it was too traumatic.

Because your mind was trying to protect you.

As Daniel started helping his dad toward the door, the blood made him remember.

Not everything in your blurs is one hundred percent the same as things in real life.

The hay baler was running.

The garbage disposal ground up your—

Then in a rush, it came back to him—images overlapping each other all in a matter of seconds, and the memory of that day flashed before him.

Your grandma is sad most of the time so when you go over there with your parents you play by yourself a lot, sometimes up in the attic, sometimes in the field or the woods near her house.

Sometimes in the barn on the neighbor's property.

One day you find a wooden box in her attic. Your parents are talking with your grandma in the living room and it isn't hard for you to slip out the back door unseen with the box.

You cross the field to the barn to sit by yourself in the hayloft and look through what's in it.

There's a lock and a key in there.

That intrigues you.

You sit on the bench up there and read through the journals, flip through the photos.

It's late afternoon and it has started to rain outside.

Then you hear a man and a boy enter the barn. They're talking, but it doesn't sound like the boy wants to be here.

You don't want them to see what you've been doing up here in the loft, so you put everything back in the box and you lock it and hide it under the bench. You don't want to get caught, so you slip behind a hay bale.

The boy starts crying.

At first it's soft, but then it gets louder.

You can hear the man tell him to stop, to be quiet, and then to *shut up*!

The boy's crying turns into terrified screaming, and then you hear the sound of the hay baler running. And when it stops, it's quiet down there in the barn.

No more crying.

No more screaming.

You're scared.

You want to leave, to run back to your grandma's house, but then you hear someone coming up the ladder.

Heavy footsteps.

It's the man.

He knows you're here. He's coming for you!

You slide farther behind the hay bale, but you can't get completely hidden and you see him reach the top of the ladder.

He takes out a jackknife and flicks out the blade.

You freeze, too terrified to move.

No, no, no.

He walks to the wall of the barn and carves something into the wood.

It takes awhile, but when he steps away you can see the words: Grady Planisek was here.

Then he goes back down the ladder and you wait a long time to make sure he's gone.

At last you climb down from the hayloft and run through the rain to your grandma's house. You leave the box in the loft so you won't have to carry it, won't have to explain anything when you get back to her house.

You don't tell anyone what happened. You keep it to yourself.

The sound of the hay baler.

The boy's screams.

The silence afterward.

No, you don't tell anyone what happened in the barn.

You throw the key into the field and you never go back to that barn again.

6:31 P.M.
IT ALL COMES TOGETHER.

That man in the barn, that man, that man—

You didn't know him back then, but you do now.

Yes, you mentioned the property to him. He knows that you piece things together.

That's why he tried to kill you.

Yes, there was a second person there on Saturday night.

It was him.

The one who drove Hollister to the house.

The one with the jackknife that—

367

Daniel could hardly believe who was actually behind all this, but he finally knew who it was.

The sound of a car approaching the cabin caught his attention.

Hollister must have heard the car too, because he called out to Daniel, "It's too late."

"Your family bought the property, didn't they?" Daniel yelled back to him. "Sometime in the last eight years?"

"What?"

"Out on County Highway N. It didn't belong to you back then."

A tiny pause. "He's not going to let you just walk out of here."

No. It wasn't Ty Bell.

He's just letting Hollister use this place.

Malcolm Zacharias called them blurs—when you first met him he mentioned your blurs.

How did he know that you call them that? There are only a few people who know that you call them blurs.

He said he had a source—

It all fit.

It's what you said on Sunday, that's why he wanted you dead.

Not Mr. Zacharias.

No.

His source.

And that's why he kept asking you about what you saw when your dad was attacked.

Yes.

The car engine outside stopped. Daniel and his dad were almost to the door when his father passed out.

"Dad, wake up!"

But his body had gone limp.

You're not gonna get out in time.

Daniel lowered him to the floor next to the knife Hollister had been holding earlier, then slid it under his leg.

And waited for his psychiatrist, Dr. Fromke, to come in through the door.

CHAPTER
SIXTY-ONE

The lock clicked, the door swung open, and he appeared, holding a gun that looked to Daniel like his dad's Glock.

Dr. Fromke stood there for a moment, the snow whipping and curling in around him, before coming inside and shutting the door.

He wore black jeans, a dark blue winter jacket and running shoes.

"I wondered if that was your car out there." He aimed the gun at Daniel. "Let me see your hands."

Still kneeling, and being careful to shift his weight to keep the knife hidden beneath his leg, Daniel held up his hands, showing his psychiatrist that they were empty.

"I'm in here," Hollister shouted from the other room. "The kid called the cops. They're on their way. I gave the sheriff Tribaxil. He's not gonna last long, not with that much—"

Hollister's words hit Daniel like a fist in the gut. "What do you mean he's not gonna last long?"

Why would they want to kill him? Why, after keeping him alive since Saturday?

They're desperate, Daniel. They're not going to let either you or your dad leave here alive.

You need to go. You need to get to the hospital.

He lowered his hands.

Dr. Fromke evaluated things, then sighed and shook his head. "Daniel, why couldn't you have just stayed in that root cellar? It would have made all this a lot easier."

"You were afraid I'd piece things together about the barn on County N. That's why you tried to kill me."

The psychiatrist called for Brandon to come into the room.

"They cuffed me to the cot."

Dr. Fromke asked Daniel. "Do you have the key?"

"I'll only let you have it if you let me leave with my dad." He wasn't sure how that would work—he was making this up as he went along. "We go to the car first. I'll give it to you when—"

"No. I'm afraid that's not how things are going to play out here."

Hollister begged Dr. Fromke, "Don't let them take me back to that institute. Remember, I know everything that's gone down here." He made it sound like a threat.

"True," Dr. Fromke said, then disappeared into the room where Hollister was. Daniel heard a gunshot and then the psychiatrist returned to the living room.

"Now," he said, "we can talk undisturbed. Just the two of us."

He killed him.

He just killed Brandon Hollister.

You need to get your dad out of here before he—

"You have a special gift, Daniel. I—"

"I know it was you. You're the source."

"Source?"

Find a way to get him close.

Use the knife.

"You're the one who told Malcolm Zacharias that I was intuitive, that I have blurs."

"Malcolm Zacharias?"

"The guy who helped me get out of the hospital."

Mr. Zacharias is at the institute right now waiting for you. It's close. He can help you. Get your dad there and—

"I was meaning to ask how you managed that." Dr. Fromke approached Daniel and sat on the edge of the couch about eight feet away, aiming the Glock directly at him.

Daniel didn't stand, just stayed crouched beside his dad, making sure the knife was out of sight, calculating when and how he'd be able to use it. "So you followed us from Beldon to the lighthouse?"

"Based on what I knew about you from our counseling sessions, I thought you might go to Nicole's place. When I got word you'd disappeared from the hospital, I tried her house, then yours, but then I figured Kyle was the next best bet. As it turns out, third time's a charm. Now let's—"

"Why?"

"Why?"

"Why did you contact Mr. Zacharias's group? Why did you do any of this?"

"You have a special gift, Daniel." He pointed the gun toward Daniel's head. "There's something up there. You see things no one else sees, pull things together in a way no one else can. There are people who are very interested in finding out how you're able to do that and let's just say they pay very well for referrals."

"So. Money."

"There are only so many things that motivate people, Daniel."

"But how did you even hear about them?"

"It's amazing what you can find on the Internet."

"But then you turned your back on them to help Hollister?"

"I accepted my payment and moved on."

"In your office on Friday I saw that certificate from the prison—you helped as a counselor there. Is that where you met Hollister? Or did you just know him from selling the property to his family?"

He looked impressed. "You really are a sharp boy. It's too bad things have to end this way."

He sighted down the gun.

"I know about Grady," Daniel said quickly. "What you did. The hay baler. I was there in the loft. I saw you carve his name on the barn wall."

A stretch of stillness.

Dr. Fromke appeared deep in thought.

"Daniel, give me your phone."

Get him closer.

Just get him close enough and then you can use the knife.

He set Larry's cell down beside his leg. "Come and get it."

"Slide it to me."

"No, I—"

Dr. Fromke fired a shot into the floor next to Daniel's dad, missing him by mere inches. "Slide it to me, Daniel. I didn't have to miss that time. I won't miss if I fire again."

Unsure what else to do, Daniel flicked the phone across the floor toward the doctor. "How many of those names in the barn were your victims?"

"You really don't remember, do you?"

"I noticed seven of them all carved the same way into the wood. It was all with the same knife, right? What? That pocketknife you use as a letter opener at your office? Did you kill all those people?"

"You're the one who killed Grady Planisek, Daniel."

"What?"

"The two of you were in the loft. You pushed him into that hay baler. I watched it all happen. I owned the farm at the time."

"What are you talking about?"

"You killed that boy, repressed the memory, and now it's resurfacing and causing you to have a psychic break. You've lost the ability to determine what's real and what's not. What's right and what's wrong."

"No."

Yes.

"You're a very troubled boy, Daniel."

You are troubled.

Yes.

You killed Grady.

No. You couldn't have!

But—

"Think back to that day, Daniel. What did you really see?"

"You murdered him."

"Did you see me do it?"

He's trying to confuse you, he's—

"I heard him screaming."

"And?"

"The hay baler was running."

"Yes."

"Then you came up the ladder and . . ."

Reality.

Fantasy.

"You killed Grady," Dr. Fromke repeated. "And you attacked your father—"

"No. That was you and Brandon. People around here know me. They know I would never do anything like that. They'll never believe you."

"But they already do. You're a suspect in your dad's disappearance, and now, tonight, you killed Brandon Hollister with your father's gun—"

"It's not going to work. No one will—"

"—and then, you shot me."

"What?"

Dr. Fromke picked up Larry's phone. "Since you're my patient I knew what you were capable of, that's why I had you committed up in Duluth. That's why I had them station an officer outside your door." He tapped at the screen of the phone, then held it to his ear.

Someone must have answered on the other end because Dr. Fromke said urgently, "He's got a gun. You have to hurry. Daniel Byers. Yes! He's going to kill me. He said he's gonna kill me. I'm at 1594 West Creek Drive. Please!"

Daniel stood there in shock.

"Get away from me!" Dr. Fromke yelled loud enough for the dispatcher on the other end of the line to hear.

Then he shot himself through the shoulder.

"No, Daniel! Why would you—"

He dropped the phone and crushed it beneath his heel.

"The next move"—he clenched his teeth, obviously trying to help deal with the pain from the gunshot wound—"is up to you."

CHAPTER SIXTY-TWO

"What have you done?" Daniel gasped.

Dr. Fromke kept the gun out, pointing it at him. "You're a mentally disturbed young man who hallucinates and does things he doesn't remember. No one will believe your word over mine. What proof do you have that I ever harmed anyone? But don't worry, Daniel. You won't suffer. I'll make sure the medications they give you at the psychiatric hospital won't allow you to feel much of anything. It's over. Now we wait."

Your dad's dying. You can't wait.

You need to get help. You need to do something.

"They'll know it wasn't me. My fingerprints aren't even on that gun."

Dr. Fromke surprised Daniel by flipping the Glock around in his hand and walking toward him.

Do it. Take the gun.

No! Your prints will be on it.

As the doctor approached, Daniel slowly reached for the knife that was under his leg.

"Here." Dr. Fromke held out the gun. "It's all yours."

Screw it. You need to go. You need to help your dad. Take the gun.

"Oh, wait," Dr. Fromke said. "They can check gunshot residue, blowback, right? You won't have any on you—unless you were close to the gun when it was fired."

He was only a few feet away and directed the Glock at Daniel's dad's forehead. "It's a shame you had to shoot your own father in the head."

"No!" Daniel snatched up the knife and launched himself between the gun barrel and his dad. Obviously taken by surprise, Dr. Fromke held back just long enough from squeezing the trigger, and Daniel drove the knife down through the man's shoe, through his foot, and into the floor.

Dr. Fromke cried out in shock and pain and Daniel went for the gun, wrestled it from his hand. It dropped.

He grabbed it.

Backed up a step.

He was going to set you up for his murder. He was going to shoot your dad.

Anger.

Rage.

Fury.

Caught up in the moment, Daniel stomped on the knife handle, driving the blade farther into the floorboards.

Dr. Fromke screamed and swung a fist at Daniel, but he leapt back in time to avoid the blow. "I'll tell them to match your jackknife, the one you keep on your desk, with the carvings in the barn," he said. "I'm sure someone who's good at forensics will be able to tell what blade made those carvings."

Dr. Fromke's face darkened.

"You were right: it is over." Daniel slipped the gun beneath his belt. "And you're going to spend the rest of your life in prison."

He bent down, slung his dad's arm across his shoulder, then lifted him—fireman's carry—and headed for the porch.

Out of the corner of his eye he could see Dr. Fromke grab the handle of the knife to try to work it free from the floor.

CHAPTER
SIXTY-THREE

In the distance, sirens wailed through the night.

As Daniel took his dad to the car, he hoped that the snow pelting against his face would revive him, but it didn't happen.

How are you going to get him into the car while he's unconscious? You'll never be able to . . . maybe the back seat instead of the front?

Moments later, as Daniel was positioning his dad in the back of the car, he heard the cabin door bang open.

Dr. Fromke stood, backlit in the doorway forty feet away, holding the shovel. He started limping across the porch toward the steps.

Go!

Daniel shoved his dad the rest of the way in, closed the door, climbed into the front, and fired up the engine.

As the wipers brushed the snow off the windshield he saw Dr. Fromke lurching across the driveway. Though he was forced to drag his wounded foot, he was already nearly halfway to the car.

Dr. Fromke's car was behind Daniel, blocking him in, but he thought he might have just enough space to get by it if he could edge along the bank of snow piled up alongside the driveway.

He locked the doors and backed up, trying to maneuver past the doctor's vehicle, but his car slid across the icy driveway and one of the rear tires lodged into the snowbank.

Dr. Fromke was now only ten feet away, and Daniel couldn't pull forward or he would hit him, but he couldn't back up either because of the snowbank.

You have the gun.

You could—

No, don't shoot him. You'd be a murderer. Don't—

Dr. Fromke arrived at Daniel's car, tried the door, found it locked, and despite the gunshot wound in his shoulder, hefted the shovel back and swung it at the windshield.

The glass shattered on impact, but thankfully remained intact, just like it's designed to do in case of a crash.

With Dr. Fromke next to the car, Daniel tried pulling forward, but the back tire didn't come unstuck from the snowbank.

Dr. Fromke drew the shovel back and smashed the blade against the windshield again, and it crunched inward toward Daniel. Another blow and it would probably give way.

You have to help your dad.

You have to get out of here.

Daniel threw the car into reverse and then into drive, and this time the tires spun for a moment, then found traction and his car jerked forward, brushing past Dr. Fromke.

Daniel stopped the car before smacking into the porch.

He could either try getting through between Dr. Fromke's car and the snowbank again, or wait here.

Sitting around waiting for the cops to arrive is not an option. Not with Dr. Fromke out there.

In the side-view mirror, Daniel could see Dr. Fromke approaching.

The sirens were getting closer.

Daniel lowered his window an inch. "Get back!" he yelled, as he popped the car into reverse. "Get out of the way!"

But Dr. Fromke was obviously more intent on attacking Daniel than staying safe, and he came toward the car, cocking back the shovel.

As Daniel tried to thread through the gap, his tires spun on the ice and the car whipped around.

Everything outside the window was whirling.

Turning.

A smear of white.

And then.

The jolt of impact as the car collided into Dr. Fromke's car, pinning the doctor between the two vehicles.

Dr. Fromke's legs might have been trapped, but when he shouted out threats against Daniel it seemed to be more from wrath than from pain.

Daniel tried to drive forward or back up—anything—but his tires spun on the ice.

The red-blue-red-blue swirl of police lights cut through the storm as a state patrol cruiser careened around the corner and came to a sliding stop on the driveway.

Two state troopers exited the cruiser, guns drawn.

Daniel left his dad's Glock in the car and climbed out, holding his hands up to show that he was unarmed. "They drugged my dad, we need to—"

"Get on the ground!" one of the troopers yelled.

"Listen, I'm—"

"Now! On the ground! Arms out to the side!"

The dispatchers couldn't possibly have believed Dr. Fromke's phone call.

But maybe they did.

An ambulance followed closely behind the patrol car.

Daniel knelt, then lay facedown and the trooper came over and cuffed his wrists behind his back while his partner went to check on Dr. Fromke.

"My dad's unconscious," Daniel said urgently. "He's in the back seat of my car. You need to get him to a hospital now."

"Sir," the other trooper said to Dr. Fromke, "we're going to help you."

"He shot me." The psychiatrist had tossed the shovel to the ground and was acting innocent. "He stabbed my foot and then tried to run me over. You need to stop that boy. He's out of control."

"No," Daniel said to the trooper beside him, "that's not—" *Sort it out later.* "Listen, tell the paramedics: Tribaxil. That's what they gave my dad. A whole syringe of it. He's the sheriff—Sheriff Byers. You need to help him."

The trooper seemed uncertain what to do.

"Hurry!" Daniel told him.

He left to talk to the paramedics, who promptly loaded his dad onto a rolling gurney.

The trooper helped Daniel to his feet, shuffled him toward his cruiser, and put him in the back seat.

"Let me ride with my dad."

"Until we figure this out you're staying with me."

The car door was still open and Daniel could see the other officer assisting Dr. Fromke, who was still stuck between the two vehicles. "You need to cuff him," Daniel called out. "He's dangerous. He—"

"We'll take care of this, son," the trooper said as he closed the door.

Daniel yelled through the window, "He's killed at least eight people!"

He wasn't sure if the officer believed him, but he did open his door again. "What did you just say?"

"He's murdered at least eight people. One of them is in the cabin."

Immediately, the man went to search the building. When he came back he spoke with the other trooper and it seemed to take forever before the officer who'd cuffed Daniel climbed in and turned the cruiser around to follow the ambulance. The other officer covered Dr. Fromke.

"Did you try to run that man over?" he asked Daniel.

"No."

"Did you shoot him?"

"No. He shot himself."

"Really." He didn't sound convinced.

"Yes, and he killed that man in the cabin."

The trooper spoke into his radio, relaying information about their location and giving them codes that Daniel didn't recognize.

Daniel prayed his dad would be okay, that the paramedics would get him to the hospital in time.

They turned onto the county road that led past the Traybor Institute and he scanned both sides of the road for any sign of Mr. Zacharias or his car, but saw nothing.

Just after they passed the facility, an explosion rocked the night and Daniel turned in time to see the building erupting in a blazing mushroom of smoke and flames.

The state trooper pulled the car over to the shoulder and muttered, "What the hell is going on tonight?"

Malcolm Zacharias wanted to take out the research station. Maybe he blew the place up.

Daniel didn't know, and right now he was more worried about his dad getting the care he needed than about what'd happened to the man who'd helped Hollister escape.

The trooper got on the radio and called for more units.

When they took off again, he drove Daniel to the hospital rather than the county jail.

So, maybe he did believe him after all.

PART VII
TWO WOLVES

CHAPTER
SIXTY-FOUR

Daniel repositioned his laptop so his dad could see the screen more easily from his hospital bed. "That good?"

"Yes." He adjusted the angle of the bed a little higher so that he was nearly sitting up.

Last night the doctors had worked on him for several hours, re-suturing his side and counteracting the drug Hollister had injected him with. It was a good thing he'd mentioned the name of it, since, from what the doctors were saying, an overdose of Tribaxil could have been fatal.

As it turned out, Hollister had done a surprisingly good job of treating the stab wound over the past few days.

His dad was still weak, but the doctors said he was "on the road to recovery," and Daniel figured that, at this point, that was about as much as he could hope for.

Daniel had spent a good part of last night and most of today filling in the deputies and state troopers about everything that'd happened. However, he did leave out the parts about his blurs so they would take the other things he had to say more seriously.

He had to go through it several times for them.

There was a lot to take in.

At first they'd kept a close eye on him, evidently still suspicious that he was lying to them, but when his dad woke up and corroborated his story, they let him spend the rest of his time with him in his room.

Dr. Fromke had been brought to the hospital as well and was being held under guard on the second floor. As far as Daniel knew, the psychiatrist hadn't spoken with the police since last night, or asked to talk to a lawyer, and he wondered what was going through the man's head, what he might be thinking or planning.

Whatever it was, Daniel did not like the fact that Dr. Fromke was in the same hospital as his dad, even if there were officers stationed outside the man's room.

He tapped at the keyboard and brought up the video chat program they were going to use to talk to his mom, who was still stranded in Alaska.

Nicole sat quietly in the chair near the window finishing a drawing of a Christmas stable scene on the last page of her sketchbook.

Kyle and Mia, who'd come back from her grandparents' house a day early, were on their way to the hospital to meet up with Daniel and Nicole and see how things were going. Kyle was also bringing a few things Daniel had requested—at least he was hoping his friend had been able to get them. Daniel had the envelope with him, but for the other two items he was relying on Kyle. From what he'd heard, Larry had come down from Bayfield and was at Kyle's house with Mrs. Goessel, Glenn and Michelle.

Daniel had already spoken with his mom three times today. Though she'd tried to get a flight out of Anchorage, that hadn't been possible, and his dad had only started feeling well enough in the last hour to have a video chat with her.

So Daniel had called her to set it up, and now here they were.

She came up on the screen, standing in front of her computer.

Champagne hair. A slight build. Worried eyes.

"Hey, Mom."

"Daniel."

She came closer to the camera, until just her face was visible.

Nicole waved to her. "Merry Christmas, Mrs. Byers."

"Merry Christmas, Nicole."

"Hello, LeAnne," his dad said.

"Jerry. How are you?" Deep concern laced every word. "Daniel said you were—oh, I can't believe all this is even happening."

"I'm feeling a lot better than I was last night. Thanks to your son."

"More like thanks to the doctors," Daniel corrected him.

His dad directed his attention to the screen. "I understand Daniel spoke with you earlier, filled you in on everything?"

"He told me about Dr. Fromke, and this maniac, Hollister, who stabbed you, all of it. It's unfathomable. Do we know how many people Dr. Fromke killed at that barn?

"They're still not sure. We have to be careful not to jump to conclusions, but my deputies are following up on the names carved into the wallboards to see how many of them are of missing persons. Daniel noticed seven names that were all apparently done with the same knife. We're checking into those first."

She let that sink in. "I can't believe I ever trusted Dr. Fromke. That any of us . . . And Ty Bell shooting those wolves? And then going after Nicole? What happens to him now?"

"Wolf poaching is a serious enough crime, but trying to attack her like that takes things up to a whole different level. He's over eighteen. He's looking at some serious time."

"Was Lancaster involved at all?"

"Doesn't look like it. Ty just let Hollister use his dad's hunting cabin."

"The same place he used as a base to go out and shoot the wolves."

"Exactly."

"And he confessed?"

"Nicole recorded it all."

Daniel's mom shook her head in disbelief. "And what about this Malcolm character?"

"I haven't met him yet. You'll have to ask Daniel about him."

Daniel hadn't heard from Mr. Zacharias since yesterday evening, but no bodies were found in the charred remains of the Traybor Institute after the gas leak explosion, so it didn't appear that he'd been inside it when it blew.

At least they were saying it was a gas leak.

Daniel didn't buy it.

The timing was just way too suspicious.

"I'll introduce you," Daniel promised his mom. "The next time he shows up."

If he ever does.

No—he also wanted to talk to you about your "gifts," remember?

He'll be back.

His mom asked about the lighthouse and while Daniel answered her, his thoughts wandered back over everything that'd happened.

This morning, after he'd told his story to the police, some officers from Bayfield went up to the lighthouse and recovered the bones from the cellar.

Then, just an hour or so ago, a forensics specialist from UW-Superior reported that her preliminary findings indicated that it was the skeleton of a female between the ages of ten and fourteen. They were doing more tests, but it looked like the story Jarvis Delacroix had written in his journal checked out.

They were going to do some DNA tests this week to determine if the girl was related to Daniel, but in either case, it looked like at last, after all these years, she was going to finally get a proper burial.

After Daniel finished summarizing things for his mom, she turned her attention to his dad again and asked him once more how he was doing.

He assured her that he was fine, then said, "Daniel told me about your talk with him the other day."

"My talk?"

"You said that you left to protect us, that you were afraid of what was happening with you."

"We don't need to discuss any of that right now, Jerry, we—"

"Listen, I want to protect *you*, LeAnne. That's what I signed up for back when we got married."

"I should've done more to help Daniel." She lowered her gaze.

"None of that matters right now. I'll do whatever it takes to make you—both you and Daniel—feel safe. Trust me."

"I do. I just don't want to hurt you."

"Being apart hurts more than being together ever could."

A pause settled between them.

He said, "When you come back we'll give things another shot, okay? We can make this work. I know we can."

She brushed away a tear, but didn't reply.

"Oh," Daniel said, "I just remembered that Nicole and I are supposed to be meeting up with Kyle and Mia in the lobby. We'll be back in a few minutes. C'mon, Nicole."

Carrying her sketchbook, she joined him and they slipped into the hall.

"Good idea," she said. "Give them some privacy."

"Yeah."

"Hey, listen, I think I understand most of what's happened—or at least why it has—but I need to ask, did you ever figure out why you went sleepwalking with that knife?"

"No. Not exactly, but it might have had something to do with my subconscious sorting through dealing with the carved names in the wall."

"That makes sense. And Dr. Fromke? Do you know why he helped Hollister?"

"Maybe because of their history together, maybe for the challenge of it all, or maybe just because he's crazy."

"I'll vote for that last one."

"No kidding."

They passed the elevator bay and he said, "Anyway, leaving my dad and mom alone gives you a chance to open some Christmas presents."

"Presents plural? As in more than one?"

"They're small. You'll see."

"Where are they?"

"On their way."

When they were almost to the lobby a husky man came striding toward them.

Daniel recognized him right away: it was the detective who'd been asking him questions when he woke up in the psychiatric hospital on Sunday morning.

"Excuse me," he said to Daniel, "but can I have a word with you?"

CHAPTER
SIXTY-FIVE

"I'm Detective Poehlman. Do you remember meeting me in Duluth?"

"Yes."

The detective faced Nicole. "And you must be Nicole Marten—you visited Daniel at the hospital under the guise of being his sister."

"What do you want?" Daniel asked.

"May I speak with you in private, Daniel?"

"About what?"

"It has to do with . . . well . . . how you left the hospital in Duluth."

"I already told the whole story to the other officers. Malcolm Zacharias helped me. Now, we're on our way to meet some—"

"It'll only take a minute."

Daniel glanced at Nicole, who shrugged slightly.

"What is it?" he said.

"In private, if you don't mind."

"Nicole stays with me. What do you need to know?"

"Well. Alright." He held up an iPad. "We've been review-ing the security video footage of you leaving the hospital. There was no one there with you, Daniel."

"What do you mean?"

"I mean you were alone when you left the building."

"Mr. Zacharias was there."

"No." The detective shook his head. "I have the footage right here."

"Show me."

Detective Poehlman finger-swiped to the video.

The footage was grainy and there was only movement in the distance, so it'd obviously been filmed from the other end of the hall, but there it was: the video showed Daniel open the door to his room in the psych ward, then pass into the hallway.

Alone.

That doesn't make sense.

The next section showed him round a corner and dart toward the cafeteria, alone. Finally, an external camera had caught him leaving the facility and sprinting away from the property on the road bordering the park beside Lake Superior.

Alone.

All alone.

No. *That's not possible.*

Either you're going completely crazy or someone edited that video, changed the footage somehow.

"Then how did I get to Beldon?"

"You stole a car," Detective Poehlman answered.

"I don't know how to hot-wire a car."

"Then perhaps the keys were in it. Look at the video."

Daniel watched the footage as it showed him rushing toward the sedan, climbing into the driver's side and then, a few moments later, taking off.

"That can't be. I climbed into the passenger's side. I distinctly remember that. I know I did."

"There was no one with you at the hospital, Daniel."

"What about the night security guard? I heard him talking with Mr. Zacharias."

"The guard on duty that night says he didn't speak with anyone."

"He's lying."

"And why would he do that?"

"I don't know."

You never actually saw that guard talk with Mr. Zacharias. You just heard them from the other side of that maintenance closet door. You could have imagined it all. But then—

"I saw Mr. Zacharias," Nicole said to the detective. "At the Traybor Institute. I was there with Daniel. He's real."

"What did you see?"

"One of the guards, the officers, whatever, was the man who'd driven into the snowbank."

Detective Poehlman consulted his iPad, obviously fact-checking something. "The man Daniel and Kyle helped get back on the road Friday night?"

"Yes."

"And you're sure it was the same person?"

"Well, I . . . I mean, I didn't see the guy that night, exactly—he didn't get out of the car, but Daniel told me he was the—" She hesitated, perhaps realizing that she was inadvertently making the detective's case for him.

"What are you going to believe, Daniel?" Detective Poehlman asked. "Your memory or the evidence?"

That's a good question. Your memory or—

Kyle and Mia passed through the automatic doors and entered the lobby. Kyle was sipping from a can of Dr Pepper. Mia took longer than she needed to stomping snow off her boots, muttering something about wishing she lived in Florida.

"Kyle can prove it," Daniel said to the detective.

"Sure." Kyle joined them. "I can prove it. Prove what?"

"You heard Mr. Zacharias, remember? I was talking with you on the phone while I was on my way to Beldon and then I handed the phone to him. He was driving. He told you he was with me."

"Yes. Absolutely. I remember."

"Really?" Detective Poehlman asked.

"Yeah, why?"

"I'm just . . . Well . . ." The detective's phone rang and he checked the screen. "If you'll excuse me for a second."

He stepped away to take the call, but Daniel heard him say, "He's awake? Okay, I'll be right there."

He hung up and finally stopped trying to convince Daniel that Mr. Zacharias hadn't been there to help him. "Thank you for your time," he told them. "I do want to follow up on a few things, though, Daniel. There's still the matter of the car that we need to clear up."

After he'd left, Mia asked, "Who was that guy?"

"A detective," Nicole said.

"From where?"

"You know," Daniel replied thoughtfully, "I didn't ask."

"So, what was that all about?"

"He has footage from the hospital in Duluth. It shows that it was just me leaving—Malcolm Zacharias doesn't appear on it at all. But I know he was real." He faced Kyle. "I let him speak to you on the phone, anyway. That proves it."

Kyle was quiet.

"What?"

"Well, I mean I spoke with someone. It could've been the guy from the snowbank. I'm not really sure."

"Who else could it have been?"

"I don't know." He shrugged. "It might've been you."

"Me?"

"I can't really say. You might have altered your voice, but what does it matter? You're here, you're safe. Your dad's okay. Things are . . ." He seemed to backpedal. "Well . . . except for the car."

"What car?"

"Yeah, I was gonna tell you, they found a sedan down the street from my house. Someone left it there. I mean, I'm sure it's nothing, but my mom did say she heard it was reported stolen from Duluth."

But Mr. Zacharias didn't abandon the car there. He drove away.

Unless he didn't.

Unless you imagined it all and you left the car there.

"Wait," Kyle said to Daniel. "You spoke with Mr. Zacharias on Larry's phone when we were driving back to Beldon."

"There you go." Mia was busy shaking a few persistently clingy globs of snow off her boot. "There'll be a record of it."

"Dr. Fromke destroyed that phone at the cabin," Daniel noted.

"But the phone company would have archives of the call, right?"

"Not if Mr. Zacharias erased them. If he's good enough to hack in and change security camera footage, I'm guessing he could alter or delete a few phone records, no big deal."

If he was real at all.

Rather than taking things any further in that direction, Kyle chose to change the subject and asked Daniel how his dad was doing.

"Better. Right now he's talking with my mom. It seems like things might be heading in the right direction. I'm giving them some time to sort things through."

"You think she'll come back?"

"Yeah. I think she might."

"Huh—Oh." Kyle held up his car keys. "The things you asked me to bring over are in the trunk. You want me to grab 'em?"

"I'll get them. Do you mind?"

"No." Kyle handed over his keys. "We'll just chillify here, wait for you."

"Did you just say 'chillify'?" Nicole asked.

"It's his new thingazoid," Daniel explained.

"Oh. Gotcha."

Since Daniel's phone had been found covered in blood at the scene of his dad's disappearance, it was still in the police evidence room, but he'd been using Nicole's for the day to talk with his mom, and now a text came through.

He showed her the screen. "No big deal," she said. "It's just Gina. I'll text her back later."

He pocketed her phone again.

Kyle told him where he'd parked, although with the size of the parking lot that probably wasn't necessary.

Daniel told Nicole he'd see her in a bit, and then headed out the door.

The afternoon was fading away, the sun barely visible on the horizon.

As he walked toward Kyle's Mustang, he thought about all that had happened this week, how things were connected there, just beneath the surface, how all the puzzle pieces locked together in a way that he never would have guessed, but that made sense now when he looked back on them.

He thought of Malcolm Zacharias, of Detective Poehlman, and—

Nicole's phone vibrated. He checked.

A text: *Answer this call, Daniel.*

While he was trying to figure out what that was about, the phone rang from an unknown number.

Daniel tapped the screen. "Hello?"

"Hello, Daniel."

It's him.

"Mr. Zacharias. What did you do? They have video footage that shows it was just me leaving the hospital in Duluth."

"How hard do you really think it is to change some footage at a state mental hospital?"

"You're saying you hacked in and altered it? That's impossible."

"Not with the technology I have access to."

He knows you have her phone. How does he know that? Is he close by?

Daniel scanned the parking lot, but didn't see Mr. Zacharias anywhere. "But the video shows me going to the driver's side of the car."

"The wonders of CGI."

"And the security guard—what'd you do? Pay him off?"

"His daughter's very sick. The money is going to a good cause."

"And I'm guessing the phone records are—"

"Expunged. Yes."

Daniel didn't know whether to feel angry or relieved talking with Mr. Zacharias right now.

He glanced at the phone's screen and saw that there really was a call coming through.

Okay, at least this is happening right now.

At least this is real.

Daniel asked, "How did Hollister get away from you, anyway? I mean, he was a killer. You wouldn't have just set him free from the institute and then let him go, right?"

"He was more clever than I thought." Mr. Zacharias left it at that.

"And you didn't know he would go to Dr. Fromke?"

"I had no idea. I wasn't aware of their connection to each other."

"But why did Dr. Fromke help him?"

"That, I don't know. And, unfortunately, from what I understand, he's not being very forthcoming."

As they spoke, Daniel was turning in a slow circle, looking in every direction, but he didn't see Mr. Zacharias anywhere. "But it looks like you got what you wanted. The institute was destroyed."

"Yes, it was."

"Did you do that? Did you blow it up?"

"I wish I could take credit for it, but it wasn't me."

Still no sign of anyone.

"I need to ask you something, Mr. Zacharias."

"Yes?"

"Which wolf are you?"

"Which wolf?"

"There's this story my dad told me once—that there are two wolves battling it out inside everyone's heart: one good, one bad. And the one who wins is the one—"

"You feed the most."

"You've heard the story too."

"Yes."

"So? Which one are you?"

"Whichever one I need to be to get the job done."

"What job?"

"Recruitment."

"Recruitment?"

That's right, remember? He came here to meet with you, to ask you to help him.

"They think I'm just imagining you," Daniel said.

Silence.

"Hello?"

No reply.

"Mr. Zacharias?"

Are you real? he thought.

"Are you there?" he said.

The line was dead.

Of course it is. Because he doesn't exist. He's—

As Daniel stared at the screen, the record of the call disappeared before his eyes.

He scrolled over to see the list of recent calls. Nothing showed up.

Nicole was approaching the car, sketchbook in hand. "You okay?" she asked.

"Yeah."

"You sure?"

"Not completely."

"You were on the phone," she observed.

"It was him. Mr. Zacharias."

"Oh." He couldn't read her tone of voice. "What did he say?"

"That he's a recruiter." Daniel took a deep breath. "Nicole, tell me I'm not going crazy."

"You're not going crazy."

"Okay, well . . . Hmm . . ."

"What?"

"That didn't help as much as I was hoping it would."

Let her open her presents. Get your mind off everything that's been going on.

He reached into his pocket, drew out an envelope, and handed it to her. "Here. Do this one first."

"What is it?"

"Your present—well, part of it."

"You want to open presents here? In the parking lot?"

"Sure. Why not? Why wait?"

"Um, okay. I do like present opening."

"I know."

She set down her sketchbook, opened the envelope, and unfolded the sheet of paper he'd slipped inside it.

"A coupon for 'Free snow anaconda lessons.' Well, I didn't see that one coming."

"It's good for a year," Daniel pointed out helpfully. "I keep the class size small for more individualized attention."

"Is that so?"

"Yeah. I like instruction to be one-on-one."

She looked at him slyly. "So do I."

He unlocked the trunk and took out the two gifts Kyle had placed in there.

"Open the next one."

He gave it to her: a box about as long as a shoebox but only half as wide, and rather inelegantly wrapped in a brown paper bag held in place with duct tape.

"Kyle wrapped it for me."

"I never would have guessed."

She unfolded the paper bag carefully, as if she were trying to protect it so that it could be used again, though with that much tape, Daniel doubted that was ever going to happen.

When she got to the box she opened it and lifted out the contents. "You got me a one-armed Batman doll."

"Action figure, actually."

"Oh. Right. Is this the one from your bedroom?"

"No, Kyle found it for me today. I'm guessing Walmart."

"And you had him tear the arm off?"

"Yup. It's so your doll, Rebecca, won't be lonely."

"That's thoughtful. It's sweet. It really is."

"And number three." He handed her the last one. "Open it."

"Hmm . . . It looks like it's about the right size for being a sketchbook." She held it up to her ear and shook it. "Sounds like a sketchbook." She sniffed it. "Smells like a sketchbook."

"Open it."

She did.

"A new sketchbook."

"You didn't see that coming either did you?"

"Not at all."

"This was your original present. I saw that your other sketchbook was getting toward the end and it works out well because I think it's time to retire the one with the demon in it."

"Agreed. Which brings me to the present I got for you."

She handed him the sketchbook she'd brought outside with her.

"What's this?"

"It's my drawings. It's for you. I ripped the demon one out."

"You're giving me your . . . I can't take this. Seriously, it's—"

She placed a gentle finger against his lips to quiet him. "You're the most special guy in the world to me. It's only right that you should have my most special drawings."

He set all the gifts on the roof of the car.

She looked at him curiously. "What are you doing?"

"The sun just went down over the trees."

"Uh-huh."

"Remember when we were standing under the Northern Lights the other night?"

"Yes."

"And then when they went away we were alone under the starlight and we got interrupted?"

"Yes."

"Do you remember what we were about to do?"

"This?" She leaned in and gave him a quick kiss.

"More like this," he said, and gave her a kiss that was not quite so quick, and was much more deserving of one shared beneath a canopy of stars.

EPILOGUE

Dr. Fromke lay in his hospital bed, his wrists handcuffed to the frame.

He thought of the irony of it—just a few days ago Daniel had been committed to a psychiatric facility. He was the one restrained, the one under guard, and now, he was the one who was free.

The tables had turned.

But they were going to turn again.

Dr. Fromke was already planning his escape.

He knew that his room was being guarded by law enforcement. So far he'd put off answering any of their questions. There was a lot for them to sort through and with his broken leg, the gunshot wound and the sliced foot, they would have to take some time patching him up before transporting him anywhere.

And it would be much easier to escape from a hospital room than a prison cell.

The door opened and another doctor came in. The third one that day.

Enough with all the different doctors.

This one looked like he was in his mid-sixties and hadn't gotten nearly enough sleep last night.

After quietly looking over the charts, he said, "So, I understand you shot Brandon Hollister?"

Dr. Fromke wasn't about to confess to anything, especially not to a man who might be an undercover cop. He remained quiet.

"I should thank you for that." The doctor set down the charts. "But I have to ask you, did he say anything about me?"

"What?"

"Did he say anything about me? About what happened at the institute?"

Now that he took a more careful look, Dr. Fromke did recognize this man from Hollister's description.

It's the guy who was in charge of the research over at the Traybor Institute. The guy who tortured Brandon, made it seem like he was suffering weeks of solitary confinement.

"No," Dr. Fromke lied. "I have no idea who you are."

The man tapped a finger against the air. "And see, I'm good at telling when people are lying. And I can tell you're not being truthful with me." He detached the bag of Dr. Fromke's IV.

"What are you doing?"

But rather than answer, he just worked on the IV bag, changing the drug it would be administering. "I'll be taking care of you from now on."

"Stop." Dr. Fromke tried to lift his hands but his wrists were securely cuffed.

"I should be thanking you for shooting inmate 176235. But I don't like loose ends, and that's what you're looking like to me."

This is not happening. This is not—

Dr. Waxford reconnected the IV bag, sending the new drug mixture into Dr. Fromke's arm.

He started feeling sleepy almost right away.

"Hey!" He called to the officer guarding his door. "Come in here! He's trying to drug me!"

Whoever was stationed in the hallway did not respond.

"We're going to transfer you to a new facility, Dr. Fromke. I have some tests I'd like to perform. It's all in the name of justice for what you did to those people in the barn. From what I hear there were seven victims. Even with my techniques, this might take a while."

Dr. Fromke called more loudly for the officer guarding his room.

And finally a man poked his head in.

It was the detective who'd been interrogating him earlier.

"Thank God, you're—" Dr. Fromke began.

"The paperwork is all set, Dr. Waxford," he said.

"Thank you, Detective Poehlman." He patted Dr. Fromke's arm. "Don't fight the drowsiness, now. Don't let that concern you. When you wake up you won't be in pain. You'll just be alone. For a long, long time you get to be alone."

• • •

From where he sat hidden in the parked car at the other end of the parking lot, Malcolm Zacharias watched as Daniel and Nicole gathered up their gifts and went back into the hospital.

He needed to make sure that he remained a ghost, even if it meant Daniel had to stay in the dark about whether or not he was real.

Yes.

Daniel had the gift.

His blurs gave him insights no one else could understand.

Well, perhaps that wasn't quite true.

The three other teens Malcolm had already recruited might understand, once he got them all together at the facility in Georgia.

He made the call to his contact person.

Yes, things were about to get very interesting, now that they had four of them to work with.

WATCH FOR

CURSE

*THE FINAL CHAPTER OF
THE BLUR TRILOGY*

COMING IN SPRING 2016

Thanks and Acknowledgments

Thanks to Liesl, Pam, Trinity, Jim, Ariel, the Northern Great Lakes Visitor Center, Erik, Dr. Huhn, Dr. Abner, Dave Strzok, Susanna, Meg, Courtney, Anna, Alex McReynolds, Katrina Johnson, John-Phillip Abner, and Eden Huhn.